Praise fo

MW00412366

"Parris Afton Bonds has the uncanny ability to insert the majesty of the English language with taste, texture, sights, sounds, and smells, making the story come alive. Masterful and memorable is a remarkable portrait of the complex young woman, Pia, who is smart, eloquent, compassionate, and who demonstrates extraordinary healing and love. I love books that make my heard dance at the conclusion."

—Elizabeth St. Michel, Bestselling and International Award-winning author of *Lord of the Wilderness*

"Bonds is a brilliant writer on many levels in all her books - characterization, plot and subplots, historical research, drama, romance with a warm lush and bewitching sensuality, crisp dialogue, sharp action sequences, a pace appropriate to the scene. But there is something else always there that some readers might miss. A sense of justice. Caught up in all its drama and action and romantic love, the stream of right and wrong, good and evil, justice and injustice is prominent in *Reluctant Rebel*, like a bright silver stream running through the novel from beginning to end and adding luster and shine and depth to the story. A powerful novel that will entertain as well as enlighten and enthrall - the heroine is a fiery wonder."

—Murray Pura, award winning author of *Zo, The Wings of Morning,* and *The Face of Heaven*

Reluctant Rebel

PARRIS AFTON BONDS

Other Books by
Parris Afton Bonds

THE TEXICANS

The Brigands • The Barons

The Bravados • The Betrayers

The Banshees (2022)

Blue Bayou • Blue Moon

The Calling of the Clan • The Captive

Dancing with Crazy Woman • Dancing with Wild Woman

Deep Purple • Dream Keeper • Dream Time • Dust Devil

The Flash of the Firefly • For All Time

Kingdom Come: Temptation • Kingdom Come: Trespass

Lavender Blue • Love Tide

Made For Each Other • Midsummer Midnight

Mood Indigo • No Telling

Renegade Man • Run To Me

Savage Enchantment • The Savage

Snow And Ice • Spinster's Song

Stardust • Sweet Enchantress

Sweet Golden Sun • The Wildest Heart

Wanted Woman • Widow Woman

Windsong • When the Heart is Right

Text copyright © 2022 by Parris Afton Bonds
All Rights Reserved. Printed in the United States of America
Published by Motina Books, LLC, Van Alstyne, Texas
www.MotinaBooks.com

Library of Congress Cataloguing-in-Publication Data:

Names: Afton Bonds, Parris
Title: Reluctant Rebel
Description: First Edition. | Van Alstyne: Motina Books, 2022

Identifiers:
LCCN: 2022931513

ISBN-13: 978-1-945060-53-3 (paperback)
ISBN-13: 978-1-945060-51-9 (e-book)
ISBN-13: 978-1-945060-55-7 (hardcover)

Subjects: BISAC:
Fiction > Historical > General

Cover Design: Venessa Cerasale
Interior Design: Diane Windsor

Dedicated to

MARY TATE ENGELS
One of our terrestrial angels, indeed

and

ENRIQUETA AGUIRRE AYALA
My precious friend-daughter-sister

Chapter One

Walter Stevenson stepped down from the Mexico Central Railroad's coach. His lengthy bones were still rattling from the train's six day crawl up from Mexico City. In one hand he carried his valise and in the other his suitcase, both items as sensible as his brown trilby, once viewed as the rich man's favored hat.

He favored the trilby because its low crown attracted less notice of wasp-whistling bullets traded between Pancho Villa's revolutionaries and General Pershing's American Expeditionary Force.

The train's hissing steam clashed with the twilight's frigid air and momentarily fogged his pince-nez. The spectacles pinched the high bridge of his nose damnably. A U.S. military mule had trampled his last pair. His eyeglasses cleared, and he strode the length of the platform.

A chilling wind, avalanching down from the ragged tail-end of the Rockies, barreled through the Rio Grande's narrow garden of green that was El Paso. Tomorrow, the desert temperature could rise to a balmy seventy degrees. One never could predict at The Pass the weather—or the wars.

Disembarking train passengers from the various platforms tugged their wraps tighter and hustled toward the Union Station Depot. Soldiers with canvas kit bags and steeple-crowned campaign hats were reporting to duty on nearby Fort Bliss, already swelled to 40,000 by troops in fruitless pursuit down into Mexico of the wily Villa. Businessmen were arriving, eager to capitalize on El Paso's brisk international trade and even more profitable smuggling.

And, of course, espionage agents filtered among the passengers. Spies, counterspies, and counter-counterspies.

The buildup of troops and government spies on both sides of the border was as good as gold for Walt, an undercover agent for the Bureau of Investigation. Not even a decade old, the Bureau was getting its feet wet in all kinds of investigative areas—not just in law enforcement, for which he was a fervent proponent, but also in national security and intelligence arenas. This federal license was stirring up fear in many of an abuse of power.

The BI had recruited him out of Mexico nine months ago where, as a war correspondent for *Collier's Magazine,* he was covering General Pershing's Punitive Expedition.

"You're what we need at The Pass," the BI deputy director told him. "A deep thinker and keen observer—with a penchant for anticipating events, if your short story a year-and-a-half ago is taken into account."

Walt doubted that short story about a rebellion led by a down-and-out ex-patriot soldier in Mexico against his hometown of El Paso predicted Villa's attack against nearby Columbus, New Mexico five months later, exactly a year ago in 1916.

However, Walt's familiarity with the area, his fluency with both German and Spanish, and his experience with the military, both at school and in the field, certainly helped gain his position with the BI.

He was assigned to work the BI's border cases and conduct liaisons with myriad Mexican and American informants and officials. He had received but limited training.

When it came to hair-raisers, the Juarez-El Paso arena was on par with any bloody bullfight arena. The area was a powder-keg, what with Mexico's decades-long revolutions and now Germany's attacks throughout Europe. Germany was looking for ways to distract American attention from the European war and Mexico was one of its focal points. Because of its strategic location, El Paso was perfect for international intrigue.

The uncertainty was as to who would light the match at the border's powder keg—Germany, Mexico, or the United States.

By discipline, he took in his surroundings in the El Paso train station. As a youth at New Mexico Military Academy and later at Pennsylvania's Swarthmore College, he had been taunted as Four-Eyes. Now at twenty-five he was grateful for those spectacles. His nearsightedness forced him to focus intently. Where other people scanned inattentively at distant things, he absorbed minute detail, even peripherally.

Without looking in any specific direction, he set his route to pass near the shoeshine stand, secluded from the biting wind in an alcove outside the terminal's entrance. One of the two high seats was occupied. A Chinaman, his black queue flapping, industriously polished his customer's pair of embossed leather dress boots.

An unfurled newspaper shielded the face of the customer, reading by the station's incandescent lighting. However, from Walt's angle of approach, a holster's black shoulder strap could be seen edging slightly from beneath the narrow lapel of the man's single-breasted jacket.

State law prohibited the wearing of arms in public areas, but few followed the law in that far west part of Texas. He himself never carried a weapon and never would, despite his authorization as a BI Federal Agent.

The Chinaman's customer could be one of the spies or counter-spies whose job was to hang out at every bar on both sides of the border. But a master spy would never employ so obvious a subterfuge—like hiding behind a newspaper.

No, El Paso's master spy would be in plain sight.

At another siding—these, electric overhead tracks—a group of young women disembarked from a streetcar. A short and slight female, no more than sixteen or seventeen-years-old he judged, swung down behind the others.

Her drab skirt swirled about ankle-high work boots. A faded purple *rebozo* warmed narrow shoulders, and a large hemp-woven bag was slung from one. Most likely, she was one of hundreds of maids from Juarez who daily crossed the Rio Grande to clean homes for El Paso's upper class.

His observation dismissed her conspicuous red hair, caught up in the popular Gibson Girl careless bouffant. Red hair and blue or green eyes could still be found in descendants of Coronado's conquistadors who had marched through this part of Mexico centuries earlier.

Her head swiveled, and she glanced absently in his direction. The prickling at his nape, a physical reaction to his remarkable intuition, could not be dismissed so easily. The energy in her arresting features was as potent as the pulque bought at any of Juarez's notorious watering holes. It was like running smack into a tree.

His quick assessment registered intelligence in eyes set below thick, pencil-straight brows and a Mona Lisa mouth that softened the severity of a square jaw. Would she be typified as pretty? He mentally shrugged. As the Mexicans would say, *Quién a fea ama, hermosa le parece.* Was not beauty in the eye of the beholder?

At that precise moment, her gaze stumbled across his. Her head cocked like a wary wren. He witnessed in her glance the same thousand-watt jolt he had experienced. For a long moment, it felt to him they both were locked in some internal struggle.

Then, as if making up her mind, she pivoted away. Her hemp-woven bag swishing with her quick strides, she headed toward her young companions and was soon swallowed up by the crowd.

You are as addlebrained as an adolescent, Walt. He was a rational man and there was a rational explanation for this experience if pondered sufficiently. He had more important issues to ponder.

Gathering his wits, he set off in the opposite direction with his valise and suitcase. In it was his valuable toilet kit, for which he received good-natured ribbing. Even in Mexico's battlefields, he shaved daily and wore clean linen.

He threaded through the crammed and noisy, high-ceilinged Union Station Depot. The train station was nearly as grand as Washington D.C.'s and designed by the same architect. He exited the street side, where the wind slithered sand across the herringboned red brick pavement.

Here, motorized taxi cabs and horse-drawn hackneys vied for passenger fares, vendors sold steamy hot tamales from carts, and newsboys hawked stories of Europe's expanding war and Mexico's latest revolution.

A pacifist—his mother had been a Quaker—he was committed to avoiding war. How sublimely ironic since his assignment as a journalist with *Collier's* involved reporting the latest Mexican revolution.

"Hey, *Señor! Garapiñados,* five pesos." A filthy old Mexican held out a brown paper pouch whiffing of caramelized peanuts and pecans. He slouched against the Union Station's brick wall that shielded him from the biting draft. He wore an eyepatch. A ragged poncho barely afforded warmth for the leathered cadaver.

The feeble man's guise was enough to turn any prospective customer's stomach, and, besides, nuts welted Walt's tongue. "They're not worth even two centavos." However, he dropped a Mexican silver dollar, an excessive sum, in the man's outstretch lined palm. "Sell your *garapiñados* to the next sucker."

His lanky body cramped from the six-day trek by train, Walt forewent transportation and welcomed the excuse to walk to the nearby Hotel Sheldon. He leaned into the blustering wind. It cleared his mind, stuffy with execrable cigar smoke from the train's closed coach, which had sardined him with a colicky baby and chicken coop, along with jobless rural campesinos and nervous hidalgos fleeing *Villista*s.

Tagging along with Pershing and his troops in Mexico, he had chosen to eschew smoking, drinking, or gambling, although the other war correspondents indulged heartily while bored and waiting for the next round of fighting. Uncertain about his literary talent's lucrative worthiness, he figured self-discipline in the fields of massacring was about the only skill he possessed. That and his single noble attribute, his integrity.

Apparently, the BI must have faith in both his literary and observation skills—that and his knowledge of the area and passable Spanish due to his stint at the nearby military academy along with his passable German from his mother's side—or they would not have come calling on him.

Being the son of the esteemed Justice Theodore Stevenson, recently retired, aided Walt's chance at being selected for the BI. Like his father, Walt was a firm believer in the law and in the enforcement of that law. Life under law was not always good or just, but life without law was bad.

And life without writing was, at least for him, the soul's abyss. Daily he reminded himself that Jack London, Zane Grey and Arthur Conan Doyle, among many other authors, had started out working for periodicals and newspapers and gone on to become critically acclaimed novelists.

However, he wanted to write within the realm of Upton Sinclair. A decade earlier, Sinclair had written *The Jungle*. The muck-raking novel had exposed labor and sanitary conditions in the U.S. meatpacking industry. It had caused a public uproar contributing to the passage a few months later of the Pure Food and Drug Act and the Meat Inspection Act.

Signing on with *Collier's*, Walt judged he could endure bullet battles if it meant the opportunity of being listed up there with literary luminaries such as Sinclair.

But that was not the purpose of his first assignment by the BI. His was merely to ferret out among the half a million persons straddling the Rio Grande there at The Pass the master spy suspected of being handled by the German, Felix Sommerfeld.

In preparation, Walt had researched Sommerfeld. The lawyer,

lobbyist, and power broker had personal access to the highest levels of the Departments of Justice, War, and State, as well as connections to the American business elite.

Two years ago, in 1915, he was purported to have told the German government he could create an incident which would provoke a war between the United States and Mexico. However, the controller of spies' involvement could not be proven, and besides, he was too important a personage to the United States to extradite.

Walt sensed the German's genius lay in his ability to provide valuable information to each country—Mexico, Germany, and the United States—while knowing which information to leak only to his German superiors.

If Walt could nail the identity of Germany's master spy operating under Sommerfeld there in El Paso, his rejected novels piling up just might be then sought after. Hell, they just might sell a million bucks.

Not that he needed the money. Between the BI's special agent salary of six dollars a day plus room and board, his income as a *Collier's* war correspondent, and the royalties from a few of his stories sporadically sold, his income adequately provided what little he required.

Then, too, his father wasn't exactly penniless. The old man's forefathers had fought in every war since the American Revolution. As the disciplinarian, Walt's father behaved with stringent restraint when it came to affectionate display. The Honorable Justice Theodore Stevenson's strong sense of duty and discipline were as ingrained in Walt's long bones as much as his deceased mother's decorum and dovishness.

No, whatever Walt accomplished in life, it would damn well be on his own and not a penny from his illustrious family.

His risk-taking war reports put to rest his recurring nightmare. Or should have, but it still weighed too heavily on his shoulders, despite their being broadened and muscled by years of routine swimming.

At the Roswell Military Institute, he had been too young, too gawky and ill at ease. But over the years, he seemed to have willed his body to grow into a responsive instrument of which he was comfortably in command.

Rather than serve in the military, as many young men were doing, he had opted, as an avowed pacifist, to report on it. And this despite the recent statement by El Paso's mayor, Tom Lea. "I have no use for pacifists. I would describe a pacifist as one who wears the yellow robe of cowardice."

As a persecuted pacifist, Walt's stance was not about to change. In one fraction of a moment, he had caused a bloodshed, taking its toll as unexpressed sorrow that reshaped his life and that of those around him.

Tugging down his brown trilby's brim with its press pass wedged behind the band, he ducked his head and, shifting his valise under his arm, he turned up his Ulster's tweed collar against the evening's bitter wind.

Chapter Two

Piedad Arellano swung down from the Sunset Heights-Union Station streetcar. As she had missed the 5:15 p.m. international streetcar outbound for Juarez, she did not expect her sister Josefina to be waiting for her.

The day before, Pia had called Trujillo's *Farmacía* from the Cardenas house telephone and asked the clerk Guido Ruiz to relay the message to their mother that she would be staying the night at her employers. Pia suspected Guido was sweet on her sister Josefina. At thirty-two, he was a good dozen years older. For Josefina's part, she appeared to ignore him.

Something made Pia pause mid-step along the platform ... that feeling of being observed. Of course, she often caught people's puzzled glance because of her rare coloring but seldom a prolonged stare.

Obeying the warning that flushed her skin, she looked around in what she hoped was an offhanded manner. All too often, a house maid would go missing, only for her violated body to turn up in the brush along the Rio Bravo days or weeks later. This despite the many bordellos on both sides of the border servicing the mounting number of soldiers, also on both sides of the border.

Her search locked on an inordinately tall man. His fedora's brim shadowed the upper portion of his face, but she could see that the lower portion was stony like a mountain and clean shaven when facial hair was the norm. His ruler-straight back hissed of the military.

He paused, turned slightly. It seemed the train station's lights momentarily refracted a rainbow off his spectacles. Then she saw those eyes single her out. The intense regard behind those lenses affected her like the shock from the Cardenas's electric toaster when she had dislodged a slice of bread she had burnt with a butter knife … momentarily staggering. Curiously, she did not feel threatened. What then was this?

Puzzled, she swerved and set off at a brisk pace to where had gathered a few of the other late-working housemaids, awaiting transfer to the next El Paso-Juarez streetcar.

"¡*Hola*, Pia!" the bosomy and blowsy Mercedes beckoned her with an urgent wave. But then everything was urgent to the two-years-younger, fifteen-year-old Mercedes.

Pia returned the wave. Still, on impulse she glanced back. Her gaze tracked the man like the sunflower did the sun. He was striding with unchallengeable authority toward the Union Station entrance.

She shook off the spell. But she forewent joining Mercedes and friends, huddled to exchange the day's gossip. Pia could catch up with it once onboard the outbound streetcar. Instead, she sought its outdoor ticket booth.

Left over from the Southern Pacific depot era, the timeworn cubicle featured double grilled windows. From behind one, the ends of Silas Wright's droopy, iron-gray mustache lifted ever so slightly at the sight of her. Beneath his visor, rheumy gray eyes belied a sharp mind.

Stepping inside the booth, she plopped her heavy *bolsa* on the unvarnished wooden counter, scored with years of burns and notches. She popped up onto the high stool behind the other grilled window.

"Well, well, if it ain't the little red-headed devil herself."

"¡*Buenas noches* Silas!" His growl put off a lot of people, but not her. She gave him the obscene *corte de manga*, slapping her upper arm, uplifted in an L-shape, then dug into her *bolsa*.

Woven *lechuguilla* with leather straps, the jumbo bag fashioned by her mother contained little, because Pia owned little. Inside were her coin purse, comb, and treasured but weighty *Roget's Thesaurus*, along with a notepad, pencil, and a few odds and ends, two of these paper-wrapped packets.

She flopped one in front of him. "Be grateful I brought you the tamales. Made them early this morning."

"Purloined 'em, did ya?" His false teeth clucked despairingly, but his age-gnarled fingers clawed open the brown parchment.

"Adelaide will never miss them. As it is, the *Señora* eats like a spider to lace her corset as tight as a banker's wallet."

The imperious *Señora* Adelaide was the German wife of the easygoing mestizo Bartolomé Cardenas. He clearly earned a fat salary as a traveling salesman for the men's clothing store owned by him and his brother, because *Señor* Bart lived with his family in the prestigious Sunset Heights.

"Where ya been the last couple of days?" Silas unpeeled the corn husk and chomped down on its rolled corn cake.

"Adelaide's son came down with a runny nose." She bit into her own cold tamale. "She had some *jaitón* function to attend." She lifted her nose in a mockery of snootiness. "So, I agreed to spend the night and care for little Richie."

Silas' grizzled brows abutted over the high hook of his long nose. "Typhoid?"

"No, no fever, *gracias a Dios*. I checked his hair for nits."

He hummphed. "Lice would be afraid of Frau Adelaide."

The recent typhus outbreak in Northern Mexico had the El Paso public running scared, despite reassurance from the Public Health Service Office for El Paso there was little danger.

The city had demolished hundreds of hovels in Chihuahita, the oldest part of El Paso. And for the last couple of months she had caught sight from the streetcar of a building that the Public Health Department was constructing beneath the Santa Fe International Bridge on its side of the Rio Bravo's banks. Some kind of a clinic it was rumored for treating those afflicted with the typhus infection.

Actually, two separate rail bridges connected across the Rio Bravo. The twin international border crossings were a continual scene of a plethora of pedestrians, streetcars, and automobiles. The traffic kept border officials on heavy active duty nearly all hours of the day.

"Then, yesterday," she finished explaining to Silas, "Adelaide's Woman's Club Meeting ran late, and one night turned into two for me."

Pia hoped Adelaide didn't expect her to be on call twenty-four hours, because she hated to be looking for another job so soon. She had only worked for the Cardenas household a couple of weeks, after walking off her previous job when the *Señora*'s husband too often found reason to brush Pia's arm, shoulder, or bottom in passing. "Is the Juarez streetcar running late?"

"Yeah, a broken wire." He wiped crumbs from his mustache with the back of his blue-veined hand. "A repair car has already been sent out."

In the winter, the copper wires often broke due to the low temperatures. More than once she had been forced to wait inside a frigid open streetcar, while the maintenance crew crawled to the top of it with insulated pliers and wound the wire together. Then the trip would resume.

"*Bien.*" She grinned. "Enough time for Code Dual, then?"

His grunt of exasperation fluttered his mustache's ends, but she sensed he enjoyed the game as much as she. "After I finish off this tamale, if there's still time." By habit, he speared a glance above the grilled windows at the timekeeper's clock and the latest schedule tacked next to it.

He was lonely. Leading a soldier's life, he had married late. As an army sergeant, he had strung telegraph wire west from Fort Davis to connect with El Paso. After he mustered out of the army in the 1880s, he returned to El Paso to work for Western Union. There he eventually met and married Millie, a retired schoolteacher.

Meanwhile, his hand and arm suffered from the repetitive stress that afflicted telegraphers. "Telegrapher's paralysis," he had explained to Pia. "The constant up and down wrist motion made my arm so weak I couldn't send dispatches. I tried switching to the left hand, but it was no better, gal. The pain went straight to my shoulder, so as I couldn't sleep a naught at night."

About this same time that his Millie came down with the grippe, Western Union summarily dismissed him. Unable to afford Millie a doctor's care, he attended her himself, until her last breath drowned in her swamped lungs.

Stripped of everything, he had taken the ticket vendor job—and with him the telegraph as a bitter memento, along with a German Luger, a canning jar containing Chinese josh sticks, and a Mexican Day of the Dead skull mask. They all resided in his ticket booth as if it were his home and they his souvenirs.

When Pia embarked on her first job at eleven as a housemaid, she would meet up after work with Josefina at Union Station. But rather than hang out with the other maids, stuck awaiting transfer to the next Juarez-bound streetcar, Pia would roam the magnificent building.

Furtively, she climbed the depot's six-story bell tower and tried to identify landmarks across the river in Juarez. Hungrily, she stood outside the second floor's Harvey House and espied *la gente decente*, the better class from El Paso and Juarez, as they passed through its door to dine—until she was shooed away. Josefina, three-years-older, always scolded her that she was too curious for her own good.

Curiosity at last drew her attention to the odd-looking machine in the streetcar ticket booth ... led her attention to the crusty old ticket vendor ... and led to his teaching her the dot-dash-dots of the machine's hand key while she awaited transfer.

The Morse code fascinated her. Like learning a secret that only a special few would ever know, not even *la gente decente*.

In the past year, she and Silas started playing games using the telegraph. They would tap out a sequence of numbers or letters where every other symbol, or every third symbol, or, more difficult —interchanging Spanish and English—might be part of a coded message the other one had to decipher. Both she and Silas were fluid in the other's native language, but she was also proficient in German.

After the Mexican American War of 1846, many German families had emigrated from Texas to settle in northern Mexico. Next in 1883 the Mexican government signed a law to encourage foreign investors to settle in Mexico.

Then, according to her mother, a decade or so later that demon dictator Porfirio Diaz dispossessed large tracts of land from the Catholic Church and awarded the tracts, not to the peons who worked it, but to these foreign investors. That was how her mother came to work as a child for the German family in the city of Chihuahua, the wealthy Heinrichs.

Reaching for a bit of the tamale, she said, "One day I am going to have my own house, a grand one like the *Señora* Adelaide's or Don Horst Heinrich's."

Pia's greatest fear was to end up like her mother, sitting on a woven mat on Juarez's *Plaza Constitución*, selling ropes, baskets, and sandals fashioned from the local *lechuguilla*. Worse now, the drought the year before, combined with this past winter's uncommonly freezing temperatures and rooting javelinas, had thinned out her mother's precious source of income.

Silas understood this. A ticket vendor's pay was poor. "Houses, they can fall down, gal. Banks can fail. Only land lasts. But land, it's limited. Buy it now."

"Buy land—me? *Está loco.*" Dispiritedly, she swallowed her mouthful of tamale. "Besides, where I dream to live is Sunset Heights—and only *los ricos* can afford that."

He tapped his temple. "Use your noggin. Go in the other direction, east, from Mount Franklin."

"Into the desert?"

"It's cheap. In a short time you could save for a down payment."

"You really *are* crazy. Why would I want to live out in the desert?"

"Not you. The damned U.S. Army."

His vitriolic feelings about it and the United States government itself did not surprise her. From his viewpoint, they had stolen everything from him.

"When war comes to America—and it will—Fort Bliss will be forced to expand even farther. It can't go west. The Rockies block it. Nor south, as the Rio Grande and the international border outlaw that. So, north or east, into the desert, it must go. The land's an investment, a down payment, for that house on the hill you want."

For the first time in her life, she felt a glimmer of hope. Something she could latch onto. Something solid. Something permanent. She thought about her twenty-two pesos, worth eleven American dollars, she had tucked away in an old Cracker Jack box. She had gobbled its entire contents of caramel coated popcorn and peanuts at an El Paso baseball game in only the few minutes the band had played the Cracker Jack slogan, "Take me out to the ballgame."

Well, eleven dollars was a start, and her glimmer of hope transformed into an elation that had her giving Silas a cockeyed grin. "You're not so loco after all, Silas."

In reality, she felt she must be the *loca* one. Else why, tired as she was, after a long three days of work at the Cardenases', did her thoughts continue to churn around a *gringo* who had merely looked at her? But it was the way he had looked at her ... or inside her. She had never had this perverse kind of uneasy yet excited sensation before, not even with Amado of the machismo deviltry.

Chapter Three

After checking for telegram and telephone messages at the front desk of the Hotel Sheldon, the principal base for reporters covering the Pershing Expedition, Walt let himself into the parlor suite he maintained. He willingly paid the difference in upgrading from a single room to the suite, which included its own bathroom rather than the communal one at the end of the hall.

He still had a late evening call to make, so he unpacked immediately. Clothes and toiletry, writing utensils, and lastly his books: the current U.S. best seller *Los de Abajo* about the Mexican revolution; a book of pacifist poetry; and a dog-eared mystery novel he had finished reading. Invariably he figured out the culprit of a mystery novel within its first few pages.

He stacked the books by size on the small round table next to the rocking chair. A rocking chair was a prerequisite for any home base of his. The one he had kept at Swarthmore was a cherished Bentwood with a smooth rocking motion.

His current rocking chair he had redeemed from disposal by the undertaking parlors of McBean, Simpson, and Wallace. The rocker had a tattered cane seat and was painted a garish red, green, and yellow. But it served its purpose, the soothing of a hyperactive mind ... or, the extreme opposite, a melancholy one.

Satisfied his living quarters at the Sheldon were in order, Walt left immediately for the home of Lionel Pollock. Pollock held the plum post of United States Collector of Customs at El Paso. El Paso was the hub of US intelligence gathering. The border city was also the point for the export of Mexican goods north whose sale was vital to the support of Villa's forces.

Thus, Pollock held the valve which could stop the flow of goods in both directions. The customs collector might despise Villa, but so long as the United States administration did not choose to recognize either of the two contenders for Mexican leadership—the revolutionary Pancho Villa or the current president, Venustiano Carranza—Pollock had to let the pipeline flow.

This, Walt had learned, Pollock most certainly did. The United States Customs Agent also turned a blind eye on small time contraband dealers numbered among El Paso's citizens, from the low to the lofty.

Pollock answered the door to his home in Mesa Gardens. Although only in his mid-thirties, gray was already muddling his thinning, light brown hair. His rimless spectacles, bridging a large, hooked nose, magnified a suspicious gaze. He held a thick, redolent cigar between fleshy fingers. "Yeah?"

For the first time since signing on with the BI, Walt made use of his authority. He flipped out his metal badge with its gold lettering: *Special Agent, Department of Justice.*

"Another one of you agency boys, huh?"

"Not just any agency. Those Secret Service fellows sniffing around here are with the Department of the Treasury. There is a world of difference that separates it from the Department of Justice—and from me."

"Modest cuss, are you?" But apparently Walt's confident attitude had gained him some leeway, because Pollock stepped aside, motioning with a jerk of his cigar toward the parlor.

Walt shrugged and grinned in passing. "No, just confident. Besides, I am the only agent the BI has in this tinderbox of a border."

He espied the rocking chair and headed straight across the hand-knotted carpet for it. Next to the rocking chair, embers flickered in the stone fireplace. "Sweet Jesus, is this a Bobbin rocker?"

"Belonged to my wife's mother. Hailed from Liverpool, my mother-in-law did." Cigar in hand, the customs agent settled into an overstuff armchair. "Only thing she brought over with her as a diplomat's bride. That and her prized Spode porcelain."

Hitching up his trouser knees, Walt sat almost reverently in the chair, tested its rocking motion—exceedingly smooth—then leaned forward, forearms braced on his knees, his Trilby dangling between them.

"I won't take up a lot of your time, Mr. Pollock. I'm searching out a master spy I believe Felix Sommerfeld planted here within the last year. A sabotage agent, who is most likely behind blowing up a munitions dump in the desert outside Fort Bliss, as well as a troop convoy and a train."

Pollock was a political appointee. He stumped for Wilson's 1912 presidential campaign and in September 1913 received his present cushy $4,500-a-year position of customs collector in El Paso as a reward.

He tapped the side of his huge nose. "If you plan to do any sniffing around you'd be a hell of a lot better off with my schnozzle. You missed Sommerfeld by a week."

"I already learned the German secret service agent passed through here on his way to Mexico City." At the time Walt had been saddled with both covering Pershing's forces, based in the Mormon colony of Dublin in Mexico and snooping out Villa's activities, especially those aimed at border skirmishes.

Walt had learned also, somewhat to his amusement, that Villa loved canned asparagus and rose each morning at 4:00 to jog. And Walt had learned even more. Sommerfeld was here and there in the North American hemisphere, creating havoc.

But it was the German's subterfuge here and now, in El Paso, that interested Walt. "What do you know about the contacts Sommerfeld may have left behind here in El Paso?"

"Oh, certain entities have kept me informed on his activities here," Pollock drawled. "Nothing of an illegal nature was reported."

"Then it's true, you have been collaborating with one of our other intelligence agencies?"

"Truth? Bah. All rubbish. Truth, like right and wrong, is mighty malleable."

Walt shrugged. "Many would agree with you."

"But not you?"

He cast Pollock a rueful smile. "I can only speak for myself. Without rules for right and wrong, I believe this planet would be one of sheer chaos."

Pollock's smile was just as rueful. "It already is. With all the fighting and killing. It's a planet afire. Look, I can tell you this. Sommerfeld's working all three sides, of course. For the sheer challenge of it. Although he cleverly never commits and so leaves no substantial proof."

"Yes, I've noticed he diligently avoids being photographed, even in a crowd, turning his head at the last moment."

"On this last visit, he had a clandestine meeting about twenty miles south of Juarez with Villa and another unnamed agent."

"How do you know this?"

"Japanese agents write their reports in invisible ink that can be developed by heating the paper with a candle. Villa's personal servant is Japanese. He, too, is playing all three sides—for the money. At one point, he'd offered to help us locate Villa on any given day ... for assassination purposes."

Walt said nothing. Listening to what was said—and not said—often accomplished more than pumping for information.

"Our illustrious government is not ready to commit bloody support one way or another to Mexico's two rival factions. But by God, Villa's revolutionaries have obliterated the lives of countless innocent victims, in both United States and Mexico."

He shrugged. "That is why I work for the Department of Justice—and justice will be served."

"Back to following rules and regulations, eh?"

"Invariably, sir."

Pollock shrugged. "My part, as customs collector on the border with Mexico is this—I only keep an eye on smuggling and neutrality violations ..." His last few words were not punctuated by falling intonation.

"And ...?"

Unperturbed by Walt's pressing interjection, Pollock delayed answering. He took an unhurried puff from his cigar first and blew out a helix of smoke. "Since the war began in Europe in—what was it, 1914?—we Americans have watched from afar, hoping to avoid entangling alliances and thinking the 4,000 miles worth of ocean is protection enough."

"Yes, but meanwhile German saboteurs are planting bombs on U.S. ships and targeting munitions plants here on U.S. soil."

"Apparently, Germany wants to buy the rights from Villa for a submarine base in Baja California ... just in case Germany goes to war against the U.S. Their German submarines will start openly sinking American ships."

"This is anticipated."

Pollock leaned forward, cigar bobbing from one end of his mouth. "Look, Stevenson, I agree with you. Most likely Sommerfeld has planted and nurtured a superspy, a saboteur agent, here in El Paso—the very one you are searching for. But you and those other agency boys are wasting your time. Sommerfeld and his agent here will outwit you all."

From down the home's hallway wafted the mouth-watering smell of roast and potatoes. Walt's stomach reminded him he had not eaten all day. And his memory reminded him of a childhood home he had forever lost. "As I said, I am not other agents. I will find Sommerfeld's master spy, Mr. Pollock. And he—or she—*will* face justice."

Chapter Four

The house where Piedad Arellano lived with her mother and sister and her sister's daughter was patched together by crumbling plaster walls, with a rear door that opened onto an alley and outhouse. Either she or her sister flushed the outhouse toilet with water pumped from a nearby well.

The absence of modern creature comforts hardly mattered. Pia counted herself most fortunate. The father of a friend, Flora, had deliberately broken her left thighbone when she was a toddler so she could earn money by begging on the streets. Luckily, six years ago a grocer over on Calle de San Francisco had hired the crippled Flora to work the counter.

Pia slung her *rebozo* and bag onto one of the stubby wall pegs and crossed the kitchen's fragmented linoleum. A time-worn, *lechuguilla-*woven rug failed to conceal completely the gaps.

First, she bent to pet Perro, wagging its raggedy tail in demand for her attention. She had made the mistake of feeding the stray puppy the month before and now could not get rid of it. Worse, it was not house trained.

Never had she seen an uglier mutt. Not much bigger than a prairie dog, it had bug eyes, and an overbite. Only patches of fur spotted its pale hide as a result of mange. Its yapping bark was annoying as fingernails on a chalkboard. In no way did she want to get attached to Perro. Not when even leftovers were necessary to feed the family and a puppy was one mouth too many. So she simply called it Perro, Spanish for dog. A name that kept it at deep caring's distance.

Next, she leaned to kiss her mother's cheek. "*Hola*, Mamacita."

Her mother, scraping the stickers off the last of the *nopalito* pads, managed a solemn smile. "*Hola, Mija*. She used the affectionate contraction for 'my daughter.' Except her tone lacked its usual warmth.

Pia was baffled. Not even a loving smile or delighted greeting this evening from her mother? What was amiss?

Six-year-old Rosita was wedged between Josefina's knees but managed a gape-toothed grin. Josefina was brushing the tangles from her daughter's inordinate length of hair, of which Rosita was inordinately proud. "¡*Hola*, Tia Pia!"

Pia blew the child a kiss, "Hey, Rosita Bonita,"

"I want red hair like yours." Rosita's bud lips pouted. "And I don't like my hair in braids, *Mamá*."

Pia's sister silently and determinedly wielded the hairbrush, nearly bare of bristles, through her daughter's waist-length dark brown hair. At twenty, Josefina was older than Pia by a mere three years but at times seemed as old as their mother. The two women shared the same warm, toasted brown shade of skin, while Pia's was much lighter.

She glanced from their mother back to Josefina. "Do your gloomy expressions have anything to do with the notice that appeared in yesterday's *La Voz de Juarez*?"

Their mother scooped the cactus pads between her work-roughened palms and limped over to the woodburning stove where she dumped the *nopal* into the salted water for parboiling. "Your sister and I were just discussing it."

Pia stole a sample from one of their mother's *empanadas*, wonderfully flavored with its tangy watercress. It grew wild alongside

22

the Rio Bravo. Their mother would transplant it, along with the citrus-minty *yerba buena*, into the galvanized tub out back beneath the casa's spigot, kept dripping to keep the herbs moist.

Of course, out back, in the alley, were also broken beer bottles, tin cans, roaches, rats, refuse, and dog shit, as well as human shit. Bordering the alley's far side were the only four dry toilets to serve five blocks of adobe, corrugated tin, and pasteboard houses.

Mamacita's own, a rented adobe, had never seen a lick of paint and jostled for space with others in the barrio. But, oh, how precious was that strip of straggling grass that separated their adobe's spigot from the alley's blight.

"Mercedes was wailing this evening about the notice," Pia said. In fact, most of the women and few men aboard the streetcar were bemoaning the degrading experience.

Apparently the Public Health Department had advised in local newspapers the day before that any Mexican workers wishing to cross into El Paso beginning the next day would be required to carry a ticket guaranteeing that they had been inspected at a fumigating facility.

Between the passengers' rantings and ragings, Pia had learned little more before the streetcar discharged her at the Avenida de Comercio stop, a little over a block away from home.

Their mother was slicing onion into the boiling water to help tenderize the *nopalito* pads, picked out of season. *"No hay mal qué por bien no venga,* Pia."

"You're wrong, Mamacita" Josefina grumbled. "Nothing good can come out of this bath house's requirements. *Nada.*" She spun Rosita about-face and began braiding her daughter's hair with an agitated flurry of fingers. "I was humiliated. We all were."

Toeing off her loosely-laced work boots, Pia slid onto one of the table's mismatched chairs across from Josefina. Perro crept under Pia's long skirt to snuggle her stockinged feet. Only the chairs and table, pie safe, and a sagging sofa occupied the main room, because the *lechuguilla's* leaves and its stalks, a good alternative for wood, took up most of what space remained.

"So, what happened exactly, Josefina?"

The prominent mole at the indentation of Josefina's upper lip seemed to perpetually weight the corners of her mouth. Today they compressed into a stringent line. Josefina nodded meaningfully toward her daughter and told Pia, "Not now."

'Now' turned out to follow a short and silently tense dinnertime, interrupted only by the clank of tarnished cutlery. Josefina returned from tucking Rosita into the narrow bed the two shared. The room's other bed was their mother's. As the casa had only that one bedroom, Pia slept on the sofa.

Their mother was, as always, busy weaving her *lechuguilla*, when at last a beaten-down Josefina returned to sit with them at the wobbly table,

Like the one table leg that was too short, so was their mother's leg. The year after Pia was born, her mother had contracted the polio virus. It had withered her right leg. Marta Arellano was only thirty-nine, but Pia thought her mother looked fifty-nine, if not older. Maybe because her heavy hair, knotted at her nape, had gone completely gray overnight—a night of which she would not speak.

Pia was poring over her *Roget's Thesaurus*. For her, it was a mark of civility. She had an insatiable appetite for information. When she could manage to leave early from whatever job she currently held, she attended night classes along with a cadre of characters—like an organ grinder, a cigar shop girl, a down-and-out attorney, and a pool hustler. Offered at the cathedral by Father Ignacio, the classes included mathematics, science, and literature.

She closed the thesaurus and folded her arms on the off-balanced table. "Was this ... this fumigation facility ... was it that awful, Josefina?"

The silence stretched too long. "Well?" Pia reached for her terracotta *jarra*. The *café de olla* was thickened with cream, dusted with cocoa powder and cinnamon, and sweetened with *piloncillo*. "Have both you and Mamacita lost your tongues?"

As there was no electricity, an oil lamp suspended from one of the low smoke-blackened beams lit the strained faces of the other two women. Usually this was the time of evening when the three gathered to relax and exchange the day's events.

During the weekdays, while Josefina worked at the Kohlberg Cigar Factory, just across the bridge in El Paso, their mother cared for Rosita of the red-apple cheeks and Rapunzel-long hair.

On Mamacita's lap was layered the long, green *lechuguilla* leaves. They were tough, and occasionally Marta's fingers still bled as they wove the fibers, so she kept a hand rag draped from her spindle chair's ear. "All Mexican workers crossing the bridge into the United States must now be inspected for lice. Everywhere, even our private parts."

"What?" Pia thought she must have misunderstood.

The ends of Mamacita's mouth tugged down the faint grooves at either side, so that her face appeared more boxy than oval. "Your sister can tell you the details."

Josefina added a liberal dose of tequila to her café de olla, took a sip, tipped back her head and swallowed.

She was still pretty, despite the weight she had put on after Rosita's birth. Like their mother, Josefina looked older than her years, twenty hard ones. Her right cheek was so swollen with an infected tooth that the brown mole appeared to be tugged slightly off center of her lip's indentation.

She stared up at the front door's low ceiling, where a ribbon of flypaper dangled from the sooted and cracked plaster. "After our streetcar passed more than half-way across the bridge this morning ... close to the Rio Bravo's opposite bank ... one of the custom officials ordered us to get off and go down a set of stairs."

She took another swig of her tequila-drenched coffee. Waiting for what may come next, Pia felt like her breath was stoppered in her throat.

When Josefina did speak, her voice was hushed, as if entering Catedral de Nuestra *Señora* de Guadalupe. "We were ordered to undress. One Public Health officer took our clothes away to be steam cleaned. Another inspected us ... for lice, like Mamacita said ... everywhere. They sprayed our bodies with ...."

Her voice cracked like the ceiling plaster, but no tears glistened in her sightlessly upstaring brown eyes. "At last, our clothing was returned. They had been sterilized ... our shoes, too ... and dried in a *secadora*."

Pia's mouth twisted. That explained Mercedes's garbled account of her melted shoes.

Their mother selected another long *lechuguilla* leaf from her lap. She appeared engrossed on plaiting the mat taking shape as a sandal sole, but her words issued like hissing steam from the tea kettle.

"The *chisme* going round the barrio ... it is said that some of the inspection officers took secret photographs throughout today ... that photographers, they installed one of those portable printing presses at the bridge to sell these picture cards ... that they are now being passed around in the cantinas ... that soldiers from both Fort Hidalgo on this side of the river and Fort Bliss on the other are paying for those photographs."

A sour taste was backing up nauseatingly in Pia's throat.

"Those of us who passed the official's inspection," Josefina continued tonelessly, "we redressed and were issued a ticket."

Pia asked, "What do you mean a ticket?"

Their mother did not look up from the sandal sole she was weaving. "It means the holder is free from lice and doesn't have to be inspected again for another eight days."

A slow simmer was building to a boil in Pia. "What? We have to go through this ... this indignity ... every eight days?" She could not imagine how her sister and the other workers had endured such debasement.

Josefina thudded her *jarrita* on the table so hard that its uneven leg tilted again, and the terracotta cup's remnants splashed like teardrops. "What would you know about indignity or humiliation, Pia?"

Pia's stunned glance darted from her sister to their mother, who uttered no reproof but merely took the washrag from the chair's ear and dabbed at the coffee splotches.

Pia was stung. In her memory, their mother seemed always to

coddle Josefina. Even now, while Pia's meager wages contributed to the monthly rent and food, a larger portion of Josefina's went toward her daughter's care. Nicer dresses than either Pia or Josefina had ever owned. And shoes. As children, Pia and her sister had run barefooted most of the time on the Heinrich estancia and in its fields they toiled the few hours they were not in school.

"I wasn't the one who got pregnant out of wedlock at thirteen, Josefina."

Immediately, she repented her meanspirited words. In the next instant, she was stunned again, this time by her mother's stinging slap. Pia's fingers went to her cheek, feeling the searing heat flushing it. Her mother had never hit her; had not even spanked her. Her lids shimmered with tears.

Surprisingly, Marta's lip quivered, and she looked about to cry herself. Her work-aged hands covered her face.

"Tell her, Mamacita." Josefina's voice ground like the kitchen's *mano* against *metate*. "It's time Pia knew. It's time to stop protecting Mamacita's Precious One."

Pia glanced from one woman to the other. "Tell me what?"

"Why do you think we live in this hovel?" Josefina's words were spittle.

"Sssh," their mother said, "you'll wake Rosita."

Obediently, Josefina hushed her voice, but her tone was a snarl. "My Rosita is not only your niece, Pia—she's your half-sister."

She blinked. Was this a riddle? Josefina's steady glare belied that, but that glare also seemed to stretch the skin around her eyes so tightly the lids surely would split at the corners.

Pia puzzled through the time around Rosita's birth. Before that, when Pia was ten-years old or so, Josefina had been a skinny thirteen-year-old, with a growing bump on her stomach. And a silent, sullen face.

Why? To Pia, life had not seemed that harsh at Don Horst's hacienda. Certainly not as impoverished as theirs was here in Juarez.

Like other valued house servants, their mother had been allotted her own itty-bitty adobe at Estancia Cascada. Josefina and Pia attended its school with other servants' children residing on the hacienda's immediate property.

Comprising eight million acres, Estancia Cascada was Mexico's largest cattle ranch. More than a thousand employees worked throughout Don Horst Heinrich's kingdom. Had one of the Estancia Cascada's young *vaqueros* gotten Josefina with child?

No, not if Rosita was also Pia's sister. That could not be. It would have had to have been a relative. But Mamacita never spoke of any relatives. Her lips were stitched as closed about her past as were any of seams of her *lechuguilla* handicrafts.

Marta also had been but barely fourteen, a servant girl, as well, when she gave birth to a stillborn. Then the next year to Josefina. Following that, another baby, a boy, who died in infancy. Then Pia. And next, another boy, Vicente, who died of cholera at three.

As rapidly as one of those new electric cash registers, Pia calculated back in her memory. She recalled male visitors at their casita, but none who came periodically, certainly none whom she could remember coming inside the casita, other than El Patron. Don Horst always patted her on the head and told her that her red hair and feisty spirit reminded him so much of himself.

"Don Horst?" she gasped. "He fathered Josefina—and me—*and* Rosita?"

Marta's heavy utterance was more a banshee's moan. Her hands covered her face, and *lechuguilla* rustled to the floor.

"Si, but I had no idea what he had done." Their mother raised eyes cracked with crimson, like red ink spilt on a shattered mirror. "After I discovered Josefina was with child by Don Horst … after she told me he had cornered her, on her hands and knees scrubbing one of the hacienda's bathrooms … I realized it was too late for her. But you … still working the fields with the other children … for you there was hope."

"*Esperanza de qué?*" Josefina wailed.

"Hope for a future for reach of us. I was determined Pia would not

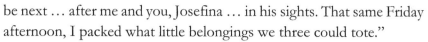

be next … after me and you, Josefina … in his sights. That same Friday afternoon, I packed what little belongings we three could tote."

Josefina clapped the heels of her hands over her ears. "Mamacita, no!"

Their mother was not to be stopped. "The truth has to come out, Josefina. *Entonces*, Pia, I caught us a lift with the Estancia Cascada's foreman. Carlos Herrera was driving up to Juarez to see his mother.

"Carlos and I shared our first kisses with one another. We had been sweet on each other since we were *niños* and conscripted to bring in firewood. From then on, we also worked barefoot together from sunup to sundown digging up the field's *cebada* used to make Don Horst's cerveza. Hail, sun blisters, mosquito swarms, snake-infested rainwater … it did not matter.

"But later, after my first bloodletting, when Horst Heinrich began paying his visits, Carlos understood I was El Patron's property. Horst was wild about me." She tapped her temple. "Loco. He could not keep his hands off me. But absolute power … it had depraved him." She shrugged. "Once safe in Juarez with you two, I changed our name to Arellano." She crossed herself. "*Gracias a Dios*, Don Horst has no idea about Rosita."

Josefina shot to her feet. "It's over with, Mamacita. Done. No more talk."

Swallowing with difficulty, Marta ignored her. "I later learned my Carlos had been taken by surprise months later. At the estancia's spring roundup, as an example of absolute power to Estancia Cascada's employees, Horst had ordered Carlos castrated, along with the bull calves."

Chapter Five

At 7:30 a.m., with the usual clicking sparks from the wires above its arched roof, the sideless Juarez-El Paso streetcar clattered on rails across the Santa Fe Street Bridge. The morning's chilly light was weak, like Pia's present temperament. She could feel the tension creeping into her muscles. Her usual pluck was deserting her.

When she and Josefina boarded the streetcar fifteen minutes earlier at Avenida de Comercio, catty-corner from Trujillo's *Farmacía,* the open coach was already filled with thirty workers, almost all young girls. Gallantly, a few males forwent seats and clung to the running board's rail support.

Usually, while waiting for the streetcar, the young men would be wolf whistling at the maids, who would appear not to notice. They would be gossiping in clusters like chickens in the coop. Skinny dogs would be barking, cats would be slinking among the gutter's refuse, and vendors would be setting up their displays while calling raucous greeting to one another.

30

But, no, an eerie silence fogged the approach to the international bridge now. If anxiety had an odor, it was the smell emanating from the passengers who did not possess the precious bath house ticket. Within minutes, the streetcar would cross the midway mark of the long bridge.

In the back of the streetcar, Josefina and Mercedes sat at either side of Pia. Both girls clutched the oblong piece of cardboard guaranteeing they had been processed at the fumigating facility and were free of lice.

Josefina's *rebozo* enshrouded her like a mummy. She sat on the streetcar's wooden bench with a stiffness that radiated both uneasiness of the approaching stop and a life-long resentment of Pia that had finally erupted the night before.

Siblings argued, Pia understood. As children, she and Josefina had occasionally wrestled and pummeled one another. Yet they had, also, pummeled any kid who threatened the other sister.

But this ... this turbulent energy vibrating off Josefina ... it was directed, not at the United States government, but at Pia herself. All these years, and somehow, imperceptibly, Josefina's sisterly devotion had converted gradually to vinegar. How had Pia failed to notice? Why had she not questioned how she came by her red hair?

Her stomach was roiling. Staying home was not a consideration. Pia's employer would be in a tyrannical rage if she failed to show up for work that morning. Worse, because *Señora* Adelaide was hosting a fundraiser that evening, Pia was once again to nursemaid the four-year-old Richie.

She would be sacked without backpay. Maids were too easy to come by.

Besides, sooner or later, Pia would have to acquire that valuable eight-day ticket. The only pay-worthy jobs were across the Rio Bravo in the United States. Every day hundreds upon hundreds of Mexican citizens crossed the border into El Paso to work in its fields, factories, and homes.

The last twenty years of revolutionary fighting back and forth across Mexico had taken a bloody toll. The only hope for a decent life was across the muddy brown river flowing below the streetcar tracks.

The tracks ran in only one direction toward Paradise, represented by the United States. They returned in the other direction via the Stanton Street bridge to the squalor with which she was familiar in Juarez. Workers and visitors had crossed and returned freely across that river … until now. And Heaven's Gate was this new Inspection Station.

She could do this. She could endure this. Just ignore the officials' probing hands. Think of something else. Of the swaggering Amado García with his easy smile.

For months now, the good-looking and strapping young man had been eyeing her on those Sundays when the two sexes paraded in opposite directions around Juarez's *Plaza Constitución*. Discreet inquiry revealed him to be a twenty-one-year-old bricklayer from over in El Paso. But his passion was drawing.

The Saturday night before last, he had claimed a dance with her at the Public Hall. Though they drew closer than tradition called for, their bodies still barely brushed. "One day, I shall also draw you—on a wall for all to admire," he had bragged. He had drawn close enough for her to smell his Aqua Velva aftershave.

Oh, there were other handsome young men who flirted and occasionally called upon her, but they had none of his charisma.

Then, five days ago, by sheer good luck, the wife of Bartolomé Cardenas, Pia's latest employer, had hired Amado to finish an addition to their majestic mountain mansion, referred to by the public as Chateau Cardenas.

Yesterday, he had boldly winked at Pia when she tossed out a bucket of water she had used to clean the home's windows, all forty-seven of them. She had counted them. And that had not included the stained-glass leaded windows in the dining room ceiling.

Returning home from work this week, she had been so tired that it had been difficult to recall the feeling of Amado's sweet passion with its promise of life stretching in front of her.

All too often, she dozed off on the streetcar rides back to Juarez.

To stay awake, she frequently visualized one day being a grand lady and mistress of a mansion like Adelaide Cárdenas's. Pia imagined running her fingertips along a balustrade, gleaming with beeswax, of listening to the tinkling of crystal chandeliers, stirred by a breeze drifting through open double-paned windows, to feeling a cool marble floor beneath her bare feet.

That kind of daydream was an absolute impossibility today, not with the moment at hand, the looming indignity.

Well past the midway point on the bridge, a pot-bellied man with a metal badge that proclaimed him a U. S. Customs Agent boarded the streetcar. He began asking for fumigation tickets.

"Off, off—¡*bájense!*" he waved to those unfortunates without one, indicating they were to fall in line behind the last load of passengers who had already formed for inspection in the plant below the bridge.

Throat constricted, she stood. Behind four other young women, she reluctantly edged toward the streetcar step-off to the platform to join the line. She got that far, to the step-off—and her feet grew roots. Heart pounding, she stared over her shoulder at the surly officer. "I can't. I can't be inspected."

He shrugged. "Then take a hike back to Juarez."

"Give me back my five centavos fare, first."

The custom agent's weary gaze ran the length of her, took in her shabby attire, and returned to stare her down. "That's your problem, not the United States'. Take it up with your Mexican ticket booth vendor."

From behind, Josefina groaned out, "Pia, for Christ sake, don't make trouble for us. Mercedes and I will wait outside for you."

Biting her bottom lip, Pia stepped from the streetcar. Her heart misfiring, she followed the other four females down the iron-grated steps leading from the bridge to the inspection building below.

There, the federal health officer in charge was separating the passengers waiting in line. Men were sent down one corridor, women another, and the children to another. Surely, their pitiful and frightened outcries at being parted from their parents wrenched the coldest heart.

What if one of them were Rosita?

But Pia had little time to spare in concern for the *niños*. She found herself grouped with several women and herded into a stuffy, damp room that smelled of new paint and harsh chemicals … and silent fear. Oblong, horizontal windows were set high in the tiled walls.

Below the windows, several women, looking officious in their white jackets and wearing rubber gloves, awaited the newest arrivals.

One older, brown-skinned woman with heavy jowls ordered, "*Todos ustedes, quítense la ropa y los zapatas. Pogan su ropa en la canasta.*" With a jerk of those jowls she indicated two rolling wire-basket carts, one in which the women were to put their clothing and shoes and the other for personal belongings.

Pia worried if any of the staff rifled through those belongings. But her *bolsa* contained only a few paltry coins, and surely her *Roget's* would hold no appeal for thievery.

She was not alone in suffering the demoralization of disrobing in front of others. Yet each woman, gaze trained on the floor's square tiles, had the consideration to spare the others embarrassment by refraining from looking around. Or maybe it was their abject degradation that kept their heads bowed.

Next the female officer barked, "¡*Hagan una fila!*"

Pia filed third in the forming line. She crossed her arms over her breasts, puckered with the chill of humiliation.

One of the female public health officers, a *gringa*, approached her. She squinched closed her eyes. Surely, her heartbeat accelerated to that of a hummingbird's.

Too soon, she felt rubber-cased fingers poking through her mass of curls to inspect her scalp, checking her eyelids, probing behind and in her ears. Next, each of her arms was lifted and fingers combed her armpit hair. Then, worse, her pubic hair.

But when the invasive fingers slipped between her buttock cheeks, their muscles bunched in resistance. Her lids snapped open and she spat in English at the attendant. "Don't you dare touch me there!"

The astonished woman paused uncertainly, then moved on past

her to the woman behind Pia. She risked a peek over her shoulder. The scrawny woman was shivering, more from humiliation than the cold.

Next, apparently the head official, a white-as-bleach woman wearing horn-rimmed glasses, passed along the line. Her magnified eyes scrutinized each nude woman. Here and there, randomly it seemed, she singled out an agonized soul to form into another line. And Pia was among those six or seven. Baffled, she moved along with those few directed into yet another room.

"Looks like we drew the short straws," said the haggard female next to Pia. Though, the young woman was likely not much older than Pia, the woman's face and neck and hands were sun-leathered and creased with dirt, indicating she was probably a migrant field worker.

"Why?"

"There's a likely reason this is called the gas chambers."

"But I had no lice."

The grisly grin the other woman displayed was also bleak. "No, you had *huevos*."

Gumption certainly was not what Pia was feeling. This room had no windows. Two more public health agents, the lower portions of their faces concealed by a mask, approached with handheld cannisters.

Pia, now first in line, was shocked when she was sprayed with some kind of cold acid chemical that smelled of kerosene and some other unidentifiable substance. The milky white fluid ran over her head and shoulders, sluiced between her breasts, pooled at her sunken navel and puddled around her bare feet.

The weathered woman, next in line, began to cough from the strong stench of the chemicals. One of the public health agents chuckled. "Gets 'em every time."

The experience could get no worse. *Gracias a Dios*, it was over for Pia. She wanted to weep with relief.

But she was wrong. The defilement was not over. At the room's far end awaited yet another attendant beside a narrow table piled with official looking documents. She was wielding one of those new razors powered by electricity.

Pia realized her head and hairy body parts were about to be shaved. Like a grenade, fury exploded all prudent thoughts of dutiful submission. Apoplectic with rage, she charged to the table, and dumped it over. The shocked agent scrambled to right the table and collect its scattered contents. Pia did not hesitate but shoved open the double doors behind the table.

The doors led to a dressing room. In it she located the hamper, empty of all but those remaining articles of clothing of the fumigated few.

She found hers along with her work boots, still warm from steam sterilization in the *secadora*. From the other basket, she plucked her *bolsa* from a scramble of possessions. Rapidly, she dressed, not even bothering to lace her boots or check her *bolsa*'s contents, then stormed outside and up the metal stairs.

There on the bridge, Mercedes and Josefina were waiting, uneasiness stamped in their tight lids and lips. "At last," Josefina breathed. "We can go now. The next streetcar is just arriving."

"Where's your ticket?" Mercedes asked Pia.

"I didn't get it."

"What?" the two squawked in unison.

The streetcar's wheels squealed to a halt on their railings. The first of the passengers stepped off, a squat, dark-skinned pregnant woman, most likely a Tarahumara Indian. Pia made a beeline toward her. "Don't go inside. Don't submit to this indignation!"

The startled woman's elongated eyes blinked. A few others spilled out behind her, followed by the furious streetcar conductor.

Pia's hands balled. "We are better than this. Better than cattle in a slaughterhouse."

The conductor prodded her shoulder. "Go on. *Sal. Pronto.* You're holding everyone up."

Caught off balance, she clutched the car's railing and balked. "No! I demand my five centavos back!"

The conductor's face flushed beet red. "What you are going to get is kicked back all the way to the Mexican side of the bridge."

Behind her, Josefina cried out, "¡*Ay, ay, ay,* Pia! For once don't think about yourself. If anything, think about Rosita and me and Mamacita."

"I am." Fear made her reckless. She charged back up inside the streetcar and began battering its motor console with her fists. All over a stupid five centavos.

"You crazy cunt!" From behind the conductor grappled with her waist, trying to jar her loose from the console.

"Pia!" Josefina screamed from the bottom of the streetcar steps. "Stop it!"

She ignored her sister's pleading and the alarmed conductor's efforts to restrain her pounding fists. She wrenched the console with its controls from its anchorage. She held it aloft. "Who's with me?"

Myriad voices from among the thirty or so passengers, most of them female, mushroomed into savage screams. Collectively, they tumbled along with her—and the conductor—out of the sides of the streetcar.

Pia hopped back from the impact of the human flood that swept the conductor along with them. Cold air smacked some sense into her, and she halted abruptly. This was madness. Nothing good ever came from opposing the *norteamericano* authorities.

Other young women surged past her to attack nearby motor cars. One housemaid ripped at an automobile's isinglass rear window, another yanked at a vehicle's lamp while another attacked its horn, and yet another clawed and tore at a roadster's canvas top. A young man's voice yelled out, "¡*Viva* Villa!"

Their fury was contagious. Console in hand, Pia made a break through the throng for the bridge, only to trip over a young woman who was struggling to stand again. Pia felt her right knee scrape the pavement, then she regained her balance. She shot out a free hand and tugged the other woman upright—Pia's frowsy friend Mercedes, no less. "Have you seen Josefina?"

The buxom young woman shook a dazed head and shoved flyaway hair from her face. "No, not since—"

Pia spun away and rushed to the bridge railing. She leaned far enough over that she could see Mexican workers lined up below, waiting outside the fumigating plant for their turn to be inspected. "*¿Qué pasa con todos ustedes?*" she yelled down and chucked the console. "Don't be stupid sheep!"

Only a few heard her. They glanced up with apathetic expressions and spared indifferent glances toward the river where the console splashed down. She groaned and spun back to the ensuing confrontation.

From out of nowhere, hundreds of protestors, composed mostly of young Mexican girls, were surging onto the bridge from both directions. Anxiously, she scanned the young females for her sister.

One of the motormen and a mail coach driver tried to make a break for it back to the American side of the bridge. Half a dozen females clung to the two men, tugged them down, and pounded them. Another motorman running in the opposite direction, toward a Chinese restaurant situated just past the Mexican sentry post, dodged a pitched beer bottle.

Others took up the assault of throwing whatever their hands could latch onto. A Customs Inspector, emerging from the brick fumigation facility below the bridge, peeked his head above the curb cautiously. From her *bolsa*, Pia extracted her lunch's orange and pitched it hard. Just in time, he ducked back down.

She next gave a fleeting thought to hurling her heavy *Roget's Thesaurus*, but it was too precious to her.

From the Mexican side of the bridge clopped horse hooves. At the forefront of his cavalrymen, Murguía the Murderer sat astride his horse. The Mexican general moved forward at a slow but purposeful trot. His Death Troop, which wore insignia bearing skull and crossbones, were known for taking no prisoners for those caught selling ammunition to *Villista*s. They drew their sabers and pointed them at the protestors.

Almost immediately, she regretted her stand, but now she had committed herself. Fear made her lightheaded. She scooped up a stone and threw it. The rock landed harmlessly well in front of the troops.

Behind her, other women rallied with no weapons but the insults they began to yell and the rubbish they hurled. The blustery morning wind did nothing to cool their anger.

Nearby, another streetcar insistently clanged its bell, intent on churning through the chaotic melee. Berserk, Pia ran ahead toward the American side. She flung herself down over the tracks in front of the oncoming streetcar. Its sonorous bell now clang a wild alarm.

Strange, although she lay across the cold railings like a stretched and quartered victim on the Inquisitor's rack, she felt merely the pain of a small rock jutting beneath one shoulder blade. But she could smell the sour, sweaty odor of her fear.

She could also feel the rails beneath her vibrating with the streetcar's thunderous advance. ¡Oh, *Jesucristo, Jesucristo, Jesucristo*!

Chapter Six

At 7:30 that morning Walter Stevenson was breakfasting at Hotel Sheldon's downstairs cafe with Colonel Robert Michie and Ed Bigelow, news editor of *The El Paso Herald*.

The café, more than half filled with businessmen, was a male enclave—inaccessible to females. The clank of silverware and clink of porcelain competed with chatter.

"Let me tell you, ain't nothing blissful about Fort Bliss, fellows," joked Bobby. He was of middling height and thinner than a bed slat. Even he admitted surprise as how at twenty-eight he had run the gamut in a mere ten years between raw recruit to Infantry Intelligence Officer, and now second in command on Fort Bliss, due to Pershing's absence in Mexico.

"But the Hotel El Paso del Norte *is* blissful," Bobby continued. "You've got to come along with me and Ellie this evening, Walt. Adelaide Cardenas is hosting a fundraiser there, and you know that, when you are on her guest list, to decline an invitation is tantamount to absence without leave."

Walt scooped clotted cream onto his cinnamon and almond scone, a fare equal to any high-nosed affair put on by his family. "And how did you score that big play?"

Bobby winced at the hot coffee he swallowed. "I wrote a proposal to the Chief of Staff that Fort Bliss be made a permanent cavalry post. Naturally, this will bring added revenue to the area—*et voilà*, Adelaide got wind of my missive."

"You want to know something, the grand dame will have the information." Ed said. Until recently, *El Paso Herald*'s hardnose war correspondent, Ed Bigelow never looked up from his huevos rancheros, its black beans smothered with melted *queso fresco*. As usual, he was badly dressed, notably so. He wore a beige, button-front, cable-knit sweater stained with printer's ink and flecked with dried egg yolk.

Between shoveling bites, he grouched. "Our social columnist is down with a nasty bout of dysentery. Satan hath consigned me to cover Adelaide's fundraiser tonight. Listening to those pompous asses. Would that the gods give me back the days of merely listening to typewriter keys smacking ink onto pages."

Stout, with a large head wreathed by a crown of thinning dark hair and a thick brush mustache, Ed was a workaholic man's man. In his late forties, he was still single and, Walt noted, was painfully shy, with an awkwardness around women. None the less, he was no slouch in the newsroom. His editorial ops found far-ranging arenas from *The New York Evening World* to the *San Francisco Call*.

The three men had met in Colonia Dublin, Mexico, where General Pershing's American Expedition Force was based. Within a couple of months, both Ed and Bobby were recalled to El Paso by their disparate duties.

Undercover, Walt remained, snooping around for the BI and at the same time ferreting out human interest stories for himself. Reuters, AP, Pathé News, and dozens of reporting agencies from around the world ignored his kind of stories as yawn inducing. They were more interested in sending back reports of war that were gruesome and sensationalistic.

Both ends of Ed's brush mustache dipped downward. "Why the

hell didn't you come to El Paso when I told you to, Walt?" He wagged his head. "You're no bonehead, boy. You know better than to let opportunities off the hook."

Brows knitted, Bobby paused in drizzling his wedge of cantaloupe with lime. "When was this?"

"A little over a week ago." Walt took a sip of his hot tea, laced with cream. He was waiting to see what Ed wanted to venture forth.

"I had telegraphed Walt, telling him to hightail it here, Bobby. He could snare an interview with that windbag Emma Goldman. She was stopping off in El Paso to deliver one of her anarchist speeches."

The same day Walt received Ed's message, he should have caught a ride on one of the AEF's convoy's headed for El Paso. Common sense dictated that decision. How to explain to his two friends that his instincts, steered by experience—subtle signals from his parents but words withheld—directed him to dog the spy-handler Sommerfeld, bound for Mexico City from El Paso.

Not that Walt's instincts were unerring. His engagement to Cordelia Schuler being one boomerang.

Walt had hitched a bumpy and hair-raising ride on a re-con flight of one of the United States' First Aero-squadron's Curtis JN-3s, also bound in the direction of Mexico City. The Jenny had fabric covered wings and that was all. No compass, no tool kit, no artillery. From 2300 feet below, a Mexican Revolutionary's .22 caliber rifle had shredded a portion of one wing.

Sommerfeld's trail vanished in Mexico City, and Walt felt foolish, chasing after a phantom on a mere hunch that there was a greater story not in El Paso but in Mexico City.

Yet, at least in this instance, it turned out his gut had been right. At the House of Tiles, he lunched with Reginald Armstrong, a British Reuters reporter transferred from covering Pershing and Villa's joustings in the desert and mountains of northern Mexico to reporting diplomatic news in Mexico City.

With a pointed nose over a tiny mustache and small darting eyes, Reginald reminded Walt of a nervous bird. The month before, the

British reporter's ankle had taken a Mauser rifle bullet from an ambush at Parral, Mexico, and Walt had helped him hobble to safety behind a boulder.

"Recently," Reginald murmured, "our British intelligence interceptted a coded telegram from the German Foreign Secretary, Arthur Zimmerman—sent to Germany's ambassador here in Mexico City. I bribed an employee of the Commercial Telegraph Company for a copy of the decoded message."

Walt waited for the waiter to set the bowl of steaming *pozole rojo* before him and depart, then asked, "What did it say?"

"Germany is offering Mexico the states of Texas, New Mexico, and Arizona if Mexico will align with Germany in the Great War."

The spoonful of pozole torched Walt's mouth and burned all the way down. His napkin stymied a cough that was the result of both the spicy Mexican cuisine and Reginald's astounding revelation. "Uh, does the United States know of this?"

Reginald's tiny mustache shifted from one side of his face to the other. "Our Room 40 is in touch with your President Wilson. If Mexico accepts Germany's offer, then I would wager Wilson will have to give in and go to war."

That afternoon Walt caught the first train out for El Paso.

The beautiful border city was a hotbed of insurrection. Here skulked the sick of all races—the curious, the insane, thieves, peddlers, newspaper reporters, and paid government informants from both sides of the border.

And it was here, on the border, that another kind of war was taking place—smuggling. Guns and ammo for opium and morphine. Cattle for American dollars. He had observed that when the Rio Grande was high, arms smuggling declined, but when the river dropped to its usual low level, smuggling increased.

But he was more interested in the valuable information smuggled back and forth. He never contemplated sharing with Ed and Bobby the tumultuous but unconfirmed news of the Zimmerman telegram.

If true, the telegram would invariably come to light within weeks, when Mexico openly declared its allegiance—either to the U.S. or Germany. Experience had taught him the less said, the better. And the less emotion shown, the safer.

Bobby often bantered that the unflappable Walt would make a formidable gambler. As for Bobby, he partook of the Saturday night poker parties with his army buddies in the same all-in manner as he did love or war.

Walt shrugged and with his linen napkin whisked away whatever scone crumbs might have clung to his mouth. "I didn't come to El Paso right away, Ed, because I had committed to following up on another lead."

Before Ed could question what that lead was, Walt told Bobby, "Count me in for this evening's shindig."

"Swell. Ellie and I will pick you up at seven-thirty and—"

Bobby halted, and simultaneously all three men canted their heads. From the upstairs lobby a muffled ruckus cascaded the marble staircase. In sync with Walt and his two friends, diners' napkins were tossed on the table and hats were forsaken beneath their chairs. Ahead of his two compadres, Walt's grasshopper legs took him three steps at a time up to the lobby.

Outside the Sheldon's glass pane windows, dozens upon dozens of the curious were hoofing the mile down El Paso Street toward the international twin bridges.

Dodging the motor cars and hackneys, Walt sprinted ahead, leaving his two compatriots behind. What he beheld at the Santa Fe Street International Bridge dropped open his jaw. A couple of hundred or more shouting people jammed this side of the bridge. More could be seen along its span and even more pouring in from its Mexican entrance.

The majority participating in the street battle were women, while the males, mostly migrant workers, stood on the sideline, urging them on.

Nearby, a dumpy woman, hooded by her *rebozo*, chucked what looked like a brass hubcap at a U.S. Infantryman. She missed, but his horse shied, toppling its rider. The women hooted and attacked the soldiers. They were powerless. The fracas was as vicious as any of the spectacles held at Juarez's *Plaza de Toros*.

At his side, Bobby yelled out, "You're on your own, Walt. I'm returning to the Sheldon. Got to reach Fort Bliss PBX for reinforcements."

Walt nodded distractedly. Stalled streetcars, motor cars, hackneys, and wagons littered the bridge. Even as he watched, the crowd of women quickly swelled to at least five hundred. Dozens of spectators' box cameras were snapping away. Nearby, at the El Paso Laundry Building, a moving-picture cameraman was setting up to film for a newsreel.

Amidst the fray, one female caught Walt's eye. Toward this side of the bridge's terminus, a redhaired young woman sat on the tracks in front of a halted international streetcar. Incandescent with rage, she was swinging her woven bag with ferocity against an El Paso policeman, hunkered over her. She braced her sensible boots against the railing and refused to budge. The policeman lunged for one of her elbows and yanked in an effort to dislodge her from her track-rail defense.

Other jeering females, as well, were following her example and now sprawled themselves across the tracks and elsewhere. But there was something about this young, working-class woman's defiant nature that kept drawing his consideration back to her.

Two policemen now held her by each elbow and, though she dug in her heels, they were hauling her toward the Paddy Wagon, not far from where he stood. At that moment, he realized he had seen the redhead at Union Station.

Her palpable energy was a catalyst's disruptive drive for change. That accounted then for how she captured his immediate interest upon his arrival at the bridge. Satisfied by the explanation, his psyche easily discounted her to move on to the volatile situation at hand.

Huffing, Ed caught up with him. "Damn, my camera's back at the office. Give me your notepad, Walt. This is an opportunity to get a jump on other newspapers."

Without taking his attention from the riot, he withdrew the small notebook from his coat's inner pocket, along with a pencil stub, and passed them to Ed. Walt was not interested in gathering facts. His mind was assimilating impressions emanating from the brawl. The working women's implacable rage burnt as hotly as any Guy Fawkes bonfire.

Something in his peripheral vision demanded his regard, and he glanced that way. At that same moment, before being shoved inside the patrol wagon, the young woman looked over her shoulder, as if searching for someone—and the desperation in her green-eyed gaze drew his like magnet drew steel.

Uncomfortably, he was reminded of the troubadour Guiraut de Borneilh's notable poem. *So through the eyes love attains the heart. For the eyes are the scouts of the heart. And the eyes go reconnoitering for what it would please the heart to possess.*

But that was inscribed in medieval times. Walt also reminded himself that even in this enlightened day and age, old Pennsylvanians still ascribed to the belief that redheads were unlucky, that they had stolen Hell's fires.

Chapter Seven

Even though the day was chilly, that far up the flank of the mountain the sunlight was more intense. A thin coat of sweat plastered the white cotton camisa to Amado García's slender torso, like the thin coat of mud he plastered to the adobe wall of the carriage house. It was being repurposed as a garage for the Cardenas's new Studebaker Speedster.

He paused in floating his trowel and squinted down the mountainside once more. Below, where the Santa Fe International Bridge crossed the Rio Grande, people had been congregating since early that morning like a swarm of ants. The crowd was much larger now. He could make out Mexican and American cavalrymen at either ends of the bridge. What was afoot?

A strike demanding fairer wages? A demonstration about working conditions?

Several years before, Mexican ore shovelers at the local American Smelter and Refining Company had gone on strike, demanding their working time be reduced from twelve to eight hours. The Texas Rangers were staged around the plant and 380 Negro workers were brought in from Dallas to help break the strike.

Like most Mexican Americans, his family had lived south of Overland Street, in the Segundo Barrio, a tenement of adobe structures known as Chihuahita. The year before, because of fear of lice infestation, El Paso's mayor Tom Lea had ordered hundreds of homes razed in the Chihuahita neighborhood. Amado's parents had been among them.

Such was the mayor's rabid fear of germs, he disregarded the El Paso County Medical Society's response that his hygienic concerns were grossly exaggerated.

Amado's potshots at the city's demolition squad had harmlessly pinged their lumbering steam shovels' large blades. Defeated, he and his parents and sisters had stood at the curb, piled with their belongings, and stared at the mound of rubble that had been their home. Dismay, followed by despondency, and finally despair befell his family.

However, another emotion soon surfaced in him, at least. Some kind of turmoil that clamored enough was enough. More than frustration but less than fury. The feeling, somewhere in between the two extremes, maybe indignation, puzzled him.

He could not comprehend why in Mexico, his class of people were treated like serfs. Here, in the United States, life was better ... but not good enough, not when the poor and disillusioned Mexican Americans were corralled into the Second Ward like a remuda of work horses.

A half dozen times now he had attended secret meetings with other social justice activists, held in the newspaper office of one of El Paso's radical publications, *La Reforma Social*.

Ay, caramba, he could barely read! Lacking the higher education of the Mexican Americans attending these meeting, he struggled with some of their phrasings but not their ideals. However, he was too hot-headed to sit and chew the fat, as the *gringos* put it.

Not surprisingly, his perturbance was expressed not only in his interest in crusading for improvements in the community but also in his passion for drawing. As a child, he had drawn on the flaps of cardboard boxes, the tops of tables, and even the walls of his parents' home.

His lighthearted subject matter of a dozing cat atop a pockmarked adobe wall or children jumping rope or an old woman puffing on a clay pipe had in the last few years changed to exhausted water boys at ASARCO's smelter, desolate kids hoeing a cotton field, and hopeless girls selling themselves outside El Paso's Rainbow Room on Texas Street. After his family's Chihuahita home was destroyed, his fifteen-year-old sister joined those desperate females.

Now another passion had entered his life, Piedad Arellano. He had failed to notice her right away, on those Sundays he crossed the river to strut with his macho chums around the *Plaza Constitución*.

How could his artist's eye not have homed in at once on her coloring, a visual expression of her feistiness? The redhaired *gringos* he had seen all had freckles and sallow skin. Her cat-green eyes and fire-red hair against skin the color of warmed honey demanded he sketch her.

And that he had, with colored pencils. On the edges of a bullfight poster, on the back of paint can labels, and—he grinned at this—at the bottom of an old $5,000 wanted poster for Pancho Villa.

He had not seen the young woman all morning, and it was lunch time. Ditching his work gloves and beat-to-shit straw sombrero, he set off toward the rear of the main house. Behind it, the gardener squatted before brilliant yellow poppy buds, whose bed meandered throughout the back acreage. "Nǐ hǎo, Cheng. Have you seen the house maid—you know, Piedad Arellano?"

The old man looked up over his shoulder. His pigtail was as white as plaster, but his stubby frame was youthful, springy like a cricket's. Amado's people decried that the Chinese, recruited for the laying of the transcontinental railroad through The Pass, had stayed on to monopolize the garden, laundry, and restaurants industries, but he had to credit the Chinese for their diligent work ethics.

"No see her today, Amado." They spoke the common language of English, although Amado understood a few words of Cheng's Mandarin dialect and Cheng far more of Amado's Spanish. "You go ask Bao—and wipe boots before entering house."

Amado found Cheng's wife in the kitchen, steamy with boiling water. The tiny woman was chopping heads off fish for lunch. He nodded a greeting. "I am looking for Piedad."

At the sight of him, Bao paused and smiled slyly, revealing a gold tooth. She jabbed a bloody forefinger in and out of the gaping mouth of a trout's severed head. "You want to poke Piedad, yes?"

Heat from embarrassment flushed all the way to the rims of his cauliflower ears. He could not chance even a crude jest reaching his employer. A few days ago, he had landed this job, thanks to his father. As one of El Paso's foremost bricklayers, his father had helped build the original home, only recently bought by the Cardenas.

Word went that *Señora* Adelaide was a perfectionist. With his father no longer able to work, due to his lung congestion from the adobe dust, the German woman had resorted to hiring Amado, sight unseen.

He thought quickly. "No, no. Pia—Piedad—was to show me a basement wall, weakened by a water leak." A feeble excuse, but he did know about the basement from his father—and was aware of something about it the new household occupants most likely were not.

"Piedad, she no here today." Bao jerked her small graying head toward the kitchen's door to the mansion's inner sanctum. "Down hallway you find basement. Second door."

Well, now what? He had to make a show of checking the basement.

He exited the kitchen door and gaped. He had never been in a house of such magnificence: granite floor and marble columns that supported coffered wood ceilings, squares of heavy hardwood paneling, and an expanse of tall casement windows that offered a stunning panorama of El Paso, the Rio Grande, Juarez and the haze of mountains and desert southward.

He started down the hallway and opened the second door on the left, which turned out to be a utility closet choked with brooms, mop, buckets, and cleaning agents.

He resorted to the door on the right. It opened to the stairwell he was seeking. It descended into darkness. He reached up and tugged on the light chain. The bare bulb lit the way to the bottom and a dank smelling room. Old chests, stools, boxes, and other stuff were shored to one side.

Then, in the faint light he saw what he was looking for—wedged off in the room's far corner—one of those low, beehive-like kiva fireplaces. Fallen-in tiles piled against one grungy, blackened side. He crossed to the heap and, stooping, peered behind the customary metal heatshield. With but a little force a panel of the heat shield could be slid to one side—just as his father had recounted.

A gap between the heatshield's panel and the adjacent sooty wall presented barely room enough to wiggle through. He peered over the knee-high, heaped tiles into shadows. He made out a low ceiling beyond. It was supported by railroad ties … this, too, as his father had described.

The tunnel had been used to smuggle Chinese railroad workers banned from the United States by the Chinese Exclusion Act more than thirty years before. Thus, the railroad ties—and the small brick-designed turtle his father had been paid to fashion on one side of the house's exterior. It was rumored the design was reproduced on a building somewhere in Juarez. In Chinese culture the turtle identified a place as a safe haven.

Satisfied, he stood, brushing the ashes and grime from his palms onto his work pants. Unless the basement underwent reconstruction, its secret passage would most likely never be espied. He had renewed respect for his father. The proud man with whom Amado shared his protruding ears might have exaggerated some of his experiences when swigging pulque after work, but this story, at least, proved to be true.

"What are you doing down here?!"

Heart slamming his ribcage, Amado spun around. A woman stood on the bottom stairstep. She could be no other than *Señora* Adelaide. It was not only her slight accent, with her 'what' sounding like 'vaut.' Not even her expensive clothing. Her bossy lift to her chin and narrowed eyes said she was accustomed to taking charge.

"I—I heard there might be a water leak." She was studying him, making him even more uncomfortable, and he stuttered on. "I was inspecting the—this brick wall." He made a vague gesture in the direction of the single wall, clear of storage whatnots—an ideal spot the artistic portion of his brain prompted to paint a portrait of Pia.

One perfectly delineated brow of the thirtyish-looking woman arched. She was not beautiful, but his artist eye saw her as striking with her dark eyes offset by upswept hair as yellow-orange as her flowerbed of poppies. Her strong features hinted she might be the obstinate kind. "I do not believe you," she said. "We had the plumbing inspected when we bought the house last year."

¡Mierda! He needed this job, what with his father laid up, his mom taking in ironing, and his sister taking … well, just taking whatever the Rainbow Room would give her for spreading her thighs in welcome for her next trick. He cast about for an explanation. The closer to the truth the better. "I confess I was searching for a friend also working here, Piedad Arellano."

Señora Adelaide's eyes, nearly black in the bulb's naked light, glinted with withering sweetness. "A friend you say? Well, your friend Piedad did not come to work today."

He fidgeted before the woman's scrutiny. He felt it did not miss his hobnailed brogans coated with dried gray mud and sand, nor his still wispy mustache he had recently started growing. He shifted uneasily. "*Pues*, speaking of work, I'll be getting back to it."

He started toward the stairs, but she made no move to let him past. She was tall for a woman, as tall as he, although he was only of average height, so she stood slightly above him on that first step. He dared to meet her eyes, and he saw their tartness soften to faint amusement. "Go get some lunch first." Her voice gentled. "Amado, isn't it?"

He nodded. He could smell her expensive floral perfume, and it made him pleasantly lightheaded.

She turned then, the ruffled mid-sleeve of one ivory forearm teasing his chest. Lifting the hem of her tubular skirt, she proceed him up the steps. He watched the slight sway of her hips and caught a glimpse of a shapely ankle shimmered by silk hosiery.

His sister had told him that girls fantasized over him, which he thought silly, but *Señora* Adelaide could definitely arouse an hombre's fantasies.

And that thought recalled another fantasy … the smart, saucy, and vivid Pia. He wanted—no, needed—to paint her. Where was she?

A story was in the making. And Walt was following upon the sensation the female rebel had created in that booming border town. He believed in shoe-leather investigation and had coaxed Bobby to arrange passes for them to attend that same day the Mexican court martial of a male in that crowd of rioters.

By noon Juárez Police Chief Maximo Torres had apprehended the unfortunate man—or boy in this case—sixteen-year-old Andres Delgado—who had shouted, "Viva Villa."

The chaps from the nearby state's capital, Chihuahua, namely the current Carranza regime, did not take kindly to that. President Carranza portrayed Villa as a sociopathic bandit in the press. However, many Mexicans in the crowd today had taken advantage of the bath house disturbance to protest the Carranza regime and voice support for his rival Pancho Villa.

When Ciudad Juarez had been under Villa's control, profits from bullfights, boxing, horse racing, and other border vices had paid for many military uniforms, weapons and provision for his revolutionary army. Gambling and alcohol concession which Villa granted to his brother Hipólito had brought in more than $100,000 a year for his troops.

Although six years had passed since Villa first besieged Juarez, in 1911, buildings still could be sighted without roofs, wires still dangled from jagged telephone poles, and some store signs and awnings remained punctured with bullet holes.

Under construction at the time of the siege, the new city hall had gone up in flames, along with the library and post office. So, today a speedy trial was held in the old city hall, the musty *Asuntos Internos Municipales*. The mayor's court was packed, and Walt and Bobby stood in the rear of the backed-benches.

The kid, Andres Delgado, his hank of brown hair still gelled to a stiff peak, sat handcuffed and quivering with fear.

Justice was swift, less than thirty minutes. As a warning, Andres was hanged immediately afterwards from a rapidly erected scaffold in the *Plaza Constitución*.

As if it were a circus, hundreds of Kodaks clicked during the lynching scene. Within hours, Anglo hustlers would be selling the grisly photographs as postcards to post exchanges all up and down the Rio Grande. Revolutionaries in conical hats and adobe-wall executions were popular among American soldiers as mementos sent to families back home.

Sickened by the sight of the slight body, jerking, wetting itself, Walt did a U-turn and stalked off. A puzzled Bobby caught up with his runaway stride. "Why then did you feel the need to attend this?"

Beneath his shoved back coat flaps, Walt jammed his hands in his trouser pockets while fighting back the nausea rising in his throat. "I thought there would be something here that might give me a clue to the leader of the riot, Piedad Arellano."

"Why, I do believe you're more than a little fascinated with this girl, Walt."

They paused for pedestrian traffic at the street corner, and Walt shot Bobby an astounded glance. "Has the mezcal's worm eaten at your brain? I have never met her—only watched as she rained holy havoc on the International Bridge this morning."

That was not the complete truth. His attention had been drawn to her the evening before, at the train station.

Grudgingly, he admitted he found the creature Piedad Arellano about as fascinating as the Devil's Claw. The local desert plant produced attractive, creamy yellow flowers spotted with purple—and painful horn-like burrs. Granted, the Devil's Claw was reputed to have medicinal qualities. He suspected, at least for him, it also contained disorienting toxic ones and should be avoided at all costs.

Bobby clapped him on the shoulder. "Seen that love-stricken look before, pal. Had it plastered to my mug, in fact—the day I saw Ellie sitting in the bleachers, right behind home plate. She and her parents had come to watch her brother play. Otto and I were both on the West Point baseball team. I was its pitcher that day. I couldn't take my eyes off her. I was love struck. I walked three batters and clunked the fourth. After that, I got pulled. I didn't know who she was then, but I knew I would make her my wife."

It was all Walt could do to refrain from rolling his eyes. "Well, Piedad Arellano is definitely not a female I would want for a wife."

"Then, pal, I think you are going to need use of powerful forces—like conjure, juju, mantra, prayer, all that stuff, to combat the power of love."

Chapter Eight

Piedad Arellano … and that was her full surname, nothing to indicate her exact parentage, like Hernandez de Arellano or Arellano de Gonzales or some variant … was a vision of flashing animation in dirtied and ripped clothing.

Walt rose from the metal chair and watched her tomboyish figure saunter into the visitor's room of the El Paso City Jail. Her patchwork ankle-length skirt rippled around her clunky work boots like a fandango dancer's ruffled skirt around strapped heels studded with nails. For an instant, it seemed light flickered around her, like evening's fireflies. He shot an inspecting glance to the overhead light. Was there was a short in its electrical current? But no, it seemed not.

She and two men had been arrested for assaulting a customs officer and an infantryman. He introduced himself and explained he worked for an American magazine and had a few questions about the riot earlier that morning.

Momentarily, her eyes flared and her lips, as pink as carnations, parted in a susurration of surprise—as if their meeting were more a reuniting after a long time. "A protest, not a riot." Eyeing him suspiciously, she slid onto the other chair at the metal table, anchored to the floor.

At three o'clock in the afternoon, the other five tables were empty. The visitor's room stank of fear and desperation and rank body odor. A new jail and courthouse were under construction. Meanwhile, this one—it had to be forty years old—was crawling with roaches. He shook one off his pants cuff, crushing the varmint beneath his shoe heel.

At his disgusted expression, her lips pursed in a smirk. Tauntingly, she began to hum "La Cucaracha." The tale of the dancing cockroach had come out of the initial Mexican revolution's border song.

His own lips surprised him by wavering at their ends, as if unsure whether to edge up or down. What a peculiar young woman she was.

He reseated himself opposite her and folded his forearms on the table. His body language was meant for her to understand he was taking the reins in this meeting. At his elbow was his notepad, although his memory retention was amazingly reliable. "Good afternoon, Miss Arellano."

Her wide, crooked grin was catastrophic to his serious intentions. "Welcome to hell, *Señor* Stevenson. I believe you said that was your name." She propped clasped hands, cuffed at her slender wrists, on the table within inches of his much larger ones.

He felt how his own hands tingled with awareness. "It is."

Without looking directly at her hands he took note that they were small with short fingers and short nails, embedded with grime. A fresh scratch limed with drying blood cut diagonally across the knuckles of her left hand. One prominent cheekbone was puffed and would doubtlessly be blue with bruising tomorrow. She was a wild thing, this one, with no respect for the law.

"You are one of those snoopy reporters, *sí?* Here for a story?"

"You speak English." This did not surprise him, as most border residents did speak both languages. Her melodic Spanish accent ameliorated the harsh consonants of her English. He was bemused that he once again felt that unaccountable and inordinate interest in her.

"And German."

This did surprise him. He feigned a glance at his notes. "Oh, yes. You gave the police Mrs. Adelaide Cardenas as your employer." As Bobby had relayed, the woman was one of the spokespeople for El Paso's German community and was influential among the city's well-to-do.

"No, I learned German from my father, Don Horst Heinrich."

"Sure, buttercup, and I am President Woodrow Wilson."

And she was a prevaricator on a grand scale. German Mexican Horst Heinrich was the largest landowner in all of Mexico. Or had been until Villa confiscated his holdings. Walt chalked off as a mistake his seeking out this young woman for an interview. She was ordinary, after all. He was wasting his time.

He went to signal the pistol-armed guard at the door but her exasperated tsk-tsk tugged his attention back to her.

Scornfully, she eyed his business suit, with its tan suede trimming at the buttonholes and elbow pads. "You are so certain you know what is right?"

"I am certain I know what is right for me. For one, truth. Honesty."

Some of the bubbly seemed to go out of her bravado. "I tell you true, Mr. Stevenson. I grew up at Cascada Estancia, outside the city of Chihuahua, and was schooled alongside Don Horst's legitimate son, Silvestre Heinrich de Salinas. It seems I am one of Don Horst's bastard offspring."

It seems? That in itself was provocative phrasing. She was not certain about such illustrious heritage? But other more important questions clamored to be answered. She was a study, this scrappy Mexican girl, with the uncharacteristic red hair and green eyes. And she was bright to boot.

"Tell me, what specifically happened to you inside the Public Health Inspection Plant to make you lead a riot this morning?"

"A protest," she corrected again. "Not a riot. My sister went inside the bath house the day before. Josefina warned me about the *vergüenza* that awaited." She shrugged narrow, bony, shoulders. "I could not do it, you understand? There are some things, like this shame, the spirit cannot endure."

Cannot or will not? With a forefinger, he nudged his pince-nez back upon the bridge of his nose, which enhanced the focus on her delicate features, a contrast to her bold attitude. "Precisely of what nature was this *vergüenza*, this shame?"

She spoke of the episode tonelessly, sparingly, and he had the feeling she glossed over the more degrading aspects. When she finished, he found himself more curious about her than the nature of the incident.

"How old are you?"

"I know my rights. I want to talk to your Justice Department."

He almost smiled. "The Texas Department of Criminal Justice is at the state capital, Austin. It is as far east of here as is Los Angeles going west. "

He saw her slender throat work up and down. "Criminal, you said?"

He rubbed his jaw. How much to tell her? He asked again, "How old are you, Miss Arellano?"

"Seventeen—almost eighteen."

"People are hanged for less than this, destroying government property and assaulting its employees. The Mexican general hanged a kid on the spot today solely for yelling out 'Viva Villa.' With war fear rampant, what you did could be called sabotage."

This time she gulped audibly. "But I am under twenty-one."

"So was the kid. Besides, if you are under twenty-one, you could escape hanging only if you plead guilty."

Her small chin shot up. Its slight quiver belied her defiance. "No. *Nunca*. Never. Pleading guilty, that will not happen."

"Tell me, what do *you* want from all this?"

"This? This what?"

"This riot you started."

"Protest, *Señor* Stevenson. *Pues*, if we are going down a street of pipe dreams, what I want is a walk in the park, as you *norteamericanos* say." She held out her scuffed hand and enumerated on stubby fingers one by one. "First, I want to get out of jail. Second, I want that damned bath house destroyed. Third, I want a mansion on the hill like Adelaide Cardenas's."

Sarcasm withered his words. "Those are not quite what we *norteamericanos* would describe as a walk in the park."

Her front teeth flashed in another off-centered smile. "For you, a *norteamericano, Señor* Stevenson, you can make at least this one thing happen—get me released from here. I would be grateful."

Here it came, at last. What the Mexicans called *la mordida*, the payoff. His tone was desert dry. "And you will be offering your virginal body to me in payment—at some nebulous point in the future, right?" Already, he was standing to leave, gathering his notepad and trilby.

Her snapped words stopped him cold. "No, I am saving myself for the worthy Amado García. You, who are closed off to feelings, you are not worthy."

He almost smiled at her putdown. "Then what *is* my payoff for providing you with your walk in the park? Merely your gratitude?"

She turned the full force of her scrutiny on him for a long moment, and he squirmed inwardly under her gaze that was both primal and sagacious. She reminded him of an oracle priestess whose prophecy was sought from the gods. She could have been a seductive seventeen or a wizened seventy.

As if reaching a conclusion, she finally spoke. "*Señor* Stevenson, you *feel* this here as I do ... " she thumped her solar plexus with her fist, " ... *siento qué un arco de luz se ha formado entre nosotros, como un relámpago.* Do not deny it."

Momentarily, he was nonplussed. He recovered himself. "Am I interpreting you correctly? You are asserting that I feel a ... a lightning bolt arcing between us ... as you claim you feel?"

She shrugged one shoulder. "Rather than like a lightning bolt to the heart, what you feel for me may be a slow burn." She was looking at him as if he were dimwitted. "Granted, we have nothing in common. I cannot even begin to imagine spending a single day with a starch-shirt like yourself."

He stared at the mischievous curve of her sensual lips and felt his throat acting strangely, tightening then going dry.

"Nor any more likely," she continued on, "could you imagine being saddled with someone as disorderly as I admit I am. But, by helping get me released from here, you get to feel again. Feel good about yourself. And admit to yourself you must feel something special for me, a slow burn though it may be."

The room was hot and stuffy. He jammed his trilby low on his head. "It's your brain that has been lightning struck. And, the only thing I *feel* for you is a wretched heart burn. Goodbye, a*dios, auf wiedersehen*, cheerio, and fare-thee-well. May we never meet again, Piedad Arellano."

Chapter Nine

Soldiers thought wars were won on battlefields, and statesmen thought wars were won at negotiating tables. Adelaide Cárdenas de Zeigel, surveying the throng gathered for the Sunset Heights Library fundraiser, knew differently. Battles were won in bedrooms and ballrooms, as testified by history.

This particular ballroom was the crown jewel of Hotel El Paso del Norte. A million-dollar, 300-room hotel, its ballroom was unequaled anywhere. It was on the mezzanine of the lobby, graced by its immense Tiffany stained glass dome.

She would have preferred to hold the fundraiser on the hotel's roof garden, with its impressive view of El Paso and Juarez's twinkling lights. However, the desert weather was chilly for nearly bared shoulders, as were most of the female guests' that evening.

Her metallic silk brocade gown, glittering with rhinestones and done in shades of royal purple and teal, had a peacock blue netting arranged tastefully at the slope of her shoulders and discreetly at her décolletage. Thankfully, at thirty-one, her breasts were still high, despite having birthed little Richie four years earlier.

Tonight was important. In recent years, she and her husband, Bartolomé Cardenas, had hosted high-toned affairs attended by upper-class Mexican refugees from Pancho Villa's raids—doctors, lawyers, bankers, and millionaire *hacendados*—who had bought homes in Sunset Heights.

These events were not attended by Bart's brother, the stodgy Miguel Luis Cardenas, who disapproved of Adelaide. Not so much because she was a Jew or a German but because she had charmed Bart, the driving force of the two brothers' clothing store, from the family fold.

During this time of revolutionary chaos in northern Mexico, city banks in El Paso had increased their portfolio by 88%. And she and her husband had increased theirs triple-fold—solely because of her.

Gregarious and with a good head for business, Bart made a nice profit as a traveling salesman for the brothers' men's clothing store. But he was reluctant when it came to risk-taking. So, she had made a fortune selling its clothing to Cisco Rodriguez, one of Pancho Villa's suppliers who equipped Villa's Division del Norte.

On one occasion alone, Villa had placed an order for 40,000 pairs of shoes and 40,000 khaki shirts, pants, and hats, when average cost for such a single military uniform was $25.

Nine months ago those glory days ended with Villa's idiotic foray in Columbus, New Mexico. The United States would not tolerate supplying a revolutionary faction in Mexico, either the *Carrancistas* or the *Villistas*, which attacked U.S soil.

Since then, Adelaide had been forced to take chances to maintain hers and Bart's standing in prestigious Sunset Heights. With Rodriguez as the middleman, she occasionally managed to trade arms she acquired from the Winchester Repeating Arms Company to Villa in return for cash and other considerations—cattle hides, cotton, even cans of opium for the addicted wife of a German hardware store owner there in El Paso.

But these shadowy dealings were barely keeping Adelaide's lifestyle afloat.

She exchanged pleasantries with the august guests—Americans, Mexicans, Germans, and other nationalities—all the while wending her way with an engaging smile plastered on her elegantly boned face toward Mayor Tom Lea. He was rabidly anti-Villa, and she was bent on fostering the mayor's continued good will.

Dressed in a polished dinner jacket, Lea lightly swirled the wine in his stemmed glass. On the short side, with a pencil-thin mustache and receding hair slicked back by Brillantine, he was explaining the morning's riot to a cluster of concerned guests. "I had no choice but to open the delousing plant—or else chance spreading the deadly typhus into El Paso."

Her sources said what Lea had telegraphed Washington D.C. was phrased somewhat harsher. *Those dirty, lousy destitute Mexicans could spread typhus into El Paso.*

The mayor had a deeply rooted fear of contracting typhus from Mexican immigrants. He was obsessed with cleanliness and racial and physical purity. How repulsed he would be if he were to discover she was not German Roman Catholic but German Jewish.

Poverty and preservation had taught her the policy of negotiation. And information was its power. When she learned his doctor informed him typhus lice did not stick to silk, she procured through Bart's clothing business a dozen pair of silk undershorts for the mayor, all on the hush-hush, per his request.

"Yes, but in the meantime the Mexicans riot and don't work," complained Alice Sturtevant, a portly matron whose thick neck sported as many ropes of pearls as its chins. "For pity's sake, Mayor Lea, cannot something be done?"

Her husband was president of the El Paso Chamber of Commerce. For all her importance in El Paso, she could do nothing for her sister in Holland, whose family was starving. Following nearly three years of intense combat since the onset of the Great War, European farms had either been transformed into battlefields or had been left to languish as agricultural workers were forced into combat with the Germans.

Adelaide could well sympathize with Alice Sturtevant's decry of the lack of Mexican workers. Her impertinent maid Piedad had not shown for work this morning. Adelaide had to fall back on Bao to care for little Richie tonight, and he threw an unholy tantrum when he learned he was being left with the old Chinese woman.

"Oh, I plan to set an example," Tom assured. "Publicly hang the ringleaders, the ones we've arrested."

One of the men, outside the semi-circle of guests around the mayor but a head above them, inquired, "Does that mean, Mayor Lea, you would execute the lone female—Piedad Arellano?"

Piedad? Her housemaid? Adelaide's eyes narrowed on the tall inquisitor. Behind his pince-nez, he was watching the mayor with an eagle's hooded-eye, unblinking glint. She searched her mental social file but did not recall this guest. He stood between Colonel Robert Michie and his young wife and Ed Bigelow, *El Paso Herald* news editor, those three whom she *had* invited.

This man had not bothered to dress for the gala's formal attire. Everything about him, from his business suit of canvas brown to his pince-nez proclaimed a meticulous, methodical man. Boring and unimaginative. Except that he had made no effort to tame his rowdy brown hair with pomade. That small quirk warned her not to make the mistake of pigeonholing the man.

"Rather a sticky situation, is it not, Mayor Lea?" the uninvited guest continued. His features—a bladed nose between steep cheekbones and a firm mouth that hinted at doggedness—were far too craggy for him to be deemed handsome. "With press attention in this evening's *El Paso Herald*, this redhead rioter could be a threat to stable society if turned loose—but adding her to a public hanging could make her a martyr and start another riot. One with much worse results, nationally and internationally."

Tom Lea shot Ed Bigelow a what-the-hell glance, but the *Herald* news editor merely shrugged. His obviously second-hand dinner jacket stretched tightly across shoulders humped like a mule yoke.

Günther von Kloss, the honorary consul at the German consulate there in El Paso spoke up. "I am in accord with your guests here." His convivial smile swept around the semicircle. His fair hair, tweeded at the temples with silver, was fashionably brushed back from its center part. With a neatly trimmed Van Dyke beard, he was the picture of restrained elegance. "Forget the matter of hangings. Domestic workers and laborers are needed back on the job. Without a cleaning woman, my consulate, for one, is beginning to look like a pigeon house."

"Let me assure you that we have this under control," Tom said. "Our Chamber of Commerce will resolve the issue promptly."

To deflect the tension, she announced with a diamond brilliant smile, "The kissing booth is now open, and Miss Lena Müller has graciously agreed to start off the evening with a kiss in exchange for a donation to the Sunset Heights Library building project."

The distinguished banker's fatuous daughter was pretty enough, and it pleased the proud Solly Müller for her to be doing the kissing booth honors.

If Müller had his way, he would be kissing Adelaide ... and more, but she pretended obliviousness toward his innuendos. Adelaide did not want to outright reject the shrewd banker. Backed by his investment on the side with her, she had cannily doubled their profits by selling barbed wire to the Mexican Federales soldiers and barbed-wire cutters to Villa's revolutionaries.

Meanwhile, Adelaide had another project crop up. She slipped her gloved hand in the crook of the mayor's arm and drew him toward a secluded corner adorned with *macetas* of tall Ficus, far enough from where band members of Fort Bliss' 20th Infantry regiment were tuning up.

Colonel Michie had obliged in providing the musical entertainment for the occasion. As he should. As a member of the Chamber of Commerce's Board of Advisors, she had offered to stage a parade for Pershing's troops, scheduled to return from Mexico to Fort Bliss sometime within the next two weeks. The U.S. military was keeping the exact date hush-hush.

"Tom, I sincerely understand the burden you bear of gentrifying these unwashed masses from Mexico. However, I want you to know I can take care of that sticky problem of Piedad Arellano for you, if you wish."

His brows shot up. "You can?"

She offered up a sigh and, admitting Piedad worked for her, suggested he arrange her bail be put at a high figure. "An out-of-reach amount for mere mortals until the bail can be dismissed and the housemaid then released on personal recognizance ... out of your magnanimity, you understand."

"But that would solve nothing, Adelaide. In no time at all, she would be back on the streets, stirring up trouble. And twenty-four-hour surveillance would be out of the—"

"Tch, tch, Tom." She inclined her bejeweled head near his. "That saucy chit of a girl can be released to *paisanos* of hers, who will take care of her. I know the perfect *paisanos* for the task."

Lea's gazed assessed her meaningful smile, then dipped to run appreciatively over her bosom. "I am in your debt, Adelaide."

She smiled at him. "Good, because I am thinking about raising funds for updating our woeful streetcars and would dearly appreciate your gaining the support of the Knights of Columbus, the Toltec Club—and oh, yes, the Moose Lodge."

She was not at all attracted to the slightly-built man. Whatever attractions she did feel, like her body's reaction to the young Mexican bricklayer this morning, she suppressed. Never would she compromise all that she had managed to achieve in her thirty-one years for a fleeting moment's gratification in toying with the attractive but callow youth.

"Mrs. Cardenas—Mrs. Cardenas!" From behind the kissing booth's counter, Lena Müller was waving her opera-gloved arms.

"Excuse me, Tom." Adelaide patted his arm cordially and glided across the grand ballroom to the kissing booth, erected by a generous haberdasher and his son. The women of the Christian Temperance Union had decorated it with red, white, and blue crepe paper hearts and banners.

In front of its counter waited Horst Heinrich, massive in both height and girth. His curly hair, red as baked brick, was a lion's mane.

The German Mexican and former governor of Chihuahua recently leased the entire top floor of the Hotel El Paso Del Norte, although he nominally was in possession still of his princely mansion outside the capital city of Chihuahua.

Despite being a refugee in the United States, the widower Don Horst continued to wield wealth and power. It was whispered his moral larceny drove his lemon-sour wife to an early death. Doña Soledad had been the sole heir of the illustrious line of the Salinas family, which possessed a fortune from mining ventures in northern Mexico.

In all fairness, Don Horst had increased the family business through other investments ranging from smelting to ranching to vineyards.

Their only child, Silvestre Salinas—his mother's maiden name which he insisted on going by—could be considered good-looking in a flamboyant fashion. He had rebelled against his father's despotic politics. Silvestre now published the *La Reforma Social*. As a rebuttal, the Chihuahuan oligarch had disowned him.

In El Paso, both American and German intelligence watched to see for which side Don Horst would place his bets to get back his land in Mexico, totaling nearly eight million acres.

He bent his ponderous torso over her extended gloved hand. "*Señora* Cardenas, I would be delighted to donate fifty pesos to the Sunset Heights Public Library."

A male's baritone voice announced, "Two hundred pesos from the German Texas Society—but for a kiss from Mrs. Adelaide Cardenas."

Everyone turned in that direction. The handsome Günther von Kloss smiled expansively.

Two hundred pesos? That was a hundred American dollars. What was behind such generosity? A gesture to allay the rampant prejudice right now against German Americans? It had been two and a half years since the war started in Europe. Even though the United States was trying to stay out of it, these days frankfurters were called hot dogs.

Despite an extraordinary experience of giddiness, she allotted only a polite smile. "But of course."

Through discreet questioning on both sides of the Rio Grande, she had learned the forty-year-old Günther von Kloss had but recently arrived in El Paso, having been appointed by the German Foreign Office to the vacant position of Honorary Consular.

She and the customs broker had a lot in common, besides their native country. Although, he exuded refinement in his royal blue tailcoat, he had in fact clawed his way up from a rag seller's son. A risk-taker, a rule-breaker, this golden-hair Apollo was.

Incredibly, she was a distant relation by marriage to the fabulously wealthy Rothschilds. Yet, she had grown up living in Frankfurt's Judengasse in a narrow tenement house little more than three meters wide.

Never again would she live like that. And never again would she tolerate being ridiculed. Nothing greater had riled her than the feeling people were laughing at her behind their hands. She had devoted herself to enforcing respect and deference. Early on she learned to bully back—but in a manner that could not be countered—with a pleasant but sly smile that confounded any opposition.

In Frankfurt, she had been getting nowhere. Speaking Yiddish as she did, she was fortunate to get hired at seventeen to work as an au pair in New York for a Jewish shoe manufacturer and his wife.

She had not realized how tedious and disgusting could be the duties of caring for a family's children. What she did realize was that she lacked the maternal instinct. Better for her never to parent a child.

There in New York, she met Bartholomew Cardenas, who called upon the shoe manufacturer. Bart was easy-going, lavished money on her like crazy, and was crazy about her to the point he did not make an issue of the sad fact she was not Roman Catholic. For that matter, she was not a practicing Jew.

Ten years ago, they married in a civil ceremony. Reflecting on that, she felt she had suffered loss of face by marrying the stocky Mexican mestizo with spindly cabriole legs. But then one did what one must in order to forge ahead.

She took Lena's place behind the counter. "I would be delighted, Mr. von Kloss." She signaled to the photographer Ed Bigelow had provided to cover the evening's event, but the big camera with a black cloth shrouding it was as outdated as the fuddy-duddy news editor was.

She waited until the photographer was ready then leaned across to offer up a chaste kiss to Günther von Kloss. At his kiss, lingering playfully on her lips, her knees nearly buckled. How could this be? This … in contrast to her experience with Bart?

She tolerated his rather repetitious technique in bed. And afterwards, his hastily swiping of any excess fluid from himself with the bedsheet before turning over to snore loudly. But how could a mere touching of lips from this German imposter impact her so completely?

Amidst the guests' applause, the tinkling of champagne glasses, and sociable chatter, she recovered herself and managed a courteous smile. "Thank you, Mr. von Kloss. On behalf of The Sunset Public Library, we are most grateful for your charitable donation."

Quickly, she cued the band to launch its music program and made to escape. But von Kloss was not to be put off. With a cant of his head, he extended his arms. "Then you will honor me with this dance, Mrs. Cardenas?"

Caution warned her to decline on whatever pretext. She could not allow sentiment of any nature, especially a strong surge of feeling like this, to jeopardize her position.

Besides, the custom broker's position as an honorary consul was not quite as prestigious as that of a career diplomat. Honorary consuls were usually resident aliens of the host country, where they lived, worked, and paid taxes. They were designated by a foreign government to look after the affairs of its citizens in the host city.

Nevertheless, she nodded and, coming around from behind the counter, glided into his arms. The sedate and popular *Sunshine of Your Smile* was playing. A few other couples followed suit.

He inclined his head so close to hers that his golden mustache, waxed to knife points, brushed her cheek. His breath whispered of both cigarette smoke and mint. "What do you want from life, Mrs. Cardenas?"

No perfunctory chitchat? No unoriginal compliments? Her feet stuttered, and so did she in excusing her clumsiness. "Uhh, my apologies, Herr von Kloss."

The flare of his heavy lids warned of her gaffe. With Germany rolling across the European landscape, *Herr* would be a verboten form of address. He lowered his voice. "Günther, please." He turned inquiring eyes on her flustered face. "So, what is that you most want, Adelaide?"

His familiar use of her given name did not distract her. She answered honestly, without a single hesitation. "To be in complete control of my destiny. To never again have to kowtow to the elite, whether in El Paso or New York or Frankfurt."

"To achieve that status would require ... what?" His deep-toned whisper at once coaxed and soothed.

"Power—money, the usual. What we all want." Briefly, she closed her eyes, seeing the fairytale palace, Neuschwanstein. She was so weary of El Paso's lacerating sun. The vision of golden autumnal sunlight or winter's snow sparkling against the pale limestone walls of the Bavarian alps palace beckoned.

"I can practically assure you of those two resources—power and money. More power and money than even you could possibly attain in this backwash of civilization."

When she found her voice, its single emittance sounded like a rusted, raspy file. "How?" Scenes from years of finessing, contriving, and beseeching merely to get her this far flashed behind her dazed gaze.

"You can accomplish that by committing your loyalty and devotion to our motherland."

She temporized. "I don't understand. I am a naturalized American now."

"Yes, you do understand. I cannot provide all the details, but Germany is offering to restore to Mexico their original territory of

Texas, Arizona, New Mexico, and California if Mexico will align with Germany's side in this war. With both German blood and a Mexican husband, you could be at the summit of the Bavarian Alps within the next year."

That was, if Germany won the war. She stalled answering until the next pattern of dance steps separated them from the nearest couples, and even then her voice sounded so unlike her aggressive temperament, rather a timid tone. "What would I ... what would it require?"

"Setting up a wireless telegraph station in your attic."

She hoped her pleasant expression covered her astonishment. "For what purposes?"

He shrugged easily. "For receiving messages—from such a long distance as, let's say, Berlin."

"That's impossible. Out here in the middle of nowhere?"

"Granted, the telegraphic plant is exceedingly costly but it is powerful and equipped with an audion detector. Your two-story house, sitting on your bleak mountainside as it does, would suit perfectly."

"What you are ... well, I ... " she was trying to assemble a coherent response. "I know nothing about telegraphy."

"You would not have to. I would attend to the telegrammed messages by way of courtesy calls on you. After all, we are compatriots—that would not be unusual or arouse suspicions."

She halted abruptly, and the silk brocade of her dress swished about her ankles. "If you know all this, then why do you not do it yourself?"

"I can and do send the occasional coded cables from my law office, but the range is limited, mostly to other—sources—throughout western Texas and northern Mexico. And I do not trust communication by telephone. Their wires are too easily tapped."

Propelling her back into the dance step, he nodded discreetly at the tall man wearing the pince-nez, observing from one corner. "Besides, I have to contend with reporters and journalists, like Walter Stevenson over there. As a German resident alien, I am often watched. But, worse as merely an honorary consul, I have only limited immunity in this country."

She thought about so perilous an undertaking. Contraband smuggling along the border, in which she participated, was commonplace. Were not black-market operations common anywhere in the world, with most law enforcement looking the other way? The U.S. Collector of Customs Lionel Pollock certainly did. She slipped him enough *mordida*.

But treason was something else. It could command the death penalty.

She halted in mid-step again. She would be far worse off if caught than Günther von Kloss. A shiver ran from the base of her spine up to her nape, where her skin warningly pricked her fine hairs. Curious, because earlier her betraying body had reacted in a bestirring way to his lips' mere brushing of her own.

Yet did she owe the United States any loyalty? Its moralism was outright hypocritical, and if anyone had a nose for smelling our hypocrisy, she did. While amassing great wealth by selling war supplies to the Allies—Britain and France—the United States turned a blind eye to Britain's blockade, which violated international law and was starving hundreds of thousands of her people in central Europe.

Hand at her bosom, she feigned breathlessness from the taxing dance. But that breathlessness came from something else, something she had never experienced—beguilement. She stopped a liveried waiter and captured two Waterford flutes from his tray. Passing one to Günther, she hoisted her own trumpet glass and smiled up at him. "*Mazel Tov!* To our success."

Chapter Ten

Pia thought it ironic that the grubby *lechuguilla* mat atop the metal bars that constituted her jail bed bore the identical weave pattern that was her mother's, with its spirit line around the edges assuring her mother's creativity would not be trapped within the mat's borders.

Here Pia was, the second day in the El Paso City Jail, and neither her mother nor Josefina had come to visit her. Not that she expected her mother to visit. It was not merely that Mamacita's gimp leg handicapped her. She also mistrusted the industrialized society that was the United States. Technology confounded her, while it fascinated Pia.

Josefina was another matter. It did not take the wizardry of technology to figure out that Josefina resented her. Now Pia understood her sister's occasional taunts, "Mamacita's Precious One."

Weighted with the uncomfortable memories, Pia shifted uneasily on her narrow metal bed, suspended from the wall by two anchoring cables. The cell, containing three other females, smelled of piss, sour vomit, and unforgivable humiliations.

She yearned to cuddle with the yapping, bug-eyed Perro. But she wanted her mother more. Strange, how more often than not, it was their mother, not God, men cried out for just prior to being executed.

Unwanted, her thoughts tiptoed around that American reporter's mention of a hanging. Sights of the dead dangling from telegraph wires or riddled with bullets and slumped against adobe walls were not uncommon.

However, she now faced the stark possibility of her own execution. She doubted, all right feverishly hoped not, that the State of Texas would take it that far. She also doubted her country would seek to intervene on the behalf of a mere housemaid, especially not one who had so disrupted the border traffic on both sides.

She was recalled from her unpleasant contemplation by the guard's announcement that she had a visitor. The journalist again? She could not get him out of her mind, this Walt Stevenson, with those stern, discerning eyes the hard gray of pencil lead in his narrow face. In no way would she call his chiseled features handsome, but there was something about him appealing ... a magnetism that threw off her inner compass.

"Hey, officer," jeered one of her cell mates, a boozy-looking older woman, "Take me, and I'll blow your hole!"

Blow his hole? Now, what was that? Shaking her head, Pia swung her feet over her suspended bedside and submitted to being handcuffed again before following the guard down the tomb-like corridor to the visitor's room.

She was astonished—and delighted—to see Amado García seated behind one of the six tables. At that time of afternoon, between lunch and quitting time, the visitation tables were empty. She slid into the chair opposite Amado.

Whatever feelings of maidenly shyness she felt were immediately replaced by shame at the sight of his nose wrinkling. She must stink like a feral hog. Not exactly her picture-book idea of romantic courtship. Tartness got the better of her tongue. "Is this the day you came to sketch me—on a jail wall, maybe?"

He looked taken aback, then he recovered himself. He wore sturdy trousers held up by suspenders and a duck cloth, collarless shirt of navy blue. She caught a glimpse of a small brass medallion of the Virgin Mary lying against his chest's spare frame.

Immediately, he yanked off his billed cap, and matted black hair tumbled out. "They can't keep you here."

Her mouth scrunched to one side. "They can do whatever they damn well please." But she could not contain her pleasure at seeing Amado. Was an angel ever more beautiful? She contrasted his good looks to Walt Stevenson's austere ones, and the journalist came up on the losing side. Still, he made her feel like a cooling drink after a fever, and she could not account for her susceptibility to him.

Amado leaned forward, folding his work-scuffed hands atop the metal table. "*Escucha*, I know people who can work to get you out of here." For the better part, he spoke English, more or less his native language, so she followed suit.

Her head tilted, her eyes narrowed. "What kind of people? Only people in power can pull strings, and yours and my kind are always the puppets, Amado."

His handsome features earnest, he lowered his voice. "I've attended a few meetings—at the offices of *La Reforma Social*—along with other men who feel we Mexican Americans are not accorded the same respect as Anglo Americans."

Surprise washed over her. Amado, who had far less education than her privileged one, cut short though as it had been, was hobnobbing with *perodistas*? She did not trust the cynical exercise of power by any newspaper, American or Mexican. Yet here, in the last twenty-four-hours, two males identified with the press in one way or another had shown up.

"Your bail is high, Pia. Three-thousand American dollars."

"¡*Hijole*!" Why such an enormous sum? When it was said the U.S. was offering $5,000 for the capture of Pancho Villa.

"*Sí*, outrageous. But if *La Reforma Social* and other newspapers like it drum up enough attention on your behalf," Amado hurried to assure her, "in the next few days we just *might* get you released."

Strange the English language. She thought about what a weak word 'might' was, while 'mighty' meant powerful. Which brought her around to her initial question. "What kind of people are powerful enough? Whom do you know?"

His vague shrug told her he was not at all sure about his contact. "I have become acquainted with *La Reform Social's* new editor, the attorney Silvestre Salinas."

Well, well, well. The skeleton in the pantry. But she only said, "All well and good, but, like most periodicals, *La Reforma Social* is likely burning through what money it has."

La Reforma Social held a pro-Villa platform and was against the Mexican President Carranza's landholding oligarchy—composed of the Catholic Church, the military, and land barons like her and her brother Silvestre Salinas's father, Horst Heinrich.

"And I've seen Don Horst Heinrich at Silvestre's office a couple of times."

She almost spat on the metal table. "Ahhh, Don Horst the puppet master, himself."

"You know him?"

"Amado, I'd rather swing by the noose than accept his help. Not that Don Horst would ever deign to help one of his bastards."

For a moment, he stared, uncomprehending. "Deign?"

"Stoop." In devouring the *Roget's*, she overlooked the fact most others of her association had no use for a thesaurus or dictionary. She loved words, whether they were English or German, Spanish or French. She found bliss in them like a Buddhist did in nirvana.

The full import of her statement hit him finally. "Don Horst Heinrich, he is your father?!"

Bile choked her grin into a grimace. "The illustrious lecher is the father of not only me but also my sister Josefina and her daughter Rosita—which makes Rosita also my half-sister." There, the pantry door was open!

A beat passed for Amado to assimilate the complexity of the relationships, then, "The fucking bastard!"

Dry humor twisted her lips. "No, it's me and my siblings who are bastards—and Silvestre the legitimate one." Her eyes narrowed meaningfully on him. "But this is a shame not to be broadcast, sí?"

For a moment, he was silent, digesting all of this, then nodded. "*Sí.*" He shrugged and said, "Meanwhile, the riot is still going on today. But this time most of the rioters are the men. They are taking advantage of your bath house protest to oppose Carranza and support Villa. And streetcar service between Juarez and El Paso has been suspended indefinitely."

That could explain why neither her mother nor her sister had visited yet. At least, that was what she would prefer to believe.

The guard yawned and called out, "Time's up!"

Amado stood and tugged his billed cap resolutely over fervent eyes. "I promise I will find a way to spring you out of here, *bebé.*"

Watching him take his leave, she could only wonder what was wrong with her. Here she had mastered decoding Morse transmissions, but she could not master society's compliance and conformance. Instead of consideration and calculation beforehand, she invariably reacted impulsively from some primordial instinct.

As a result, she had alienated herself even further from Josefina; she had landed herself in jail; and she had done the most asinine thing yet in her reckless, impulsive life … she had fallen in love at first sight with a man who could not possibly cherish her caprice with all its flaws—and it was not Amado García.

Barely had she been returned to her cell and begun repenting her defiant stance, than she was singled out yet again an hour or so later. However, this time she was escorted not to the visitor's room but farther along the corridor. She followed the guard to a door labeled Discharge Room.

This was peculiar. Had Amado already wangled a way to spring her so soon? Of course, he could. Was he not Don Quixote's ideal of the knight in shining armor? Still, where would Amado have come up with such an astronomical amount of money? But then she was not that familiar with jail processes, American or Mexican. And who was she to question the gods?

Several male clerks worked from behind a long, defaced wooden counter. One clerk in a green visor signaled her forward. "You're being released, gal."

With elation bubbling in her throat, she signed off on the return of both her *rebozo* and *bolsa* from the property room. She rumbled through her bag to make sure both her few centavos in her coin purse and her *Roget's* were still inside.

Josefina certainly thought Pia's time was wasted on the thesaurus. "Improve your English for what?" she had once scoffed. "So you can become First Lady of Mexico?" And Pia had responded, "No, so I can become President of Mexico." Which, of course, elicited whoops of cackling. "But, why not?" something inside her protested.

She next signed a plethora of release papers.

"Your custodian is there."

"My custodian?"

Not far behind her a voice rumbled, "*Sí, Señorita* Arellano, *me llamo* Cisco Rodriguez."

She peered over her shoulder. A man of average height rose from one of the benches girding the room's walls and removed his filthy sombrero. From a swarthy, cherubic face, his dark eyes crinkled with his smile. His companion, a burly man with deep frown lines and a concrete-block jaw, looked bored. Both wore the common vaquero clothing—sombrero, bandana, chaps, and boots with roweled spurs.

Cisco Rodriguez switched to English. "We are to take you home."

She looked askance at the scruffy two—reminded herself one should never judge a person's worth by outward appearance—then looked back to the visored clerk, whose shrug telegraphed the matter was out of his hands now.

Why not, she was too wrung out to quibble.

Chapter Eleven

Walt hunched over his notepad. "Typhoid Fear Shuts Down America Border." How insipid. He scratched out the heading of his article to be submitted to *Collier's Magazine*.

He was to join Bobby and Ed at the Hotel Sheldon's bar below in fifteen minutes. The late afternoon's respite would provide easy conversation and conviviality with the two—and eavesdropping on information from other tongues loosed by liquor.

He should be refreshing himself for the cocktail hour meetup. A clean collar would be prerequisite for his brown-striped shirt, with sleeves presently rolled to his forearms. His stubble-shadowed jaw needed a second pass at shaving that day.

Instead, with a disgruntled sigh he deserted the narrow secretary desk and crossed the suite's sitting room to settle in the rocking chair. He rocked, the calming way his grandfather had rocked him.

He let his mind drift. Invariably, little by little, solutions to problems came to him through just the rocking motion. Not just a specific solution he might be seeking but other solutions to issues he might have overlooked or forgotten.

So, minutes later he was not particularly surprised when the perfect title to his story emerged at the forefront of his mind. He rose and recrossed to the desk. His pencil seemed to take on a will of its own. It scribbled on his notepad, "Amazon Redhead Versus American Regulation."

Bemused, he sat at the desk and stared unseeingly at his precise, vertical handwriting. Reviewing all the facts and findings presented in his article, it was clearly evident his article was not about the riot but about the rioter, Piedad Arellano.

He pushed back from the desk and, hands locked behind his nape, gazed sightlessly up at the gently swishing ceiling fan. This was unlike him—his interest to be caught up wholly by a female. True, he had thought himself in love with his college sweetheart, Cordelia Schuler. Still did suspect he was, for that matter.

But never had he experienced this sole preoccupation with a female, either before or after Cordelia. And even his courtship of her had been more of romantic affection rather than physical passion, out of respect due her, of course.

While the debutante slouch with hollow chest was the rage, he had been attracted to Cordelia's lush curves, for which she made no apology. After all, she was one of the Mayflower descendants.

Further, he could ascribe no outstanding attribute to this Mexican housemaid. Beautiful? Not necessarily. Intelligent? Yes, but not exceptionally so. Not like Cordelia, a graduate of Bryn Mawr. Accomplished? Not like Cordelia either, a violinist virtuoso. Kind of heart? Not if he considered reports of the housemaid pummeling a streetcar console like John L. Sullivan bare-knuckle boxing any of his unlucky opponents.

So, what was it? What inexplicable force of Piedad Arellano attracted Walt's attention, his interest, his preoccupation? Right now, he felt that distinctive, innate warning that came when something was amiss; and this, this signaled as if nearing the edge of a personal precipice.

With Cordelia, he had felt … well, settled. As if he had found his place in life. His niche. Apparently, she had not felt the same. Had felt he was not totally invested in their affair of the heart. "Not sufficiently enough for mine, at least," she had relayed in her curt Dear John letter.

The terse note had sounded more wounded than what it was intended to be—wounding. Well, he had licked what wounds she inflicted and trooped on.

Was he lacking in passion? A small and tight, self-derisive smile deepened the crevices bracketing his mouth. Did not reviews for his stories and mail received at his various publishers laud his stories as impassioned. Did not those affirm his passionate nature?

And then there were the trysts with a scattering of women here and there, usually socialites seeking him out for their literary parties. With those few he had partaken of sensual revels, and they had continued to seek him out, even after he had lost interest.

The clincher was that he was *content* with life's small pleasures but never *satisfied*.

Giving serious reflection to Cordelia's charge, he had to take in account she knew him better than anyone ... at least, anyone alive, now that his grandfather had passed.

Self-examination produced no explanation where he might have gone awry within his courtship. Granted, he had comported himself as a gentleman and had not compromised her with passionate inveiglements before their wedding vows.

If he was not 'sufficient' as he was, did it not correlate that her love for him was 'insufficient,' as well?

While he had waited for a mental breakthrough to this quandary, his work-in-progress about the tragic and mysterious murder of El Paso's Senator Albert Fountain and his son in the desert years before had gone untouched. Walt had simply lost interest on the unsolved murder of the acknowledged kingpin of western Texas, as obviously had local authorities.

Covering Pershing's expedition into Mexico and back, while also working for the BI, had given him something else on which to focus, a transitory purpose until his writer's muse decided to revisit him and his long-neglected manuscript.

Now, this Mexican Amazon made him feel … unsettled again. He wanted to wash his hands of her. But here he was, descending the only elevator in the city, preparing to ask Bobby and Ed for the preposterous.

At the bar, conviviality hardly described the features of his two glum friends.

"Already ordered your hot tea and creamer," Ed said, lifting the Lone Star bottle for a swig.

Hunched over a snifter of the famed Pass brandy, Bobby lowered his voice, although no one occupied the tables closest to them. Farther away, a few businessmen were clustered here and there with their drinks. "Ed was just telling me about an explosive telegram the press room received today."

Snapping open his linen napkin, Walt schooled his expression to mild interest. Had news of the Zimmerman telegram already been made public? "'Explosive' is a provocative figure of speech, Bobby. Has Villa dynamited another one of the Carrancista troop trains?"

His jest made no impression on his companions, so consumed were they by the import of the news, whatever it was.

Ed's brushy mustache dipped deeply on both ends. "Congress just passed the Immigration Act after all—and within days following this riot. Takes effect on the 1st."

Two days off. "What a fiasco," Walt muttered. Though the bill had been originally intended to stem the tide of the 'Yellow Peril'—as newspapers labeled the Chinese immigrants who came to work on laying the transcontinental railroads—now for the first time in history Mexicans also would need a passport to cross the Rio Grande, something both sides of the river had done freely from time immemorial. Moreover, Mexican laborers would be required to pass a literacy test and pay a head tax.

"If this bath house melee made international news," Bobby drawled, "wait till all the merchants, industries, and housewives this side of the border learn of the bill's passage. They'll be in an uproar.

I'll have to order out the cavalry, infantry, and aero squadron to keep peace."

The white-jacketed waiter placed the matching porcelain saucer and cup with teapot and creamer in front of Walt. "Thank you, I'll serve myself."

Then, after the waiter departed, he said, "Well, the Immigration Act will make the Mexican merchants happy, at least."

They had been losing business, since the first mule-drawn streetcar began traversing the long bridge before the turn of the century, making it too easy for Mexicans to cross and do their shopping on the United States side.

He poured tea into his cup and added his hefty dollop of cream, giving his offhanded remark time to allay some of the table's tension before forging ahead with his purpose. "Look, you two, I want to arrange for the female who started the riot—Piedad Arellano—to be released from jail."

Both men's brows jacked up. Ed said, "You interviewed her in jail yesterday, right?"

"Right. I think her story could capture world imagination. I'd like to follow her. See if she's Mexico's Emma Goldman. Find out if she's the real deal. A feminist, an anarchist, and a champion of the downtrodden—or if she's merely a flash in the pan."

He would give her this, the raging and ranting Emma Goldman had merely exhorted her El Paso audience to demonstrate several years ago but had not risked her life to take part, as had done this riled and rallying Mexican housemaid.

Bobby grinned. "Just as I said, you're keen on her."

Walt was not going to let his friend's remark irk him. "I am after what I think could make a great human-interest story. She is one of those impossible radical activists."

For the life of him he could not say why in that short half-hour interview he came away with that impression of her. Well, yes, he could. Radicals could be the most difficult activists to deal with. They did not trust the government and its laws to protect the people, and that certainly defined her belligerence.

"Oh, you mean she is not an idealist like you," Bobby kidded. "You know the kind. The ones who expect—and demand—a perfectly law-abiding world."

Walt cut his eyes at Bobby, took a sip from his teacup, then continued. "I'm concerned the young Mexican woman won't get a fair shake if Mayor Lea has anything to say about it."

"Evidently, you're right." Bobby finished off the last of his Pass brandy. "Lea's pal, the judge, established an outrageous bail. Three grand. So good luck with that. Can't help you there. Ella and I don't have that kind of money. Not on my soldier's pay. Our bank account is at low tide."

"That bail money is not so much the issue." With some financial finagling of his various bank accounts, Walt could likely manage to lay hands on the money. That was not what concerned him. "Why the high bail, guys? The investigative journalist part of me is piqued. And I am hoping one or both of you can put in a good word with Lea, use your clout to persuade him to dismiss the bail. If he won't, I'd be mighty interested in his reasoning."

Ed, who had remained silent during all this, said, "You're a little bit late, chum."

Walt plunked down his teacup. "Exactly what do you mean 'a little bit late'? What do you know, Ed?"

"She's already been released. About an hour ago. One of the *Herald*'s tipsters who hangs out at the courthouse passed along the info."

"Did they say who bailed her out?"

"She wasn't bailed out, so to speak. Her bail had been dismissed. Apparently, she was released to cohorts of hers."

"Did you get their names?"

"Yeah, one of them. He is a chief arms supplier for Villa." Ed made a sound like he was about to hawk and spit. "Cisco Rodriguez."

Bobby frowned. "That makes no sense. The mayor hates the *Villista*s. He wouldn't tolerate them one inch this side of the border."

Walt whisked his lips with his napkin. "It makes a lot of sense. Let the *Villista*s do the dirty work—rid him of what could be a thorn in his side. No finger pointing at his camp." He folded his napkin neatly and laid it to the left of the saucer. Collecting his trilby, he stood. "Ed, can I borrow your Hudson?"

The man's bushy brows shot up. "It's my baby."

"Your baby's older than Methuselah." He held out his hand.

Ed grudgingly dug into his sweater's chest pocket and dropped the clunky ignition key into Walt's palm.

Union Station, not El Paso's commercial district, was the hub of the city. Taxis, horse-drawn carriages, streetcars, trains—they all originated here, as did information.

In researching his novel about the Fountain murders, Walt had created contacts with many of the old timers and drew on their reminiscences. Once he was recruited by the BI, he continued to draw on their knowledge.

Outside Union Station, he hunkered before the gnarled and filthy Mexican, peddling the brown paper-wrapped caramelized peanuts and pecans. "Pablo, what do you know about the *Villista*, Cisco Rodriguez?"

The old man lifted his eye-patch, revealing an eye with better sight than Walt with the aid of his pince-nez. He hacked brown sputum on the pavement. "A Juarez middleman. Plays both sides. Trades mostly cattle rustled from Mexico's *hacendados* in return for American cash for arms and ammo for Villa—with a take on the side for himself, of course."

"Do you know where I can find him?"

He shook his shaggy head. "No, but Silas might."

Walt next set off for the streetcar ticket's booth, on the depot's far edge. At the grill, he nodded crisply at the grizzled old man. "I need to find Cisco Rodriguez. Now. Time's short." Already the sun was deserting the sky, taking its warmth with it.

Silas nodded back. "Give me ten minutes."

The immediate tap-tapping of Silas' telegraph key receding in Walt's ears, he headed toward the shoeshine stand's alcove. Bootblacks could offer other services besides shoeshining and shoe repair. The Chinaman liked to shoot the breeze, and Walt worried this would be one of those times. "I'll be getting my shoes shined."

Wang Wei grinned. "I see you twice in forty-eight hours And I see your two-tone scuffed oxfords, too. I take care of them, you see."

They had not seen a polishing rag since he had boarded the Chicken Coop Express from Mexico City. Taking a step up onto the high seat, Walt hiked his cuffed trousers. "Who works with Cisco Rodriguez this side of the border?"

The black-clad Wang Wei flipped his dangling, equally black queue over his shoulder, out of his way. With a flourish of his rag, he cleaned the dirt and dust from Walt's right brogan, "Many, many. Any and all who can. Rodriguez, he controls underground economy."

Walt shook out a newspaper left in the adjacent vacant seat. The *El Paso Morning Times* headline announced: 'Bath Riots Renewed at Santa Fe Bridge.' And below it was a caricature of Pia Arellano, appearing for all the world like the statue of the Winged Victory of Samothrace. Had her noble Amado García, the bricklayer with artistic aspirations, according to Walt's informants, penned the caricature?

"Names. I need names, Wang Wei."

The Chinese informant dolloped wax paste on one dress shoe and began polishing it. "From that flower girl over at depot doorway to that Missy Adelaide Cardenas at turtle house. From former mayor, that Mickey O'Bannon, to that banker Solly Müller."

"Adelaide Cardenas, you say?" Few these days knew that the turtle shape, fashioned of brick on one side of the Chateau Cardenas, had once signified a safe house for Chinese illegal immigrants. "Tell me what I don't know about Adelaide Cardenas."

"Missy Adelaide, many, many would like to hump her."

"Like who?"

Wang Wei set to buffing the other brogan clean. "Many, many.

Any and all who hump."

"Is Lea one of her lovers?" That might confirm his suspicion of the mayor's involvement in the housemaid's disappearance.

"No, no." He applied wax paste to the brogan, then his polishing rag. "Flirting, that Missy Adelaide allows. But no more than that. Many, many careful, she is. Many proper."

He tipped Wang Wei handsomely and strode briskly back to the streetcar ticket booth. "Well?"

Old Silas shoved up his soiled visor. "Word's out Rodriguez has kidnapped the gal, the one who started the bath house riot, from right in front of the magistrate's eyes, so to speak."

"How do you know she didn't go willingly, that this wasn't family or friends she went with?"

Silas looked at him as if he were slow-witted. "'Cause I know her. Pia Arellano. A smart gal she is. Good at telegraphy, too. And I know about Cisco Rodriguez, a cutthroat smuggler."

"So, what else did you find out?"

The geezer's knotted fingers leafed through a slew of mustard-colored papers. "This one—a telegram from a contact at Fort Hidalgo. Rodriguez's Model T passed Delgado's Wheelwright Shop. He's the father of the kid who was hanged over in Juarez."

"How long ago?"

"Oh, the kid, he was hanged about—"

Walt controlled his impatience. Self-control he was good at. "No, how long ago did the Model T pass by the wheelwright shop?"

The old codger glanced back down to the telegram. "About forty-five minutes ago."

"Where is this shop?"

"On the way out of Juarez, on the road to Chihuahua City."

"That's not much help. Nothing but desert lies between there and Chihuahua City."

"It's rumored Rodriguez runs his smuggling operations out of caverns, somewhere about twenty or so miles out—just past a paloverde split by lightning, where a rutted trail runs toward the cliffs.

They could be headed there. Or for that matter somewhere else."

Just swell. The Model T had an hour's head start on a gravelly road that spanned 265 empty miles. The odds of catching up with it were about as good as his seeing 20/20 again. Enigmatic, how his vision had rapidly dimmed after that fatal day in his childhood.

He cranked up Ed's Hudson. It was a foolish idea this, to pursue the housemaid for a mere human-interest story when he should be concentrating on Bureau work.

Besides, if the mayor was, indeed, behind her disappearance, the human-interest angle could turn out to be another stymied political story like his current one about El Paso's Fountain murders.

No, it would be wiser to stick to his BI duties. Nailing Sommerfeld's spy operating there in El Paso—especially before the Zimmerman telegram was made public—was paramount. After that, the master spy, whoever it was, would most likely have accomplished Sommerfeld's objective ... whatever that was.

And that worried Walt—the 'whatever that was' part.

Walt headed toward the Second Ward—the Segundo Barrio where cheap secret agents and ex-deputy constables nosed around.

There he might find a lead on the Japanese male who was Villa's personal servant—while finding the red-haired Amazon was not his responsibility. He needed no more responsibility in his life. What he already had was sometimes a cross too heavy to bear.

Chapter Twelve

Outside the old, red brick El Paso County Courthouse, the sun, already sliding down the far side of the Rockies, had left the air chilly.

Pia had followed Cisco Rodriguez's clinking spurs a couple of blocks over to a sand-coated Model T that looked like it had toppled down the side of Mount Franklin. At the Ford's front, Jaw Man cranked the engine half a dozen times before the engine caught.

Inside the wheezing cranker, she had been crunched between the taciturn two, smelling most likely as foul as she. Instinct whispered she may be jumping from the frying pan into the fire. "Uhh, whom do I thank for posting the bail?"

Cisco's beatific smile wrapped around yellow teeth. "An anonymous donor."

Paranoically, following both the bath house and jail house experiences, she had suspected yet another nasty surprise. Her misgivings eased their twitching somewhat after the Model T, passing the bridge's Mexican border easily, had rattled on into Juarez. However, she had been expecting to be dropped off, if not at her mother's house, then within walking distance, at the Palazio Comercio.

She swallowed a hard knot of anxiety. "Uhh, you missed the turn off to my home. It's back a couple of blocks."

"We've another stop first," said Cisco. He hinged open the glove box and retrieved not gloves but a six-shooter and knife, its blade a dull red with rust … at least, she hoped it was rust. He shifted his weight from one side to the other to holster each weapon, with the firing arm the one to grind against her thigh.

Genuine alarm rang its warning bell. Goosebumps having nothing to do with twilight's chill pimpled her skin. She tugged her *rebozo* tighter to warm flesh that might never feel warmth again.

Wedged between the two, she could not jump from the motorcar. And at such close quarters, she had no hope of prying loose Cisco's pistol and getting off a shot.

For that matter, she had never shot a pistol. Had nearly been unable to wring a stray chicken's neck that first year of hard living in Juarez.

"A necessary deed that has to be done if we are to eat," her mother had explained and made Pia take the wildly flapping chicken by its hockjoints, grab hold of its feathered neck, and twist it hard, snapping it.

But could she bring herself to kill a human being?

Cisco took a second pistol from the glove box and passed it behind her to Jaw Man. Shoving it with one hand into his hip holster, he kept driving … past the commercial district with its multitude of restaurants, bars, and watering holes, past the adobe residential district, past the outlying citadel that was Fort Hidalgo, and then past the few straggling jacals, mere wattle-and-daube structures with tin roofs.

In the motor car's deathly silence, the two men could surely hear her heart hammering. Her fingers gripped her *bolsa* on her lap. She had a cold premonition.

Against the gradually receding sunlight, eerie shadows of desert vegetation arose—clusters of thorny cholla and twisted mesquite amidst deep arroyos and abruptly rising sand banks.

About half an hour out, Jaw Man made a sharp right just past a tortured paloverde tree. The Model T easily negotiated a road that was little more than a sand-furrowed trail. When he purposefully swerved the wheel to squish flat a gopher, which had the misfortune to pop up at the wrong moment, she knew for certain her companions were not of the altruistic kind.

Shivering in her skin, she turned to Cisco and grinned wider than a jack-o-lantern. "You know, you can let me out here, *Señor* Rodriguez, and I'll walk back. It's no problem."

He grinned back, an unfeeling grin in that angelic face. "No *hay problema, Señorita*."

Her goosebumps morphed from chilling fear to a prickling heat of dread sweeping from chest to cheeks.

He leaned forward to better see Jaw Man. "Hey, Pablo, this is as good as any place to stop."

At a remote patch cut by the trail, Jaw Man braked so sharply dust and grit flurried inside, sending her into a spasm of coughing.

Once Cisco shoved open the door and stepped outside, she wasted no time in edging past him. "Thanks for the lift. I'll be on my way."

His hand latched onto her forearm. "*Perdon*, but this is your final destination." He actually looked a trifle regretful. But next an expression of slow and intense malice dawned in his swarthy face.

Whatever hope she held out for human kindness from these two *Villista*s evaporated quicker than the scant inch of rain the area had received the last six months. She had been set up. And why? Why the concern about an insignificant housemaid?

She had no desire to continue rioting. Her anger had flared and fizzled. She wanted nothing more than her life to return to its normalcy. She wanted the promise that a simple life with Amado held. Because no promise whatsoever of a life was offered with the stone-hearted Walt Stevenson.

Her stomach quivered like a spoonful of her mother's to-die-for caramel flan. And because apparently Pia was going to do just that, die, she summoned the strength to transmute panic into alert focus. "*Oyes, mi amigo*, El Paso's *polítocos* may want me out of the way, but I'm one of you. Below Mexico's moneyed and social class, I'm doing my best simply to survive from day to day."

She might as well have been speaking Swedish. Cisco's eyes were as cold as a grave. "*¡Que lástima!* Survive, you won't *mi paisana*." He poked his six-shooter against the center of her forehead.

She heard the first click of his pistol's hammer thumbed back. On her tongue, she could taste fear, sharp and metallic. She could barely draw enough saliva to beg, "*Por favor. Por favor* don't."

His forefinger curled around the trigger.

It was said that one's life played out like one of Alameda Theater's moving pictures, which she had never seen, but she had only the instant to feel regret that she had never kissed Walt. What a jolt—Walt, not Amado. Walt of the inscrutable eyes.

Then came the hammer's second click.

And nothing. Within a clock's second-hand tick, she realized the six-shooter had failed to fire. Cisco looked as astonished as she felt. He went to pull back on the hammer again.

She flung her *bolsa* against his head. The wallop her heroic *Roget's* delivered jarred him but momentarily. She sprang past him and plummeted down into an arroyo. He must have got off another shot, because she heard something zing just above her.

Like a jackrabbit, she streaked along the sinuous arroyo. If she were a jackrabbit, he was a greyhound. She could hear him huffing ever closer. Cloud-filtered moonlight hampered her flight. Chest bursting, she sped up around another bend of the arroyo.

She was quick afoot, but his legs were, of course, longer. And her *rebozo* and *bolsa* kept catching on the arroyo's scrabbly chaparral. Did not matter; she was not about to let the *bolsa* go. That large bag contained her lifeline, her precious thesaurus. It was her desert island book over a bible.

A shot, winging but a hair's breadth above the cradle of her neck and shoulder, plowed with a spray of gravel into a thorny clump on the steep wall just ahead.

She tripped over a lava rock the size of one of her mother's bread loaves. She went skidding. Her palms were painfully scraped. She scrambled to her feet and took off again.

She risked a glance over her shoulder. Cisco was striding fast and gaining on her. His peaked sombrero, restrained by its neck cord, bounced wildly against his back. She outpaced him for maybe a dozen yards more.

Then, his hand lassoed one of her ankles. Her *bolsa* went sailing. She slammed face-first into the baked ground. Pain vibrated from her chin to her nose to her forehead. Kaleidoscope colors danced a jig behind her lids.

He flipped her onto her back and rammed his knee down into her stomach. Her breath whooshed. She lashed fists at his chest, his head, anything solid. He jammed his pistol against her temple this time.

A corpse could not have gone as lax.

"A little pleasure I'll have with you first, I think."

The brutish look in his eyes told her he could not be persuaded against his intent. Still, she tried begging again. "*Por favor, por favor ...* you don't want to do this."

His free hand wrestled with the folds of her long skirt, tangled between her legs. She screamed. Rational thought disintegrated and reflexively she swung out with her fist. She walloped his shoulder and heard his grunt. The six-shooter spun away and thunked in the sand off to her right. Out of reach.

With one hand, he anchored her wrists above her and with the other shucked his knife. He scratched his head with its hilt. "Por que, you no make this easier for the both of us?"

"For God's sake, don't do this. Let me go. I'll never say anything about you or your amigo."

"That you won't." Ignoring her plea, he proceeded with his knife to rip the strings of her underdrawers from their seam. Then, he straddled her. Like a bull in the *Plaza de Toros*, she thrashed and twisted and heaved. He loosed her wrists and, hauling back his left fist, punched her in the face.

She felt blood and snot spurt from her nose. Behind her lids, streamers of light rocketed. Stunned, she lay there.

With his free hand, he was unbuttoning his flap, setting loose his private parts. Hindered by her lowered underdrawers stretched above her knees, his own knee could wedge no wider her thighs. Solving the problem rapidly, his knife slashed the muslin fabric, nicking her.

The pain was negligible compared to her fear. He would rape her dead—or alive. She preferred to be alive and continue to be so. Though still dazed somewhat, she grappled for the knife.

He jammed its tip up into the underside of her throat. She felt the pain, quick and sharp. Immediately, she desisted.

Eyes pleading, she looked up into his face. It was a mask of frenzied lust. He shoved himself inside her. Or tried. It took him several attempts. Her whimpers accompanied her body's involuntary writhings. The knife tip pricked deeper. She felt blood dribble from the knife's tip into the hollow of her collarbones. The monster would cut her throat, even as he violated her.

What he proceeded to do was maddening. At first a ramming, then quickening, his thrusts scooted her backwards in increments on the abrading sand. She could not prevent her sobbing yelps echoing off the sides of the arroyo.

Unexpectedly, his sexual frenzy froze above her in mid-thrust. Next, her insides were awash. Following that, gasping, he collapsed half atop her.

She lay rigid. Then, as if wakening from a nightmare, she shook off its horrific miasma. No time to shed tears over a precious lost maidenhead. As he lay atop her and still shuddering in noisy breathing after-spasms, she grabbed the knife, lying loosely in his fingers. With more violence than she realized she possessed, she corkscrewed the blade up into his gut, then yanked the knife out.

Astonishment flashed in his face. Only a whispering of a gargled groan escaped his salt-dried lips. His eyelids fluttered but never completely closed over glazed eyes.

Fear enhanced her strength. She thrust his dead weight off her.

Unsteadily, she stood. At once, she dropped the knife, as if to rid herself of the evening's entire bloody episode.

The way her stomach persistently heaved up against her throat, she felt like she was going to vomit. She doubled over, hands braced on her knees, and heaved nothing but spittle.

Straightening at last, she tried to think clearly. Foolish to return to the Model T Ford. She had no idea even how to start much less drive it and would most certainly be ineffectual going up against its driver, Jaw Man.

She glanced around and tried to get her bearings. Purple mountains sailed ahead of her, but were they the El Paso Franklins to the northwest or the mountains southeast of the Rio Bravo, the Sierra de Juarez? With clouds intermittently obscuring both city lights and the rising copper moon, she had nothing to guide her. But she needed to get a move on and fast. Jaw Man would soon be wondering why his *pistolero* compadre had not returned.

She paused only long enough to refasten the savaged strings of her sand encrusted underdrawers. Suddenly, a hand latched onto her ankle. Her instinctive scream was shrill. Cisco was using her hose-torn calf to pull himself upright. "¡*Puta*!" he snarled.

She tried to shake him off. She stumbled, and they both went down. On his knees now, he loomed over her. The knife, smeared with his own blood, was once again in his hand. Crazed eyes glinted from beneath his half-masted lids.

She swung a fist, but Cisco savagely knocked it away. Her flapping hand struck cold metal on the ground behind her. Her fingers latched onto the butt of his pistol. She cocked it. At the same time he plunged downward the knife, her forefinger yanked on its trigger.

Like a cannon boom, the shot reverberated between the arroyo walls. He toppled off her. Gasping, she squiggled free and stood, wobbling. Like her mother's flour sifter, she had been shaken forcefully.

She looked down at him. The failing twilight leached the swarthiness from his face so that it was bone white. His body still twitched. Specks of blood bubbled over his lips. Just in case, she fired the pistol again, giving the coup de grâce ... that terrible after-shot some called 'mercy.'

Except in this case, it was not. A black-powdered hole plugged the outer corner of his right eye socket, the eye itself a pulpy black-and-red mass. Blood and brain matter puddled behind his head. She still didn't feel quite satisfied. Damned lucky for Cisco he was done in.

So, she could kill someone. Quite easily. Solemnly, she crossed herself and parroted aloud over the corpse her mother's instructional comment in regard to dispatching a chicken. "A necessary deed that has to be done."

Nauseated, she bent aside and this time vomited. She wiped her arm's torn sleeve across her bloodied nose and mouth and the nick beneath her chin. With resolution, she then set off on tottering legs across the high desert, revolver in one hand and her retrieved *bolsa* slung across one shoulder. Left behind, half beneath Cisco's corpse was her *rebozo. Ni modo.*

Her destination was the main road bisecting the two mountain ranges ... and her hope was that Jaw Man would not return by it to Juarez.

She was freezing. Night's chill congealed her sweat, her nostrils' bloody trickle, and Cisco's sticky body fluid seeping down her thighs. Her head was throbbing, and her lungs were so constricted she could barely draw in air. She realized her physical and emotional pain were dulled by shock. However, she registered at some level the horror of what had happened to her, although she doubted she was fully processing it all.

Directly over her, a bat skimmed so low that she could feel the thrumming of its wings and the air moving her hair. From nearby came a burrowing owl's shrill whistle.

Fervently, she hoped she was heading north—and fervently hoped she met up with neither scorpion, diamondback, nor Gila Monster. And especially not Jaw Man. She kept looking over her shoulder for sign of him and listening intently for the spooky rumble of the Model T.

Her teeth chattered from the high desert's increasingly cold temperature and joined forces with her body's shock and her innards that boiled with anger.

She would not let this reduce her to a sniveling coward. Josefina had suffered the same, and at only thirteen years of age. And then she had borne Rosita alone, with only Pia and Mamacita to help.

From somewhere, a coyote howled. Pia fought her quivering jaw's guttural rejoinder to that plaintive howl. Instead, she softly hummed "La Cucaracha."

"La cucaracha, la cucaracha ... all she wanted was to dance. La cucaracha, la cucaracha ... and she would never miss the chance. La cucaracha, la cucaracha ... the legs on her back she tore. La cucaracha, la cucaracha ... all is fair in love and war."

Chapter Thirteen

After pulling the spark lever and adjusting the throttle of Ed's Hudson, Walt steered it toward the Second Ward … and passed by his destination. He kept driving. Across the Rio Grande, over its bridge, beyond Juarez, and into the gathering dismal dusk.

Once past Juarez's scattering of hovels, he folded down the windshield from the Hudson's roof to divert the sand. From here on he was on his own. Unarmed, as he preferred, and for companions only the cacti, an owl or two—and the usual bloodthirsty banditos who prowled under the cover of darkness.

It was unlikely an American military convoy up from Colonia Dublin would be traveling this rutted Mexican road at this time of night. But not so unlikely any number of Villa's Dorados. They would know every pothole.

The Hudson's headlights coned narrowly but a few yards ahead. His eyes strained through their pince-nez. Only a trio of javelinas scampering across the road interrupted the Hudson's progress.

A quarter of an hour later, the motor car began to limp along on one of its rims. Tarnation!

The horse was still the favored form of transportation in that desolate area where Mexico, Texas, and New Mexico triangulated. And with eight to ten nails per hoof there were, of course, nails everywhere on roads.

The Hudson was covering mere feet in its forward progress and threatening to eject him with each revolution of the flattened tire. Mentally groaning, he nosed the clunker to the edge of the road, turned off the engine, and got out. The high desert air had turned colder. His breath frosted.

It was doubtable a tire patch kit was tucked underneath the seat. Still, he hunkered and groped beneath it. He found the prerequisite jack and tire chains. That was all. No tire patch kit. This time, he groaned audibly.

"Can I be of help?"

He almost jumped out of his skin. He wheeled about.

Impossibly, there she stood. Piedad Arellano. The wallop of electricity he felt was instantaneous.

And she looked as if she had been electrified, too. With a mass of corkscrewed red hair shooting out, dried blood tracking from her nostrils, a swelling cheekbone, and a bruising eye socket, she was a pint-sized Medusa wraith.

He discounted the electrical sensation he felt as one of those phenomena of nature attributed to factors of weather and geography. Still, he was slightly breathless—probably, he told himself, due the handgun she clutched. "Yes, you can get us both back to civilization. Any suggestions?"

She was still dressed in the same clothing, only it was even more tattered, her skirt filthy, and one sleeve had been ripped from her peasant blouse's shoulder seam. Dirt smeared her everywhere … and she was trembling. "Us?" She managed a half smile, somewhere between the macabre and the forlorn. "This from a man who told me, 'Goodbye, *adios, auf wiedersehen,* cheerio, fare-thee-well, and may we never meet again!'?"

"That may be, however, my aim now is to get us safely and quickly back to El Paso. However, a flattened tire has made for a rather slow and rough ride."

"I have no wish to go back to your El Paso. Ever."

Exasperation grunted from him. "All right then, buttercup—to your Juarez."

"Easy enough, then. We remove all the tires."

He blinked in astonishment at the simplicity of the solution. "Why didn't I think of that?"

"When you're poor, riding on rims is often the only option."

Given the road back was gravelly sand, friction against the rims would not be a problem. Ed would be. He would have every inch of Walt's skin flayed.

"Uhh, do you mind putting down the handgun?"

Gingerly, as if the handgun were an eggshell that might crack, she placed it atop the Hudson's fender. He shrugged out of his herringbone jacket and draped it around her quivering frame. The jacket swallowed her.

Glaze-eyed, she stared up at him with incomprehension, as if she were unaccustomed to gallantry.

He removed his cuff links, passed them to her, and rolled his sleeves to midarm. Hunkering before the automobile, he jacked the damaged tire only high enough that it could not escape. The removal of it and the next two tires was not too laborious, but by the last one his shoulder and back muscles were protesting. He was out of shape. He needed to get back to his swimming regime. He would have to check out the El Paso YMCA's swimming pool.

He passed her a grungy nut.

"A milking stool would be wonderful, wouldn't it?" she said, a little too snidely.

Sweating despite the cold, he looked over his shoulder up at her. He did not think he could tolerate her a minute more. Except there was something both pathetic and boldly brave about her shivering silhouette. "What happened back there, back there with Cisco Rodriguez?"

Surprise surfaced on her fey features. "You knew? That he and the other man took me from the jail?"

"That's why I am here. What happened?" Her cuts and blood and bruises were not suffered solely from flight through the desert.

The muscles in her jaw spasmed. Her body vibrated like a plucked violin string, and her throat hummed a taut almost inaudible strain.

His heart softened. He pushed himself erect, brushing off his hands. He knew better than to touch in solace her grubby fist that held the nuts. "They hurt you, Pia?"

She nodded. Only nodded but her eyes glistened. Then she gulped. "He ... I was ... despoiled. I shot him dead."

He swallowed. Nodded. "And the other man?"

"Out there somewhere."

Strange, he wanted to take her in his arms, console her. Foolishly, he did just that. Enveloped her shoulders with one arm and encircled her waist with the other. He tugged her to him and held her taut elfin body against his, lending her his warmth. His body rocked them both ever so slightly, like the comforting motion of a rocking chair.

Her cheek was pressed at the base of his sternum. She mumbled, "And I was saving myself for Amado García."

That Amado García again. Whoever the hell he was, if her maidenhood was a factor, she was too good for the fellow. But, wisely, Walt said nothing.

Cordelia had taught him this, that he did not have to solve a problem of hers. Just listen. And that was something at which he had always been good. Or he would not have chosen the literary career he had. He simply stroked Pia's hair, snarled like a miscast fishing line.

After a few moments, her shuddering stopped. Her eyes peering up at him were shadowed with the same strange conflicting feelings he was experiencing ... the body's simultaneous distaste and demand.

"Well, best we get going," she murmured. "Jaw Man, he could be out looking for me."

He refrained from smiling at her nickname for Rodriguez's companion. "A brute, eh?"

She nodded shortly. "A Neanderthal."

That bit of information, coming from her, startled him, that this Mexican housemaid was that erudite.

She was turning toward the Hudson's fender to reclaim the handgun, when a woman's pained shriek in the near distance halted Pia midstride.

Goosebumps raised on his flesh, even though he was aware of the shriek's source from his time spent with Pershing's expedition deep into Mexico's interior. A mountain-lion in heat. Cats were nocturnal animals ... and dangerous.

Both he and Pia glanced at each other, then back toward the scrub, suddenly rattling close by. A pair of yellow eyes gleamed low within it, as if the mountain lion was about to pounce.

Walt was closer to the handgun. Pia nodded at it emphatically.

He shook his head.

Thick brows arched, she stared him down.

He shrugged.

She grabbed the handgun, closed her eyes, and cocked the hammer. The brush rustled apart. At the same time she fired, an armadillo waddled forward. Surprised, it instantly leaped straight up.

"Missed execution by a high jump," he said, watching the armadillo vamoose on its short legs back into the chaparral.

She glanced at him with a horrified expression. Then she started chuckling. So did he. Next her chuckling burst into uproarious laughter and, as he watched in dismay, that deep-bellied laughter subsided into spasms of tearful hiccoughs. "Had it been a mountain lion, we could have been mauled and—"

"We weren't."

Her demented glare was brittle. "But what if it had been?"

He understood what she was intimating, his timidity. "Well, it wasn't—and I am against the spilling of blood. Killing goes against my nature, you understand?"

She shut up. On the return trip, she sat sternly silent, though he noticed she shawled her vibrating shoulders beneath his coat with her cupped hands, warding off the cold wind sweeping inside the rattletrap Hudson. At last, she spoke, her voice a whisper. "Why did you come after me. Really?"

Either answer he could give was the truth … that he wanted to use her to infiltrate El Paso's spy community. Or that he was unaccountably and certifiably insanely drawn to her. He chose the former.

"Like I told you, I am a journalist. Looking for the story of the century. I want to ferret out a master spy for Germany, operating in El Paso right here under the nose of the United States. You speak German and English fluently. And the streetcar ticket agent says you understand telegraphy, which is a plus."

Her eyes narrowed. "Why would you be talking to Silas Wright about me?"

He loosed an impatient sigh. "It is a journalist's job to ask questions. Look, like a lot of businesses and homes now without maid service, the German consulate in El Paso needs one. The master spy, whoever it is, will eventually but assuredly make contact with its honorary consul, Günther von Kloss. I want you to spy on von Kloss."

"Spy?" She spit the word as if it were dung in her mouth. "Why would I want to spy for the United States?"

"Well, I can think of several reasons."

In the darkened motor car, he could not see her features clearly, but her tone was plainly sneering. "Whatever they are, my single one is better. Because of your United States' law against protesting, I was jailed and faced swinging by the noose. Now, you tell me why I should help the United States."

For a moment he was silent. America's democratic laws had their faults, but they were better than other countries and certainly better than no law at all. That would be retrogressing to the serfdom of the Middle Ages—or the serfdom that Mexico still was, for that matter.

He wanted to remind her the bath house protestors had vandalized public property, disrupted public services, and, worse, injured innocent bystanders. Picketing, petitions, parades were one thing, but destruction was another.

However, remonstration would not gain his objective. What could he say that would be persuasive? Once again, he fell back on the truth. Honesty accomplished so much more, when to lie only gave away one's power, one's control. And control of oneself was paramount.

"You should help the United States because your country's current corrupt government favors Germany as an ally and is willing to give a free hand for it to delve into Mexico's good earth and mineral wealth. Which *means* you could risk German occupation right here in Juarez. From what I hear back from Europe's battlefront, life under German rule could be a lot worse than what you are experiencing now."

"Well, let me tell you something else—never ever again will I set foot on the Santa Fe Bridge as long as it *means* being ... being stripped naked and poked in my private parts, sprayed like a cow with ticks, and my hair shaved."

That would be lamentable indeed, he thought, with hair as riotously glorious as hers. "Listen, no country is perfect. Since your country's myriad revolutions began ten chaotic years ago, hundreds of towns have been destroyed, and a quarter of a million of your people have lost their lives."

"A new constitution is being approved this very week, in Queretaro—with land reform promised."

So, she was steeped in current political events. He smothered another sigh. "Whether it is your current president, Carranza, or Villa who winds up running the show, there will still be Germany to deal with."

"I can't believe you are asking me to work against my country."

"Not against your country. Against its policy favoring Germany."

"I am not at all interested."

Juarez streetlights twinkled just ahead. "Twenty pesos a week."

A pause of a beat. So, her principles were not etched in stone. He repressed a smile. There was a certain piquancy in the dichotomy that was Piedad Arellano.

"Pull over at this next intersection. My mother's house is just off it."

"Well, does the twenty pesos interest you?"

A street's lamplight briefly illuminated her dead-in-the-gunsight-glare. "I may owe you for the ride. However, my soul is not for sale." With four fingers she hurriedly crossed herself, indicating she was most likely a devout Roman Catholic, more the pity. "Keep your filthy money."

At a darkened corner she indicated, he stopped the Hudson, and she opened its door to get out.

He leaned across the seat toward her. "I'm at the Hotel Sheldon, should you change your mind."

"Goodbye, *adios, auf wiedersehen,* cheerio, and fare-thee-well. May we never meet again, *Señor* Asshole Stevenson." She slammed the door.

Chapter Fourteen

The battering Pia's body had suffered was now taking its full toll. She found the shear act of placing one foot in front of the other excruciating. Like walking on nails. Dry eyed and drained of all emotion, she entered the hovel that was her mother's *casita*.

Seated at the table, her back to Pia, her mother was weaving the *lechuguilla*. Josefina, facing the wood-burning stove, was stirring with a broom handle clothes washing in a large pot's boiling, sudsy water.

Silently, Pia hung her *bolsa* and Walt's jacket on the wall pegs. She turned to find Rosita staring at her with eyes round as billiard balls. "Tia Pia! Your hair—your clothes!"

Pia had thought she was empty of feeling, but immediately she swept Rosita into her arms and rained the child's face with kisses before releasing her.

At the same time, the *lechuguilla* fibers fluttered from her mother's fingers. She pushed unsteadily from the wicker chair. "You are out of the jail, *Mija*!"

Dipping her head, concealing her anguish, she knelt to cradle the excited Perro against her chest. "Awww, you missed me, *mi perro precioso.*"

Josefina dropped the broom handle. The sweaty face she turned to Pia was not only swollen on one side from her abscessed tooth but now was reddened. "How did you get out?" Her dark brown eyes took in Pia's disheveled state. "*Dios mío,* Pia, what did they do to you in the jail?"

In her uneven gait Mamacita crossed hurriedly to Pia. "*Mija,* I am so relieved you're alive!"

When their mother stooped to plant a kiss atop her head, she crumpled. Perro scampered away just before she rolled onto her side into a fetal position. She began to gasp choking tears. "Mamacita, Mamacita." Over and over. That was all she could get out. "Mamacita."

Their mother knelt and curled her bony body over Pia's. "It's all right, it's all right, *Mija.* Whatever it is, *esto también pasará.*"

"I seriously doubt this, too, shall pass, Mamacita." Each word felt like a chunk of lava rock squeezing through the knot that was her throat. "I was raped."

"Oh, *Mija,* no, no! Not you, too." She rocked Pia in her arms. "*Mija pobrecita.*"

Rosita was staring wide-eyed, and from beneath the shelter of a chair, Perro was whining.

"Rosita," Josefina ordered, "it's bedtime."

"But, *Mamá,* it's only—"

"Go to our bedroom, get ready for bed." Once her daughter was out of the room, Josefina asked, "Are you all right, Pia?"

She gagged on her snot. "All is divine, Josefina—or shall I tell you how I really feel?"

The concern in Josefina's voice abated somewhat. "Spare me. I know. I've been there, remember? First things first. Should you conceive, my Guido can provide a compound from the *farmacía* to rid you of … it."

Astonished, Pia stared up at her sister, speaking in such a matter-of-fact manner, though her words were muffled somewhat, most likely by a peppermint compress her mother had fashioned for toothache.

Josefina brushed her plump palms back and forth against each other, as if swiping off crumbs, and exposed the sweat stains beneath her sleeve's armpits. "Back at Estancia Cascada, Mamacita and I did not have as safe means as this,"

Pia pushed to a sitting position and backhanded her scalding tears. "But neither you, nor I, nor Rosita would then be here had you or Mamacita access to such *safe* means."

Their mother intervened. *"Tranquilas, niñas!"*

Josefina ignored her and spat with angry satisfaction, "Just deal with this, Pia. Stop acting like you're something special and get on with your life—not that your bricklayer boyfriend will want you when he learns that you are spoiled goods."

Her sharp inhalation burned all the way down to her chest. Even if word of her rape failed somehow to get back to him, could she keep the secret should their relationship proceed as far as a marriage proposal? A man might be quite willing to bed a despoiled woman, but he would ironically want a virgin for a wife.

"Shut up, Josefina!" Mamacita snapped. Rubbing one veined temple, she spouted her usual homily for dire consequences. *"No hay mal qué por bien no venga."* Nothing can happen without some good coming out of it.

"Forgive me, Mamacita, my lack of faith," Pia said acerbically. What a broken family they were. All this time. The secrets ripping them apart. The hurting that had turned them on each other.

"Ask forgiveness instead for being self-centered," Josefina snapped back.

Startled, she said, "How can you possibly accuse me of being selfish, when almost everything I earn goes to keeping us in home and food?"

"I did not say selfish, Pia. I said self-centered. Remember when you were crusading with those other silly suffragists in front of *Plaza Constitución?* How it rained, and the dye from your yellow sashes streamed down your white skirts? Someone said, 'Look at that rain-soaked goddess,' and you assumed it was you they were talking about.

Someone else said, 'Look at that *idiota* in the rain,' and you reacted the same. It's always all about you, damn't, Pia!"

She pushed erect and made her painful way to the pie safe below the single window with its potted bright red geranium.

Next to the window was tacked a cheap wall calendar advertising Trujillo's *Farmacía*. All three women, Pia, Josefina, and their mother kept track of their monthly menstrual courses on it. Pia could not bring herself to search for her last initialed notation. If Cisco's rape impregnated her ... she could not bear to think of such a consequence. Not right now. Something of more import demanded her attention.

Atop the pie safe were tin canisters of flour and ground coffee, a lard can of aloe vera their mother used for her arthritis pain—and Pia's old Cracker Jack box, its trivial prize plundered the year before.

If she wanted to get out of this pothole that was her life, she needed to make a drastic change. That timeworn cardboard box's twenty-two pesos, now intended for investment in United States real estate, would instead serve as her ticket out.

She would catch the next train bound for Chihuahua City, where there would be no border to cross, no probing or shaving or spraying of her naked body.

And, as Walt Stevenson had pointed out, she was not only multilingual but also accomplished in telegraphy. Surely, sufficient qualifications to land a job. And best, real estate in Chihuahua City was even cheaper—albeit this was due to homeowners' life expectancy drastically reduced by the multiple revolutions.

She reached into the Cracker Jack box ... and encountered nothing. She dug in farther, her fingertips clawing along its cardboard folded bottom and sides. In slow motion, she pivoted toward Josefina and their mother. "Where is my money?"

Like gunpowder in a flash pan Josefina's dark eyes fired defensively. "The last two days, I couldn't cross the Rio Bravo to go to work."

"And?"

"Kohlberg Cigars could easily let me go. There's always a hundred girls willing to work the box-stuffing line. And besides, we needed food. There were barely enough scraps left over for your Perro."

Aghast, Pia stared. "A couple of pesos would have provided more than enough food." She glanced at her mother, who appeared equally surprised by Josefina's statement. Pia glared back at Josefina. "Where's the rest?"

Josefina had the grace to look sheepish. "You know Rosita needed a new hairbrush, and I—"

"I know, I know, and you needed your tequila."

Tears welled in Josefina's eyes. She reached into her skirt pocket and flung out a handful of coins. Several centavos bounced and rolled across the chipped linoleum. "No, I needed a dentist to pull my tooth."

Pia felt crummy, but she could not summon any charity at the moment. Wanting to weep, she grabbed up her *bolsa* and Walt's jacket from the wall peg. "Keep the money, Josefina. You need it more than I do."

Slamming closed the casa door on her mother's beseeching cry to stay, Pia started walking, her body bowed forward, bracing itself against a rogue wind that stung her ears.

Her impulsiveness—would she ever temper it? Would she ever refrain from making snap decisions? Always walking away she was, it seemed. So many housemaid jobs she either walked away from or was discharged from because of her insistence of autonomy. So many relationships—friends, *novios*, and now family—she walked away from because they impinged on her sense of fairness.

The frigid night air restored some sanity. From this point forward her future would be different than her past. She knew now where she was going and what she was going to do. She was resolved she would yet have a grand house on Mount Franklin. She would never give up on that intention.

Chapter Fifteen

Walt glanced in the bathroom's oval mirror, frowned, and scrubbed his craggy jaw, bristling with a five o'clock shadow. He reached for his watch chain. Nearly nine p.m., too far past the closing time of the hotel barbershop below.

Tracking down Pia Arellano and getting her back had made for a hell of a day, and the hotel's Turkish bath beckoned him. Grabbing up his room key and his trilby, he realized Pia had his suit's herringbone jacket. He was about to retrieve a corduroy field jacket from the closet when a rap-rap on the room door interrupted him midstride.

What now? Frowning, he opened the door. A bellboy in a red cap and braided red uniform extended a folded paper. "Telephone message for you, Mr. Stevenson."

Walt tipped him from his pocket change, a hefty ten centavos, and shut the door. He unfolded the paper.

Hello, hola, hallo, cheerio, and hail my new employer. I am waiting at Trujillo's Farmacía. In irregular scrawl, the note was signed 'Pia Arellano.'

He rolled his eyes. What cheek.

Ed's parked Hudson was not rolling another mile without new rims and tires. There were no taxicabs outside the hotel. Walt hailed a Hansom cab, the kind used for a romantic tour along the river or through El Paso's farce of an Old Town.

When he told the driver the round-trip destination to Juarez, the old black man perched up on the driver's seat said politely, "No way, sir."

"What do you mean?"

"You haven't heard? About the riot?"

"Yes, yes, of course."

"Then you are aware that I might get us over to Juarez by way of the Stanton Street Bridge, but returning on the Santa Fe Bridge, it's blocked by authorities on both sides."

"I know. I just crossed it." Pulling from his hat brim, he flashed his press pass. "This should suffice."

The driver's white teeth gleamed. "Giddy up, gal," he ordered his gray nag.

Pia was still wearing his herringbone jacket. Her arms hugging herself, she was standing before the lit-up pharmacy, the base of its stucco wall rimmed by wind-blown litter.

He stepped down from the carriage and opened its door for her. Ignoring his proffered hand, she scooted to the far side of the squab's split upholstery. Once again, he felt that inexplicable acceleration of his pulse. After the cab started up, he said, "I thought you swore never to cross the Santa Fe bridge again."

Her teeth were clicking like castanets. "I said I would never set foot on it. Besides, there is less chance of running into Jaw Man on the American side."

"Double talk. What changed your mind? Other than the lure of filthy money."

She ignored his caustic barb. "*Mire, Señor* Stevenson—"

"Walt, please."

"Look, we Mexicans are not like you Americans and Germans with your silly squabble between one another, *gracias a Dios*." She shrugged.

"I will do this one thing, spy at the German consulate. If it serves to disrupt the sumptuous lifestyle of the German-Mexican who threw away me, my mother, my sister—my *sisters*—like we were used toilet paper, then so much the better."

He raised a brow at the word 'sumptuous' being a part of her vocabulary but only said, "I am hazarding a guess here. That would be the man you claim is your father, Don Horst Heinrich?"

"Who is also the father of my sister—and my niece Rosita, which makes her my half-sister, if you can follow me. He raped his own daughter! So that should tell you something about the caliber of man that piece of shit is."

He was not amazed that he could almost feel the heat radiating off her spewed invectives. The heat and the hurt. She was not one of those half-measure women. For her it would be all or nothing.

"Does your mother know that you will be … uh, working for me?"

A streetlamp momentarily cast its garish glow on her face. Tight lipped, she shook her head.

"Won't your family be worried about you?"

"My sister Josefina, she is already angry about the rampage I caused." A tiny sigh fluttered from her lips. "And if not about that, then it would be something else."

"I see. So, you are on the outs with your family?"

More stolid silence from the little stick of dynamite.

He presented his press pass to the Mexican border guard, who gave it a cursory glance and waved on the Hansom cab.

While it clip-clopped across the bridge to the American side, Walt was thumbing through his options quickly. El Paso had no YWCA. And boarding houses were full, what with all the refugees from the revolution crossing the border.

What a half-baked idea of his this was. Tracking down Pia. Where was he going to put the wild child?

He fingered looser his collar and cleared his throat. "Tomorrow, I shall start looking for a place for you to stay, but until then you can sleep on the settee in my suite's sitting room."

"At home, I had to sleep on the sofa. So, I get the bed this time." Her words were rigid as her posture.

"Not so fast. It's not a sofa. It's a settee. Far too short for my gangling frame, but suitable for your short stuff, Goldilocks."

"What?"

"Never mind."

The American side of the Rio Grande was more heavily guarded by troopers out of Fort Bliss and his press pass more closely examined. Once through the barricade, he said, "You'll need more presentable clothing tomorrow before you apply for work at the consulate."

She stared sightlessly out the up-and-over glass window. The cab's faint lamplight fell on a shattered spirit. While she could in no way be described as a classic beauty, he had to admit she possessed an unconventional comeliness.

The sound of steel horseshoes clanging against brick pavement gradually reduced to a halt before the Sheldon. Walt paid the driver through the rear of the roof's trapdoor, then got out and held up his hand to help Pia descend the carriage step.

Her gaze glanced at his hand then flickered up to meet his. Swiftly, her lids lowered over her distraught expression. Lifelessly, she placed her palm in his. He was struck by how work-hardened her palm was, how small it looked laying in his larger one, and how disconcerted he was.

He ushered her past the lobby's ornate marble columns and front desk. Large vases of fresh flower arrangements intermittently arrayed the counter's expanse of pink granite and partially screened his hasty passage to the elevator.

When both the door and its hinged scissor-gate slid open, she stopped short. Her naturally pink lips formed a perfect O. "An elevator!" she breathed ecstatically, the way some females would upon viewing a diamond engagement ring.

He placed a hand at the small of her back and gently propelled her forward. "Hello, Joe," he told the elevator operator.

"Good evening, Mr. Stevenson." From behind his thick, beer-bottom spectacles, the operator's bleary eyes rounded at the sight of Pia's bedraggled appearance.

She stiff-legged past the old man in royal red livery, and Walt pivoted her around to face the front. "War orphan," he told Joe.

Joe's chin, stubbled with gray, clamped shut. Undoubtedly, the elevator operator had seen gentlemen bring up to their rooms their *filles de joie*—but ones always better dressed than this girl in scuffed working boots, raggedy clothing, and draped in Walt's now rumpled and too-large jacket.

Staring straight ahead, the old man pressed the large, wheeled lever on his right to the forward position, and the elevator jerked upward with grating protest.

Pia's palms clasped against her concave stomach. Her cheeks flamed. Her eyes widened. "Ohhh!" Her exclamation blended both terror and wonderment.

Caught up by her impassioned emotions, Walt blurted, "You should go up in an aeroplane with me. It is powerfully elating."

She glanced askance at him, as if he were speaking Greek—while he wondered what had possessed his run-away tongue.

Once inside his suite, he watched her register the sitting room's ornate furnishings. Her gaze moved from the desk, neatly arranged with his notepapers, pocketknife, pencils, and barrel pen; past the sideboard with coffeepot and tea service; to the tall wardrobe; then on to the settee with its teal-colored silk bolsters at either end. Faltering footsteps took her through the next doorway, and her gaze settled on the double bed topped by a tufted turquoise counterpane.

He felt sorry for her. She had been through a hell of a lot in the past forty-eight hours, including the unimaginable, being raped. The last thing she needed was worrying about his jumping her bones.

"Listen, you may feel better after a bath." He nodded toward the adjoining door. "It locks."

The gratitude reflected in her eyes at this simple gesture nearly bowled him over. After she closed the door behind her, he could hear moments later the tub's water running.

He hung his field jacket and waistcoat on the coat peg, tugged loose his tie, then shrugged down his suspenders and unlaced his oxfords, stowing them neatly side by side. Lastly, he placed his pince-nez on the bedside table and flopped on the bed.

He clasped his hands at his nape and stared up at the European-designed ceiling. Which brought him around to thoughts of the Madrid-born Dulcinea del Jardín. Twenty-three years old, she had immigrated to Mexico five years ago and become Juarez's famed *matadora*, a female bull killer. She was sexy, savvy, and strong.

They were compatible in and out of bed … with the one vital exception: he could never countenance killing, especially for the sport of it. After attending a performance of hers in Juarez's *Plaza del Toros*, one that was at once as breathtaking as a Russian ballet and as violent as one of Villa's executions, Walt was conscious their relationship would never progress beyond the boundary of a bed, although he was aware she continued to hope it would.

But then so had Pia killed, admittedly in self-defense. Thinking of the two females gave him an idea. Yes, perhaps he could unload Pia on Dulcinea. Have her shop for clothing for Pia, then finagle her into boarding the Mexican wraith, the expenses which he would be delighted to cover.

And thinking of the Mexican wraith, he wondered what was taking her so long to bathe. It had been over a quarter of an hour. He listened for the sound of splashing. None. He began to worry. He knew nothing about her. She said she had been saving herself for this Amado García and now she had been violated. She did not seem the kind to take her life. Still … .

He thought of his straight razor, the folding kind where the blade slid into the handle. It was with his strop and shaving mug on the washstand. He scrambled from the bed faster than he had ever scrambled from beneath the enemy's barbed wire.

He rapped on the bath door. Silence. He rapped again. Still nothing. He tried the knob. Locked. He debated which was quicker—knocking down the door or jimmying the lock with his pocketknife.

Resorting to the latter, he was inside within less than a sweating minute. He came to an abrupt halt. Her nude little body lay in the large clawfoot tub, her red hair fanned about her face, pale as old ivory. Her thin arms were outflung, as if she were merely drifting upon a current.

God Almighty! In two strides he was bending over to scoop her from the now tepid water. Anxiously, he scanned her features for some sign of life—and was rewarded when her lids fluttered open.

Startled fear widened her sea-green eyes. Her frail body thrashed against his arms. She began screaming.

"Hush, hush. I'm not going to hurt you, Pia."

Her fists drummed his chest. Her moans were the same tortured sounds he had witnessed from those victims who wore the freshly, incised Masque of Villa—their ears and nose cut off.

What to do? He had no experience with hysteria. All the people in his life tended to be placid and phlegmatic. As he passed the bed, he yanked off the counterpane and strode into the sitting room. He dropped into the rocking chair. With the turquoise spread he cocooned them both and began to rock.

Rocking. Creaking wood. Rocking. Creaking wood. Rocking. And his soft whistling, a lullaby his grandfather had often played on his harmonica. Rocking. Creaking wood. Whistling.

Gradually, her piercing moans deteriorated into a cascade of tears, accompanied by a violent shuddering of the waifish, naked body. He cradled her tighter to him. And continued his whistling and rocking.

She curled against his chest, buried her face into the hollow of his shoulder and collarbone, and began to weep silently. Within minutes, the front of his shirt was sopping.

Rocking. Whistling, this time the lullaby "Cuddle Up a Little Closer." Rocking. Creaking wood. Whistling. And more rocking. Haplessly, he patted her back. "There, there." Actions, wordings, and feelings invoked from his childhood, from his grandfather's comforting surfaced in him. Rocking. Rocking. Rocking.

At some point, her weeping dissolved into a soft hiccoughing.

Eventually, gradually, with a faint sigh, her body went limp within his clutch. The kind of clutch a toddler bestows on its favored stuffed toy.

He risked a glance down at her upturned faced. Like snapped-open fans, her thickly-lashed lids were spread in exhausted sleep. Her lips were parted in baby breaths. That close, he, who noticed the minute, was mildly surprised he had somehow overlooked the light sprinkling of freckles across the bridge of her nose and cheeks.

His own sigh was knitted with relief and exasperation. Gently, he rose and laid her slack body upon the mattress. Noting that her flesh was goose-bumped, he retrieved his pajamas from beneath the far pillow. He tugged her arms into the pajama top. It engulfed her.

He was disgusted that, while he buttoned the gray flannel, his gaze nevertheless absorbed her small breasts, the dusky pink of their nipples, turgid with the cold, and the burning red bush at her groin. As fast as his fumbling fingers could manage, he finished buttoning the top and rolling up each sleeve.

Then he retrieved the settee's bolsters. By damn, he was not going to forego a night of sleep with his rangy body scrunched on the settee. Rationally, he understood his anger was directed at himself. But he was not a rational man these last few days.

After he saw to the care of her discarded clothing, he undressed, donned the pajama bottoms, and climbed onto the bed's far side—with the bolsters aligned down the middle of the bed, separating him from temptation.

Pawning Pia off onto Dulcinea could not come quickly enough, because, by some quirk of nature, his heart was always with those who dealt with temptation by surrendering to it. While his own rigid mindset had hitherto forbidden him to do so.

Innately, he perceived that he was of the ilk of writers who had to balance upon the wire that was both suspension and tension, a wire that was a woefully woven silken thread of reality and illusion.

Chapter Sixteen

January 31st, 1917

Vague recollections of the night before fleeted through Pia's mind ... how in the huge bathtub she had scoured her skin, as if she could scrub away her defilement ... the safety and security of Walt's arms as he had rocked her to sleep ... later his intermittent snoring from his side of the bolsters, aligning down the plush mattress like a turquoise brick wall ... and then this morning awakening to find him sitting at her side and extending to her a saucer containing a muffin and cup.

"Time to face the day, buttercup. I'll introduce you to my friend, who will get you outfitted." He had shaved and was already dressed in a three-piece narrow-striped, tan suit. Its morning coat's shoulders, which she doubted were padded in the current fashion, emphasized their breadth.

Her feminine instinct raised her brow. "A female friend?" So this was the woman who held his heart. She sat up and took the saucer.

"You'll be staying with her." He stood, brushing his palms and brushing away Pia's intrusive question. "Then it's off to seek employment at the German consulate tomorrow."

She took a sip from the cup and, closing one eye, winced. Not coffee, but tea. And it had cream in it. Gag. "Does the hotel restaurant have strawberry soda pop by any chance?"

Behind his pince-nez, his eyes glinted with amusement. "Strawberry soda pop?"

"*Sí.* Rosita got me started on it."

"Ahh, yes, your niece—er, and half-sister."

"What if I do not want to stay with this … your friend?" What Pia wanted was nothing more than to curl up against the bastion that was Walt's chest while he rocked her once more. And wanted him to feel the same sweet unfurling of the senses she did within his arms.

"Dulcinea del Jardín is her name. And it's out of the question your staying with me."

"*That* Dulcinea del Jardín? The *matadora*?"

"One and the same." He went to the bureau and picked up a paper-wrapped package by its bundling string. "Last night I sent down your clothing to be cleaned and re-seamed."

Nibbling on the buttered muffin, she mumbled, "First, I want this week's twenty pesos." Better to get the terms upfront and agreed upon.

His mouth looked like it was struggling to fight off a smile. "Have you heard the English bromide, 'Beggars can't be choosers?'"

She shrugged, and his pajama top slipped off to expose her left shoulder, where hair pins loosened during her sleep had plummeted lengths of unkempt hair. At once, his gaze skittered away, when the night before he had to have seen her fully nude body in the bathtub. What an enigma he was.

"And have you heard the biblical passage," she replied, "'Ask and ye shall receive?' I want a bank account opened. In my name." No more would her hard-earned savings be pilfered from her.

"I'll wait in the sitting room while you dress." He crossed to the door adjoining the sitting room. Hand on the knob, and looking over his shoulder at her, he added, "Despite the similarity of desert landscape, El Paso is not the Holy Land," then firmly shut the door behind him.

Well, she had to agree with him on that. Quickly she washed and donned her refurbished clothing. In the sitting room, he was twirling his trilby's brim between his fingers. "On our way to my friend's place—"

"Does your friend, Dulcinea del Jardín, know we're coming?"

"Yes, and before I drop you off there, we'll stop off at my bank. This is a business deal, and nothing more, you understand?"

She wanted to throw her arms around his neck but resisted the impulse.

His fingertips at the back of her waist, he propelled her into the elevator again. She recalled the prior ride in the magical cubicle. Her stomach had plummeted the same way it used to do whenever she saw Amado. She managed a nervous grin for the operator. "Hello, Joe."

Both Joe and Walt looked at her with surprise. "Good morning, Miss," Joe said, smiling back despite his effort to maintain an employee's reserved decorum, and snapped open the cage.

Walt was coaching her in the taxicab they caught at the corner, but her nervousness increased to outright anxiety, and she barely listened. One male had violated her, but this male, by asking nothing sexual from her, made her even more uneasy. His preternatural dispassion rattled her. There was no way to breach his stone wall.

"My objective is to find out to whom here in El Paso von Kloss reports." Walt was numbering off his points on one long finger after another, and she was imagining what it would be like for them to stroke her cheek—or even merely to hold her hand, entwining their fingers.

"One, listen in on any telephone conversations made while you are there. Take mental notes. Two, see if you can find a budget or an account ledger of some kind—that would provide invaluable information. Three, search for any written references of local individuals, like receipts, et cetera—even if the references seem unimportant—that you may come across. A code of some kind could be involved. Four, speaking of codes, check the office teleprinter for …. "

As he continued to rattle off his points, she studied his face, carved with crevices too deep for one so young. She judged him to be in his mid-to-late-twenties. Dark brows marked his sensual face. He smelled fresh, the same scent of the brick of expensive wood-barrel soap she had discovered in his bathroom.

At the bank, the ingratiating balding teller tried to mask his dismay when Walt summarily informed him an account was to be opened in her name. She could barely assimilate all that happened to her in the last three days. From jobless to jailed. From cherished by Amado to violated by Cisco. From holding an empty Crackerjack cardboard box to holding a deposit-noted bankbook.

Once outside the bank, she asked Walt point blank, "Do you love her, this Dulcinea?" Jealous feelings, with which Pia hereto had been unfamiliar, swarmed around her now, buzzing loudly like disturbed bees.

He opened the rear door of the taxicab he had paid to wait and looked down at her with a solemn scowl. "I have committed my heart to only one other woman—back East in Pennsylvania—and that apparently was not enough. And I am not prepared to give any greater—my heart *and* my soul."

Oh, so here was another clue to the *Norte Americano's* stolidness. His forceful and imperturbable approach she might find off-putting in others, but somehow she was drawn to it—and to him. Here was a man of honest arrogance in comparison with the hypocritical humility she recognized in some of her wealthier employers. "You are so pigheaded, Walt Stevenson."

His soulful solemnity gave way to blistering mockery. "I wouldn't expect you to understand. You, who last night sang the value and virtues of your soul, exchange it today for a bank account."

She should be affronted, but she cared too much. Ignoring his nod to get in the taxicab, she stood on tiptoe and cradled his face between her palms. "I understand this—that I am the one your heart *and* soul need, Walt Stevenson."

"Although the owners of The White House Department Store are Germans from Alsace-Lorraine," Dulcinea purred in throaty Castilian Spanish, "I still prefer its merchandise over The Popular Dry Goods, despite what Walter may suggest."

Pia was somewhat in awe of the vigorously fit *matadora*. Posters of her were pasted on street posts, columns, and walls on both sides of the Rio Bravo.

The much taller woman paraded Pia along one of the aisles and grasped a hangered pink satin blouse from one display, a pencil slim black skirt from another, and a few items of clothing that were more work-related. All these she passed blithely to the clerk who trailed in their wake. "Walter may say he wants clothing fit for a domestic, but he doesn't understand the female sex."

"Uhh, but he *is* paying for all of this."

Dulcinea shrugged muscle-striated shoulders. Incongruously, she was wearing a shirtwaist and man's tie above a hobble-skirt. And she looked stunning. "Money is nothing to him. But his writing is everything." Dulcinea's red-painted mouth screwed up. "*Pobre de mi*, I can barely read my own posters." She shrugged again. "*Ni modo.*"

Pia was determined to make him see her in another light than the current opinion he held of her. She had already decided he was the one for her. However, it was obvious he had no idea that everything to this point had been preparing them for one another.

"You love him—Walter Stevenson?" she ventured to ask the beautiful Spaniard.

"Far too much." Dulcinea stopped and turned toward her. A stylish, pinless hat resembling an upturned flowerpot barely contained her upswept mahogany hair. Without looking directly at Pia, she fiddled with the fingers of her kid gloves. "I love him enough to know that it must be me he wants. Totally."

"A warning?"

With that Dulcinea's eyes bore straight into her. "Exactly. I want everything up front, no dark horse coming up on me from out of the stretch. So, I want him to see you at your best—and see if it is enough to best me. That is also why, while I find it very inconvenient, I will put you up at my place—most grudgingly howbeit—rather than tempt him with your presence at his hotel suite. Do we understand one another?"

"*Perfectamente.*"

So, were the two lovers? The thought deflated Pia, deflated her conceit in believing she was what Walt needed to release his vice-like grip on restraint of his feelings.

The *matadora* beamed back. "Good. Then we are *d'accord* as foes. I suggest we collect our packages and then adjourn to the Elite Confectionary to celebrate our pact."

Elite Confectionary had been one of sweet-toothed Pancho Villa's daily hangouts during his exile in El Paso until he fell out of favor with the U.S. government a couple of years before. With a $20,000 center soda fountain, the place was always packed, summer and winter.

Today was no exception. There was not a table empty nor a stool at the fountain available. Then from the back, an arm waved, hailing them, and Dulcinea exclaimed, "It's *el perfumado*—Silvestre!"

Pia mentally winced. There could be only one Silvestre who was a sweet-smelling dandy. Her five-year-older half-brother. She remembered him as being at once both kind and high-handed, much like his father in the latter. Otherwise, the two were in no way or manner similar. From sexual persuasion to political affiliation. They were at odds with one another, Silvestre being the black sheep of the *familia* Heinrich-Salinas.

Wearing an Ascot cap and wielding a gold knobbed cane, he threaded his way from the back and in between the small, round tables. Short and slender, he wore rings on every finger, including his thumbs. With fine features and black pomaded hair and pointed beard, Silvestre looked more like his deceased mother, who had been cursed with a faint mustache.

He dropped a kiss on Dulcinea's extended gloved hand. In a high and nasally voice, he said, "Come join me and my friend, *mi preciosa*."

She turned to Pia. "Let me introduce you to Piedad Arellano. Pia this is Silvestre Salinas."

Intelligent and inquisitive eyes surveyed her, noting her shoddy clothing, and she noticed he did not offer a gallant bow. "I know you?"

While she wanted to grit out, "Yes, I am your illegitimate half-sister. One of three," this was not the time to do it. If ever. Why make matters worse? She often wondered if they shared other siblings in the pueblos dotting the eight-million-acre Estancia Cascada. She merely replied, "My mother, Marta, and my sister Josefina and I worked for your father as housemaids."

Sudden recognition played across his face. "You and your sister Josefina—she was closer to my age—you two attended our estancia school with me."

"Until Don Horst sent you off to Paris for a higher education."

She was hoping he would not remember anything else, but he did. Those studious brown eyes narrowed. "You were the one who put the tarantula in my satchel."

She refused to shrink beneath his glare. "Only after you had stuck the end of one of my braids in your desk inkwell."

He shrugged. "I did not like red hair at the time." Even then, most everyone at the hacienda was aware he and his redheaded father butted heads with one another. "I still don't. But it looks good on you now, Pia Arellano." His haughty manner lessened somewhat, and he executed a slight smile along with an even slighter bow.

As he escorted them to his table in the back, heads turned to watch the statuesque Dulcinea. She carried herself with assurance, in the same way Walt carried himself with the air of success, regardless of the odds.

Pia's lips twitched. *Mierda*, the two were a well-matched pair. She could only hope Walt was unaware of just how well he and the sure-eyed Spanish woman matched.

Toward the rear of the confectionery, the conversational noise was less voluble. Silvestre halted before a table at the very back, and Pia's jaw dropped. Amado sat there, spooning a dip from the scoop of chocolate-covered vanilla ice cream.

At the sight of her, he dropped his spoon and shot to his feet. "Pia!

Dios mío, I went back to the jail, and you were gone!" He caught her hands. "You are all right, *bebé?*"

She felt the heat of a flush rising up her neck to her cheeks. What could she say in front of Silvestre and Dulcinea? *No, I am no longer a virgin.* She could not bear to see the disappointment in Amado's eyes. "A little worse for the wear, I am."

Next, Amado's gaze, tinted with the hint of a fan's idolization, landed on Dulcinea. "I have seen your posters everywhere, but I never thought I would have this opportunity to meet you."

Dulcinea cast him the kind of smile one did for an amusing child. "Now, here's a handsome young man who knows how to make a woman feel good."

The rims of his protruding ears flushed. He quickly helped deposit the garment bags and shoe and hat boxes atop one of the table's empty chairs.

While she and Dulcinea ordered what Amado was eating, a Baseball it was called, costing a substantial ten cents, the two men were exchanging hushed words.

Silvestre's peanut brittle lay untouched. After the aproned waiter left, Silvestre peered at her thoughtfully. "From what I understand from my friend here, you're the girl he has been wanting me to help, the one who instigated the bath house slugfest."

She shrugged, feeling uncomfortable with the three's attention focused on her. Apparently, Amado had not divulged the sibling relationship she shared with Silvestre.

Silvestre said dryly, "Obviously, then, you haven't changed a bit since we were kids. Still a little renegade are you?"

The Texas Department of Criminal Justice would undoubtedly apply another term to her misconduct.

"But how did you get out of jail," Amado persisted.

She smiled weakly. "A couple of Villa's elite Dorados got me released and set me loose outside Juarez." Far outside. More sins of omission. Father Ignacio would have her doing Hail Mary penances the rest of her life. He already declared her incorrigible in the evening collegiate courses he taught.

Amado frowned. "Why would *Villista*s take up your cause?"

"Most likely anything to aggravate the United States," Silvestre suggested. Then, "How do you know Dulcinea, Pia? I thought I was familiar with all her friends."

Dulcinea flicked her a look that said you're on your own.

Her swallow of the heavenly ice cream was more a gulp. "*Pues, Señor* Walter Stevenson, a journalist for an American magazine, he interviewed me in the jail. So that I could more easily find another maid's job, he has kindly arranged a place for me to stay on this side of the border." She nodded toward the *matadora,* who with a droll smile was listening closely to Pia. "With his friend here, Dulcinea."

Amado asked, "Is there anything I can do to help, *bebé?*"

The adoration she saw in his eyes … it was a yearning so strong it almost broke her heart. She started to shake her head sadly, and then came the prompting thought. "Yes, please—go to Trujillo's *Farmacía* and ask the clerk, Guido, to fetch my dog Perro from my home."

Dulcinea glared. "No dogs in my house."

"You'll love Perro," Pia asserted, but, honestly who in their right mind could care about such an ugly dog?

"My cat Leona won't."

"Come on, Dulcinea," Silvestre coaxed, "Leona doesn't even like humans, so what does it matter?"

Pia could see the woman's resistance teetering and held her breath. Perro was all she had left that was hers. She had lost everything. Home, family, what little money she had saved—and her maidenhead.

"Nothing permanent, you understand," Dulcinea grudged.

At long last, Pia thought, things in her life might be changing for the better—as long as Jaw Man stayed on his side of the Rio Bravo.

Chapter Seventeen

E xhilaration zinged through Amado. He sat next to Dulcinea, who was driving her Ford Model T Speedster with the same grace and split-second skill she flourished her cape at bulls.

The roaring wind flapped his black poncho into raven's wings. It loosened some of her pinned curls and threatened to swipe her yellow motoring cap. The weather had warmed considerably, making both her matching duster and his poncho unnecessary.

The speedster's green frame was lowered to only a couple of inches of ground clearance, and the road noise along the river road was deafening. The late afternoon sunlight transformed the sluggish brown of the Rio Grande into a shimmering topaz and the denuded cottonwoods and willows into sleek woody creatures.

A grin following the curve of her goggles, Dulcinea turned to him and shouted, "Like taking risks, do you?"

Was that an invitation? He could smell the scent of her arousal. But he did not know if he was responsible for it or it derived from the thrill of the power and danger of the motor car's speed.

He was not sure of anything recently. In the last few weeks, he seemed to be attracting females like shit did horseflies. But these kinds of women were like butterflies … Pia Arellano, *Señora* Adelaide, and now, Dulcinea del Torres. Was this a newly realized virility—or was this mere vanity on his part? "As much as you do," he yelled back.

"That is why you are involved with Silvestre—and this revolutionary periodical of his?"

He shrugged. "You are a *matadora, sí?* Better to die on your feet than to live on your knees, no?"

She nodded briskly. "*Claro qué sí*—and you are a rabble rouser, I think." She refocused her attention back to driving, gearing down to cross the international bridge.

Pia and Silvestre had stayed behind at Dulcinea's place. Were the two catching up on old times? Amado felt a pang of jealousy—unaccountable, given that surely Silvestre's preference in love affairs ran toward his own sex.

Amado could not contain his curiosity. He leaned into Dulcinea to make himself better heard. "Why is Pia staying with you? Really?"

Her athletic shoulders shrugged, and her red-painted lips crimped. "What Walter Stevenson wants, Walter Stevenson gets."

Pia had mentioned the name, of course. But the name was already vaguely familiar to Amado. He searched his memory. Yes, he recollected it now. The name of Walter Stevenson had been brought up in one of *La Reforma Social* meetings he had attended. A reporter for *Collier's Magazine*, this Stevenson was.

That wounding arrow that was jealousy once more targeted Amado. Did this Stevenson, this intellectual, have a romantic design on Pia? Reluctantly, Amado had to admit that she might well be intrigued by this highly educated and accomplished *Americano*. But after the initial fascination wore off, what then? The two had nothing in common.

At Trujillo's *Farmacía*, Amado learned that Guido was off work but the on-duty clerk gave directions to the Arellano casa. Dulcinea creeped the speedster along the potholed dirt street leading off of Avenida de Comercio. One of the hovels they passed looked as if it had been pancaked by more recent revolutionary fighting. She braked in front of the postage stamp-sized house that belonged to Pia's mother.

Pia's sister Josefina answered the door. A dark haired, cinnamon-skinned young woman, her prettiness was diminished by petulant lips perpetually downturned beneath a dark mole centered directly below her nostrils.

"*Hola*, Josefina, I am Amado García—remember, we have met at the *Plaza Constitución,* the Public Hall, and a couple of other places."

She looked taken aback. "*¿Sí?*" she asked cautiously. Above her head dangled a flypaper sticky with desiccated flies.

"Uhh, Pia asked if I would bring Perro to her."

From behind Josefina, an older woman inserted herself to the forefront. Her abundant hair was knotted in an untidy gray bun. She had to be the mother. "Pia is safe?" She was wringing her hands. "Where is she, *por favor?*"

Dulcinea pushed her goggles up atop the short brim of her motoring cap. "*Mira*, the girl, she is staying with me. She is safe enough."

Mouths open, the mother and daughter stared at Dulcinea in sheer awe. "You are Dulcinea del Jardín, sí?" Josefina breathed.

She allotted a smile, and he had to wonder if she ever tired of the public's adoration. "Last time I looked in the mirror I was."

Yet another individual squeezed ahead of the Arellano females. The middle-aged man was as wide as he was short with glossy black hair greased back. Under one arm he cradled an ugly mutt.

He stuck out his free hand to grab and pump Amado's. "Guido. Guido Ruiz." His grin displayed a missing bottom front tooth. "For the love of God, *por favor*, take Perro." His round brown face a portrait of relief, he shoved the yipping pooch at Amado.

The mother's bird-like hand latched onto his poncho. "*Por favor*, tell Pia we love her. We want her back, home here with us."

"Speak for yourself, Mamacita," Josefina said.

The ride back across the Rio Grande was fast and silent—until the nervous little dog between Amado's legs pooped on the floorboard and Dulcinea screeched, "Hell and damnation!"

The *matadora's* fashionable Mediterranean apartment on Palms Court perched just below the demarcation of astronomical wealth, Sunset Heights. Pia flung open the front door and whooped at the sight of the stinky dog Amado held aloft by the scruff of his neck.

"*Mi preciosa!*" she cooed and happily hugged the squirming animal to her. Nevertheless, Amado could not help but note how wrung out she appeared. Shadows haunted her eyes. Her mouth that he wanted badly to kiss had lost is mischievous tilt … all in the space of the little time since he had last seen her.

Behind her, the dapper Silvestre looked on with concern. Had they discussed childhood memories on the Cascada Estancia—or, worse, their father Don Horst Heinrich?

"Come on in," Dulcinea told Amado, tugging off her goggles and hat and shrugging out of her duster. Beneath she wore what he estimated had to be an expensive brocaded bolero jacket. She drifted to a small bar built between the adjacent kitchen and main room. "Coffee with a splash of brandy, everyone?"

"I'll start the coffee," Silvestre said, heading for the kitchen.

Amado joined Pia, cuddling Perro on the cushioned banco, the built-in bench stretching the entire length of the wall. But for a knee-high carving of a rampaging bull, its horns lowered to the floor, the starkly white room was bare of adornment.

Well, nearly. In a high niche, where one would expect a statue of the Virgin Mary or a saint, perched an orange cat. Looking like it had been stuffed, its fur stood out, as if electrified. It glared down at Perro.

Amado's eye traveled past the riled cat to the room's longest wall. A portrait of the vivacious Dulcinea should be its focal point, he mused. And both she and Pia were exactly that, vivacious. Not merely existing but gulping down life's water, be it stale or invigorating.

His fingers itched to pen India ink over a graphite underdrawing of Pia, to capture the fulsome way she laughed—her head tilting back, her wide mouth open, gulping in life, her amusement bubbling up from deep within. He could well imagine her head falling back in much the same way but caught up in the throes of passion's release.

"There is something you should know, Amado," Pia began and set aside the dog.

In his mincing gait, Silvestre came round the corner from the kitchen. "Beware, *mi amigo*, Amado. That kind of announcement always heralds an unpleasant change."

Her lids lowered, she combed trembling fingers through Perro's matted fur.

He could tell whatever this admission was, it was costing her a soul's worth. When she raised her gaze, moisture glistened her eyes. She looked from him to Silvestre to Dulcinea, listening intently from the bar, then back to him. Her chin jutted. "Silvestre convinced me I should tell you."

"Tell me what, Pia?" Regardless how awful it might be, he wanted to know. He did not believe in secrets. His parents had been married since Adam and Eve, and they shared everything. *Every thing.* Which made for great battles and great makeups. He knew. He had heard enough of their frenzied lovemaking afterwards through paper-thin walls.

She looked down. Then looked up at him. Her eyes glowed like the ghosts of All Hollow's Eve. "I am no longer a virgin, Amado. I was raped out in the Chihuahuan desert by one of Villa's arms buyers who got me released from jail."

His stomach clenched. He tried to connect with the agony in her hoarse whisper. But, being a virgin himself, his own imagination could not comprehend this kind of violation. It was too much for him. He did not know how to respond.

The room's silence screamed at him.

Mercifully, Dulcinea responded for him. She came around the corner with a tray of jarras she placed on the coffee table. Her mocking smile singled out him. "*Mierda*, a maidenhead, Amado—it is unimportant."

He had not expected the *matadora* to be as pure as the Holy Virgin, but *Dios mío*, he had expected Pia would be.

Startling him, she loosed the ratty dog and shot to her feet. Her hands fisted at her sides. "Si, Dulcinea, I am more than a thin cylinder of fleshy tissue."

She was staring directly at him now, awaiting, measuring, his reaction. He could feel the hectic color invade his cheeks and ears. Which infuriated him. Hell, he knew which end of the crowbar was up. "I understand that, *bebé*. I was stunned about ... by what that man did to you." His tongue could not get out the word rape. "I am just glad you're alive—and safe now."

His last words tumbled out with an ardor—and truth—that took him by surprise. The small, slight Pia with her large, luminous eyes and wide sensual mouth was smart and strong and added sparkle to the drudgery that was their people's existence.

Her iron-hot glance swerved once more from him to an intrigued Silvestre to an amused Dulcinea and back to himself. "My maidenhead may be gone, but not my dignity. Never! What is most important to me, Amado—Silvestre—Dulcinea, is to never have to pass through the Public Health's bath house again."

"I know only too well what that humiliation, that indignity, is like," Silvestre said. "Such things cannot continue to be allowed, not here in the United States."

At that point, the defiance seemed to go out of her like a much battered and, at last, punctured pinata, and she slumped back onto the banco. Her sigh was the rustle of dead leaves. "Then it's time things changed."

"Oh?" Dulcinea drawled. From the coffee table, she took up a match box, along with a tin of Pall Mall cigarettes and withdrew one. "And you have suggestions for change, Pia?"

Watching Dulcina light up, he was entranced. His grandmother had smoked cigars, but he knew no women of his age who smoked. "You have already, haven't you. Dulcinea—changed the way things are done?" he asked. "Fighting bull—what only men do."

When the flame danced against her fingers, Dulcinea shook out the match, slowly exhaled a helix of smoke, then smiled in that seductive way that tripped up his thoughts. "Si. So, Pia, what would *you* do?"

Pia shrugged and joked, "Run as a candidate for deputy of Juarez's constituent assembly."

He joined in the chuckles circulating around the room, as women were forbidden to hold public office in Mexico, but at that moment, Dulcinea yelled, "Shit!"

All three glanced in the direction of her glare. Perro had taken a dump between the dipping horns of the carved statue of the bull.

The man scooted the hangers one by one along the wooden dowel rod. He was searching for the right housedress from his dead mother's clothing. A behemoth she had been. Any of her clothing could accommodate his dumpy frame, although his broad, humped shoulders could stretch some of her wardrobe's shoulder seams.

His mother's expectations and a society hostile to what newspapers reported in their arrests columns as 'sexual deviants' or 'perverts'—mentioning them by name, ruining their careers, and their lives—had conditioned him to repress his needs and desires. At least openly.

The dress he chose was a florid dark purple. From a chest of drawers, he withdrew her girdle, corset, bloomers, and hosiery. As he donned each, finishing with a pair of her low heeled, sturdy lace-ups, he felt a rush of pleasure close to euphoria.

The ultimate, the gratification, came next, when he swished into what had been her parlor, now his office. Settling behind her heavy, black walnut secretariat, he felt the dress's flounces shimmying down around him. With a sigh of satisfaction, he began to leaf through each of the folders, containing dossiers he was building.

Mickey O'Bannon: Part of El Paso's corrupt Democratic politicians known as The Ring. Practicing bossism. O'Bannon and his Mexican supporters had illegally paid poll taxes for large numbers of both El Paso Mexicans and Juarenses in order for him to win the previous mayoral position. Now, without a political office from which to tap funds, his own were in the red.

Lionel Pollock: a bigoted enthusiast and member of the Ku Klux Klan. Nevertheless, the man was reported to 'visit' negresses and Mexican whores occasionally.

Günther von Kloss: a German operative, his personal physician's medical notes include a venereal disease. Felix Sommerfeld wanted to make use of von Kloss, but the man's weakness for women could sabotage this most far reaching of all Sommerfeld's stratagems.

Horst Heinrich: reported to have raped one of his underage female house servants as well as one of their daughters he had fathered. The German Mexican had lost most of his holdings in Mexico and stood to lose his wealth now transferred here should word of his indulgences be revealed. He would be persona non grata anywhere, in any country.

Colonel Robert Michie: 'heartily bussed' his sister-in-law at last New Year's Eve party. Siphoned $150 from the Officer's Club. That had been to help cover its Chinese cook's emergency appendectomy—which would make no difference to the U.S. Army.

Walter Stevenson:

The stuffy young man's file was blank. So far. But eventually his weakness would be discovered. Every single person had their shameful secrets, some of them more sinister than others. Which was a shame, because the young man was likeable, a decent sort. He was a respected cultural and political journalist. But everything about him hinted at phenomenal competence—and ergo a threat.

Blackmail was invariably the best tactic. Maybe that was why lashing out at degenerates like Silvestre Salinas was in a sense liberating … if he could but bear to admit it, because he himself struggled with the vile feelings of homosexuality.

His mother had once accused him of paranoia. Forever suspicious of others. But then later it was she who suspiciously accused him of heartlessness as she lay slowly dying, unattended by a physician or a friend. Only by him. He had done what he could for the mastodon.

Sitting there in her dress and reviewing the folders, the man felt that accumulating pleasure slithering throughout him. A pleasure derived by dominating others in way he openly could not.

That kind of pleasure came close to combating the dominance his mother had wielded over his childhood, and manhood. And the pain—and pleasure—as a result from it that was as deep as his mother's grave.

Yet that pleasure of power he experienced, when dressed as he did, was not nearly close enough to counter the power Sommerfeld now wielded over him. Sommerfeld knew his own nasty secret and would expose his abomination if he should ever fail to work in Germany's highest interest.

Chapter Eighteen

Adelaide refilled her husband's snifter with brandy from the sideboard's decanter, then took a sip from her own. Copper warmers over alcohol lamps on the serving table kept the coffee heated, as well as the lunch's bockwurst and chorizo.

Bart sat across from her at the alcove's wrought-iron, glass-topped table. The bay window's afternoon sunlight filtered through the gauzy rose curtains and shone mercilessly on his thinning dark hair, which he combed from the swarthy crown of his head to the front.

"Bart, dear, General Pershing's troops are due to return from Mexico to Fort Bliss next week. Mayor Lea has suggested the Chamber of Commerce plan a celebration for them. You know, a pageant of sorts, with the American flag draped from every building—bells tolling and factory whistles blowing for five minutes, that sort of thing."

Her paunchy husband glanced up from the newspaper, forked another wedge of chorizo in his mouth, and smiled beatifically. "What a splendid idea, Adelaide."

She delivered a steely smile at the newspaper he once more held before his face. The fact that Bart and John Pershing were both members of the Adventurer's Club, an elite all-male fraternity was even better. Its forty-odd members ranged from the mayor to machine gunners to soldiers-of-fortune.

"Do you think Cardenas Clothing could donate the cost of bleachers for the parade? I thought it would be a patriotic deed, supporting General Pershing, while promoting Cardenas Clothing."

"Splendid," Bart said from behind the newspaper. "Have the bills sent to the store." He might dote on her, but he lacked Günther's devastating sensuality. Luckily for her, Bart was rarely amorous. When she had complained his snoring made sleep impossible, he had consented to separate bedrooms.

"Montgomery Ward's has red rubber balloons we could use for the parade," she continued. "Günther von Kloss has offered to cover that outlay through his law firm." She dappled her linen napkin over her lips. "He's coming later this afternoon to discuss the number needed, the cost and such."

"Splendid, Adelaide. Did you see this news item?" He lowered the newspaper again. "The Public Health Service nabbed a professional bather." He started chuckling. "Get this—in one day the young man went through the Fumigation Plant five times and sold the clearance tickets issued him. What an enterprising hombre. Now that's someone we would dearly like to have working for Cardenas Clothing."

The bath house fiasco and the sand gathering on the windowsill reminded her she had yet to find a maid to fill the last one's position. The last Mexican girl—Piedad Arellano, that was her name—had been efficient but impudent. And what chutzpah! Starting a riot, all for nothing—only to be dropped off like a feed sack in the middle of the Chihuahua Desert. If she survived, one could only hope she learned her place.

Either one had class or did not. The Rothschild blood running through Adelaide's own veins distinguished her from the common masses and assured her a place among society's elite. Blood will always tell.

After Bart returned to the clothing store, the hour wait until

Günther arrived was interminable for Adelaide. She could occupy herself with a few domestic duties. Polishing the silver or running the sweeper over the carpets she could do. Clean the toilets she would not.

The only help available came from this side of the Rio Grande, but these domestics were already employed and those who were available were using the leverage of the bath house riot to demand an arm and a leg.

Which reminded her of the young bricklayer she employed. She went in search of him, following the poppy-bordered, graveled path to the old carriage house, now a garage. He was almost finished with his bricklaying assignment, lacking only a day or so. As she approached, he paused to eye her speculatively, as did most men.

She smiled engagingly. "Amado, a baluster has come loose from our balcony banister. When you finish here, I would be willing to pay you for the banister repair—and any other household tasks that need tending to—on a fulltime basis. You understand?"

Tarrying, he removed his filthy sombrero. A slow grin surfaced. "*A su servicio, Señora.*"

Amado's frisky innuendo was not lost on her but compared to the worldly Günther he was a mere boy.

Back inside, she went to stand in front of her triple-paneled cheval mirror and turned to view herself from all angles. With Germany invading Russia, its peasant style clothing had become the rage—hip-length tunics and skirts softly draped to the calves. Best, with the fading of the Edwardian rigid tailored lines so, too, had faded the need for tight-fitting corsets.

Free of the odious constriction, she shifted her stance to better feel the erotic pleasure of the silk chemise feathering back and forth across her breasts. Her lids fluttered closed. Never had she felt this much excitement that came from anticipation. But then never had she entertained the thought of a paramour. Bart had been her first sexual experience, a calculated one at that.

Although Bart traveled often on business, she never took the risk of an occasional partner to assuage her feminine needs, which Bart's

140

clumsiness invariably and miserably failed to alleviate.

Nonetheless, after all these years she could not help but feel a tendresse for her good-humored Mexican husband. He was unfailing gracious to her, granted her whatever whim was within his means, especially after she had dutifully given birth, painful birth, to a son for him. But Bart was utterly without imagination.

From below came the sound of Günther's voice and that of Bao's tinny one, admitting him. Adelaide's lungs squeezed off her breath as tightly as if had she, indeed, worn a corset.

Today, in true cloak-and-dagger fashion, he would be setting up the wireless station in the attic, which would let the Kaiser's high staff in Berlin communicate freely with Günther.

The thought of what would happen to her if the United States authorities discovered the transmission set had tripped her heartbeat far too many times since she had agreed to Günther's dangerous proposition. Fear stalked her like a hungry wolf.

The last woman found guilty of treason and hanged might have been half a century ago, but Adelaide was fully aware that third-degree torture still continued to be a practice on both sides of the border by all three countries—the United States, Germany, and Mexico.

Günther was watching her descend the stairs. Appreciation flickered across his sensuous face. For her part, the stirring susceptibility she felt to his virile potency threatened her primary rule of self-preservation. Flirt, allude even to a potential tryst, but never, never violate duty and dignity. She should have pleasured herself beforehand.

He gestured over his shoulder at two peons toting a rolled carpet on their shoulders. "The Aubusson you admired in my law firm. A gift from the German consul, *Señora* Cardenas."

He paused, and after a beat, she divined his ploy. "Oh, thank you, Mr. von Kloss. How thoughtful of the Consul. In the attic will do for now until I can decide which room it best suits. I'll show you the way."

Bao, whose shifty eyes never missed anything, stood near the end of the hallway. At Adelaide's dismissing nod, the old woman trotted on once-bound tiny feet back to the kitchen.

Up two flights Adelaide climbed, feeling all the while from behind the heat of Günther's gaze. He was at once intractable, sexy, ambitious, and stimulating, and all this appealed to her. However, she recognized in those Nordic blue eyes a ruthlessness that could burn like hot ice if one had the temerity to cross him.

At the top was an unused maid's quarters. She continued past it, farther down the hall to the attic door. She pulled on the bulb's light chain. Beneath the rafter beams a cubicle emerged from the warm and musty darkness. The place was cluttered with a rocking horse, an old desk, various picture frames, a badly bent golf club of Bart's, a stuffed moose head, and other odds and ends.

Günther indicated a vacant area to deposit the rug and, with a snap of his fingers, sent the two men on their way.

Alone with him, she felt nervous and was conscious her nervousness had nothing to do with the incriminating item rolled within the carpet. She rotated away from him, stepping to the old desk and with a swipe of the back of her hand cleared away the dust bunnies, along with a sooty chimney brush. "You can put the telegraph station here."

From behind, his hands captured her shoulders. Her head turned, and, looking up into the dark hearts of his eyes, her resolution crumpled. How could this happen to her, she who was always so practical and proper and cautious? Günther had come into her world and disrupted all her careful planning, disorienting her entirely.

"Adelaide, you are all that I can think of. My brokerage business, my consulate duties, they go barely attended."

She pivoted, meaning to step away, but in his grip she was fully facing him. She pressed her hands against his chest, trying to create space. Space to think clearly. "I don't feel ... that way ... the same as you."

"Yes, you do. I understand you. More than you think."

"Why? Because we're cut from the same cloth, you and I?"

He blinked repeatedly, and she was not sure if it was pain or surprise or both she saw in his eyes. "I infer this reference to cloth has to do with my past?"

She framed his angular face with her hands. "I know all about you, a rag-picker's son, and it makes no difference to me, do *you* understand this?"

"I understand this—that this is what we both have never really had." His head lowered, and his mouth claimed hers, moving over it back and forth, as if seeking the solace neither of them had ever experienced.

Instantly, she was consumed by his kiss, blistering her lips like sunburn. He nudged them apart, and at the taste of his tongue sparks flew throughout her, incinerating her flesh into ashes. Her whole world crashed.

Helplessly, hungrily, she returned his kiss. Let the devil take tomorrow. Today, she was Günther's, wholly and completely.

"Mama—Mama!"

She whirled toward the door. His thumb in his mouth, Richie stood there, staring agog. She broke free of Günther's embrace and navigated the storage items to kneel before her tow-headed son.

His thumb slipped from between his slobbering lips. "That's not Daddy."

Chapter Nineteen

B eneath dusk's dusting of ice-blue stars, Walt strolled the short distance from the Hotel Sheldon to the El Paso Del Norte Hotel. Here stayed the wealthy, like the owners of the Cusi mines in Mexico and the Guggenheims who owned one of the ASARCO smelters.

After *Villistas* shouted "Death to the *Gringos*" the year before and executed eighteen Cusi mining men, riots had erupted in El Paso between the Anglos and Mexicans. The local police could not adequately restore order, so General Pershing had no choice but to place El Paso under martial law. However, he was prudent enough to assign his soldiers to keep order side by side with the El Paso Police Department.

The General was known to be strict and rigid, but Walt admired him. When Walt had interviewed him last year about the Cusi Mine riot there in El Paso, the two had recognized they shared a mutual respect for law and order.

Two years earlier, while Black Jack Pershing was called away to duty, his wife and three daughters had perished in a house fire. Tragedy was something both Walt and Pershing had endured and had transformed their suffering to a more bearable stoicism.

Tonight, Walt was embarking on a mission to assuage his conscience. The El Paso Del Norte Hotel provided a service few other places did—boxed meals. Originally, Pershing had ordered these for his staff whenever out on reconnaissance, but the general public had hopped on the idea for picnic outings, train travel, and such.

Walt headed toward the bar off the hotel's main dining room to pick up his order—a five-pound rump roast, a loaf of freshly baked bread, and cans of artichokes. "Throw in a box of Nabisco's," he told the white-aproned bartender. "Oh, and a couple of bottles of strawberry soda pop."

"I'll get that from the restaurant right away, sir," the man said and vanished through the swinging doors in the back.

"Well, aren't you a rare bird," a male voice said.

Walt allowed his head to turn now in the direction of the far end of the bar. He had been aware the entire time of the debonair man, the only other patron present. He sat hunched over his tulip-shaped pint glass. "So I have been told, Mickey."

While mayor, Mickey O'Bannon and his cohorts had formed what was known as The Ring, which was every bit as corrupt as New York's Tammany Hall. Mickey had supported open gambling and prostitution, was on back-patting terms with everyone, and had a finger in every pie. White politicians needed Mexican votes, and this Irish Catholic politician called himself a friend of the Mexicans. "So what story are you sleuthing out now, Stevenson?"

Hands in his trouser pockets, Walt strode to that end of the bar. Fumes of Guinness enwreathed Mickey. He wore a bow tie and spanking white buck shoes.

The Irishman loved media attention. Walt played on that. He smiled blandly and laid a finger beside his nose in a gesture of confidentiality. "Chasing tales of that *mujeriego* Villa's latest dalliance this side of the border."

"Hell," he boasted, "I disarmed Villa myself once, when he vowed to kill General Giuseppe Garibaldi."

So, what was Mickey now up to? Word was that without the city's treasury as a resource, he was running low of funds. "I would imagine as former mayor you have heard your share of stories about El Paso's sub rosa activities."

Mickey hoisted his glass but even in the bar's dimmed light, Walt did not miss the startled glint of suspicion in the man's eyes. As if wondering what exactly Walt might know. "Well now, Stevenson, I guess you heard about Villa's grand prank—he brokered a deal to return silver ingots he had stolen in a train robbery in return for Wells Fargo paying him a Finder's Fee. Doesn't that take the cake?!"

"Old news, Mickey, but thanks anyway." He gave the ex-mayor a two-fingered salute.

Taking the sack the bartender returned with, Walt made a mental note to investigate the sleazy Irishman a little more thoroughly, but at the moment there remained a mission to fulfill. An uncomfortable mission.

The taxicab rattled over the International Bridge, and the driver, a local Tigua Indian Walt learned, managed to hit every pothole on the street where Pia's family lived. In the twilight, a pig snuffled beneath the bougainvillea holding up one adobe wall of the family's dilapidated household.

Walt told the taxi driver to wait. Toting the sack, he approached the lopsided turquoise door and knocked.

A small girl, she had to be Rosita, opened it. A braid, almost as long as she was tall, draped over one shoulder. Behind her, an older woman with hair the gray of mist appeared and Walt passed her the sack. Obviously, she had once been exceptionally beautiful. Tonight, she looked worn down by life, but when she peered inside the sack, her mouth dropping open, her face took on a Rembrandt luster.

"Abuelita," the girl implored, tugging on the woman's apron strings, tied in front, "let me look in the sack. Let me look!"

Without taking her quizzing gaze off him, the woman passed the sack down to the little girl. "Who are you, *por favor?*"

He tipped his trilby. "My name is Walter Stevenson. I am a reporter for *Collier's Magazine*. I was just dropping these off. Your daughter Pia had mentioned picking up the strawberry sodas and other items in the sack." Well, more or less. It was not an outright lie.

Another woman, younger and plumper, appeared behind the mother. She had to be the sister. She eyed him sourly. "How did Pia get money for food like this?"

"Uhh, she now works for me … involving telegraphy and reports. You know, when I need to send off a news item. Things like that."

"That's Pia for you. Like a cat, she lands on her feet every time."

The little girl was examining the sack's contents. Withdrawing the soda pop, she squealed with delight. Hugging the bottle close to her flat chest, she did a pirouette, then dug back into the sack. "And look, cookies!"

Feeling like the worst kind of heel, he retreated back to the cab. He was preying on Pia's weaknesses. And one of them was quite obvious to him. Her family. Clearly, she was close to these three.

Despite her intrepidness, she needed cash and immediate security, while he was conscious she wanted more from him. More than a gift of a sack of food for her family. And for him to entertain that idea was ludicrous.

Born Beatriz Lopez, at sixteen she pirated the name Dulcinea from some famous novel a much older inamorata had mentioned. For her surname she had taken del Jardín, because she thought the idea of a garden conveyed beauty.

Where she had been born and raised had not been one of beauty—quarters behind a butcher shop next to Madrid's bull ring on Carretera de Aragón. Her father, the butcher, catered to an avid populace seeking not only the freshly killed bull's meat, but also its treasured testicles and blood for fertility and prowess.

Growing up near the arena, she absorbed the art of bull fighting by watching the flamboyant matadors in their pink socks and tight pants. In her quite willing exchange for sex, because she genuinely loved men, she practiced with a wiry picador, who performed during the first stage of the bull fights. From him, she learned the vital skills of survival in such a dangerous occupation.

Early on, since she could barely read or write, she understood that bullfighting would be her ticket out of squalor. When she turned a knife on a jealous lover, a highly-placed governmental official who had attacked her, a flight from a charge of murder in Spain became imperative.

Making a name for herself in Juarez as a female bullfighter had been difficult, but she had been lucky, and she always figured better to be lucky than good.

She had succeeded in a male-dominated occupation, not without a few scars. A livid scar hooked the underside of her wrist and extended up her forearm to its bend at her elbow. Another scar, invisible, singed a trail across a small portion of her heart.

She had gone and let Walter Stevenson distract her from her determined path of fame and glory there in Juarez. She found beautiful men tediously vain. Whereas Walt wore the forceful mantle of one of those bare-knuckled fighters who sparred beneath a cluster of trees at Peace Grove, near Hart's Mill.

Oh, she had experienced sexual passion with any number of men since that picador, but never that blaze of coming free of the body that she did when with Walter. He had that singular gift of fully concentrating his libido on his intended result—his partner's intense, sustaining pleasure and the ultimate, shattering release.

Que lástima that she was not the one his heart needed. Ahh, but for the errors of Cupid's arrows.

Well then, she herself would outperform Cupid here in El Paso.

Soothingly stroking a hissing Leona, Dulcinea glanced over at the mangy mutt indulgently. "You go for it, Perro."

She consoled herself over her loss by cosseting a fantasy about the young idealist Amado. Yes, she felt certain she could take the good looking but inexperienced bricklayer in hand and teach him how to pleasure a woman the way Walter had her.

148

Fighting bulls had taught her this much—some fights you win, some you lose.

Horst Heinrich's heavy flatfooted gait took him across the narrow cobblestoned street, littered with trash. The street was the permeable border between the Chihuahita tenement south of Overland Street, within a short distance of the Rio Bravo, and the Anglo neighborhoods, rising north toward the Franklin Mountains.

He lumbered through a cubicle courtyard and up an outside, paint-flecked wooden staircase. Each step groaned. At the landing, he opened the door. The room smelled of disuse, underlaid with the stench of older odors, like rotten food and piss and stale smoke.

Two men sat at a rickety table. Cards and coins were jumbled atop it. At his entrance, the men's guarded glances announced more was at stake here than their peso antes. They both nodded a terse greeting.

A third man, his back three-quarters to them, stood at the room's single window, its pane blotched by smut. His paunchy figure was silhouetted by weak, wintry twilight. The man glanced over his shoulder at Horst.

He inclined his head in acknowledgment and took a seat, the chair shifting seismically beneath his weight. In his youth, he had cut a dashing figure, a tall and slender hidalgo with hair flame red. Time and excesses of pleasures had exacted their price. In his youth, females had been wild about him, but he had been wild about only one. She had escaped him. Time and poverty's hardships had exacted their price on her, as well.

He eased back the flaps of his suit jacket, so that the Smith & Wesson he always packed was within easy reach—necessary, as he no longer had personal bodyguards at his beck and call. There were far too many who would like to see his body dumped in the ASARCO plant's molten steel.

To his right, Günther von Kloss was rolling a gold Azteca coin across his knuckles, back and forth. He was sharp. And a fool to stake his all—his career, his life even—on allegiance to the Fatherland in his seesaw hopes to elevate his social status upon his return to Germany.

To Horst's left, El Paso's previous mayor, the fiftyish Irish Catholic Mickey O'Bannon, snapped off the end of his Havana with a cigar clipper. He wore a fashionable fedora pushed back to reveal fair skin sun-spotted by too many years spent in The Pass. O'Bannon could present the most danger in this intrigue because he was a hothead. He wanted his power back, whatever the cost.

However, Horst was most circumspect of the hump-shouldered man in the tatty sweater at the window. He deserted his spy post and claimed the table's remaining seat. The latest news editor of *The El Paso Herald*, Ed Bigelow was a brilliant man stuck in a flunky job, but a job that allowed him to eavesdrop on the vagaries of humanity, from society's derelicts to its wheelers and dealers.

He was said to snoop and keep secret dossiers on the high and the low, and Horst had reason to believe this. The curt phone call summoning him to this clandestine meeting in this backwash of El Paso had lightly touched upon the financial gains of a certain project to be discussed—and had with the mentioning, as if in passing, of a news item that had recently come across his desk.

"Did you know the most severe penalties for incest are in Texas and Massachusetts? Twenty damn years. Hell, Heinrich, those Puritan degenerates up in Massachusetts have nothing over the slop-bucket ones here in Texas, do they?"

Horst had yet to calculate what motivated this man, who was like a sewer that collected dirt, but Bigelow, regrettably, was all too aware of what motivated *him*.

Granted, under Carranza, the current revolutionary president of Mexico, Horst stood to lose his eight-million-acre Estancia Cascada. However, he still owned his hacienda and its vast accompanying grounds outside Chihuahua City.

The hitch was Villa's bounty on his head. He could not set foot in Mexico to reclaim it until Villa and his army were routed. German occupation of northern Mexico could not only accomplish that but might also restore Horst's eight-million acres.

Hunching over the table, the newspaper editor locked his thick fingers, stained by printers' ink, and said with biting insincerity, "I am honored you gentlemen have found it to your benefit to accept my invitation to discuss a certain project."

"And this project," prompted von Kloss, a nerve in his temple ticking, "would require what exactly from us?" The man wasted no time.

So, Horst thought, Bigelow had each of them at that table by the *huevos*, exploiting their most precious dream and frightening nightmare.

"Of course, you three understand Imperial Germany's objective is to get America embroiled in a war with Mexico, thereby keeping America out of the war in Europe. Alas, the methods to accomplish this have proved ineffective thus far."

Enlightenment flooded Horst's brain. The insignificant news editor was operating as the hub of clandestine activity for Imperial Germany there in El Paso. Well, be damned if he would let this wart on a horse's ass intimidate him. "*Für die Liebe Gottes,* get to your point. What do you want from us?"

The pinch-browed Bigelow sneered. "As if you were familiar with either love or God, Heinrich."

Horst refrained from chomping off his head. Not yet, anyway. He would wait and see what cards the man led with. As if bored, he hmphed a grunt and, pulling his penknife from his pocket, began cleaning his nails.

"What my ... contact ... has in mind," Bigelow said, "is the assassination of General John Pershing."

A susurration of collective shock stirred the room's stagnant air. The coin dropped from von Kloss's grasp. O'Bannon's cigar bobbled. Horst left off paring his nails.

Bigelow's hooded eyes flicked from von Kloss to O'Bannon to Horst. "The mission is to be carried out during the parade planned for the return of his Punitive Expedition—in five days, February 5th."

Horst wondered who the hell the man's contact was. Certainly, someone in a higher authority than that of the news editor.

"The assassination," Bigelow continued, "should shake President Wilson from his initial pledge to keep America out of a war—but it would be a war with Mexico, not Germany's in Europe."

Von Kloss's eyes narrowed. "I have heard nothing about this plan from my superior—the German Foreign Secretary, Arthur Zimmermann."

O'Bannon smirked at von Kloss. "That shows how low you are on the totem pole."

Bigelow drilled his stare on the Irishman. "O'Bannon, your job will be to provide unrest and protestors from among your Mexican political supporters. I want them everywhere along the Army's parade route."

Horst thought pridefully of one of the offspring he had sired by Marta, the girl Piedad. If only his sole legitimate child, the pansy Silvestre, was half the warrioress she was. Her recent protest at the fumigation plant could put to shame his son's feeble literary protests.

O'Bannon chuckled. "We'll shove a boot so far up the army's ass they'll be tasting leather."

Bigelow glanced at the German honorary consulate. "Von Kloss, the same. Use your influence—and charm—to galvanize the pro-German Carrancistas in the area. Also, it is essential to know the exact cavalcade route and its timing at each point." His pause was like that before a boxer delivered a surprise gut punch. "You can obtain this from your latest love conquest, Frau Cardenas."

"Fuckary!" O'Bannon snorted his surprise.

Shock flushed von Kloss's fair complexion. "My ... source isn't privy to that information. Only the Chamber of Commerce's president has the details."

"Get them."

Horst frowned at Bigelow's dictatorial response. However, Horst was bothered more by what as yet had not been said. "And who is to be the assassin?"

With the dangerous expression of a cat smelling out a baby mouse, Bigelow at last looked at him. "You."

He digested that like it was a *chiltepín* pepper, burning all the way to his stomach. If the mission failed, he would be the one to pay. A refugee in the United States, he no longer had a thousand or so underlings who would carry out his orders unquestioned. "Surely, you can find someone short on cash and long on guns willing to kill the general?"

"Come on," von Kloss said, "you know the fewer people involved the better."

"I won't do it."

Bigelow said nothing. But looking into his eyes, Horst got the message.

He lowered his own eyes and put away his penknife. He stood to gain all that he lost in Mexico by carrying out his part of the mission. And stood to lose everything, even his freedom, maybe even his life, if he refused.

Chapter Twenty

February 1ˢᵗ, 1917

Pia fretted a lot lately, so unlike her. While hurriedly dressing, she fought off a barrage of pestering questions.

Would she be able to glean any worthwhile information for the hard-ass Walt from her maid service at the German consulate—if she was lucky enough to secure the position this morning?

Would Dulcinea grumble for the second day in a row about Perro's *popo* piled here and there throughout the *matadora's* pristine apartment.

Did Amado still want Pia now that he was aware of her maiden's status—or lack thereof? Which was irrelevant, she supposed, when she had gone and fallen in love with Walt.

Would Josefina ever forgive her for striving farther and further than had Josefina, saddled by a baby at fourteen? Did she resent Pia's lighthearted, reckless and feckless life, when she herself had to act responsibly … and, *Dios mío*, when she had to bear the shame and the secret of rape by their father? Pia stood in awe, wondering how their mother had endured Horst Heinrich's continual violation … and, later, how Josefina had carried on after the rape.

But most importantly right now, most worrisome for Pia … was she carrying a child as a result of her own violation by Cisco Rodríguez? *Ojalá*, his bones were bleaching white as wedding cake there in the desert arroyo.

It was well past the break of daylight, nearly seven o'clock, and still Dulcinea slept. Before leaving the apartment, Pia made one last foray, scooping Perro's *popo,* using a monogrammed sterling silver pie server knife—it was the only serviceable shovel available—then disposed of the *popo* in the crapper.

She hustled to catch the streetcar down to San Jacinto Plaza, the center of El Paso's business district. Two blocks down from the Elite Confectionary, at the corner of Oregon and San Antonio, rose the imposing First National Bank Building.

Günther von Kloss kept his customs brokerage office-cum-honorary German consulate on the 4th floor. Three years before, Villa's *Consulado de Mexico* had occupied the same floor. On room #412's frosted glass pane was stenciled:

Günther von Kloss
Broker ~ Consular

She set down the pail and mop Dulcinea had grudgingly provided. Tentatively, she knocked. Waited. Knocked a little more forcefully. Waited. Now she was suffering misgivings. When even the sharp-eyed Walt could not nail von Kloss himself with spy activity, how was she to ferret out a master spy connected in some way with the German consular? She inhaled and rapped the door harder.

The grating sound of a bolt sliding jerked her to attention. The door was yanked open. A good-looking man with mussed yellow hair and a stiletto mustache with tuft on chin frowned down at her. His plaid wool waistcoat was unbuttoned and his white dress shirt's cuffs hung loose. In one palm he held pearl-studded cuff links and studs and in the other a cigarette. "Yes?"

"*Señor*, I'm applying for the maid service you advertised."

Confusion shadowed sleepy eyes that widened as they raked her from her blue bib overalls down to her work boots. "I did not advertise for maid service."

¡Santo Cristo! When Walt coached her, why had she not paid more attention? "Yes, you did, when you told friends your office needed maid service. Friends told friends and passed the word along—and here I am."

His gaze turned critical, his tone suspicious. "Maid service, you say?"

She realized she had made a mistake in her manner of speech. She reverted to pidgin English. "*Sí*. Your office, *Señor*, I clean *muy bien*."

His eyes wandered from her face up to her red spools of pinned-up hair with wholly male interest. But his assessing gaze returned to search her face—her eyes, especially. He shook his head. "Uh, I—I had someone older in mind."

No, he was looking for someone dull-witted, some disinterested maid who would be unlikely to give thought to what went on within his office.

Pointedly, she let her gaze drift around the office, a wall-to-wall wastebasket. Behind the outer office would be, of course, another room or two, often used by renters for personal living space. She effected a guileless smile. "Maid service, it is hard to come by, sí, *Señor* von Kloss? Not many want to get the bath house ticket we need to cross over."

"Uhh, but what I have in mind is someone without young children demanding attention at home."

"I have no *niños*." He was grasping for excuses. How to convince him she did not introduce a risk to his clandestine activities, if any?

"Someone responsi—"

Before he could protest further, she plopped her bucket and mop against the wall and edged by him. She could feel his flabbergasted look as she bypassed a pair of worn, button-tufted leather armchairs and dropped her *bolsa* next to the candlestick telephone on the large desk.

It was already cluttered with papers, an ink blotter, inkwell, fountain pens, and an array of folders.

"Look," he protested vehemently, "I am not interviewing right now."

She ignored him. Behind the desk was a credenza. On it, next to on office's essential teleprinter, telegraph station and headphones, was a couple of grungy drinking glasses and an empty bottle of malt liquor. The room was stuffy with cigar smoke, and someone had missed hitting the spittoon several times. "Your office, *Señor* von Kloss, it is pig sty."

Stooping to collect paper wads from the hardwood floor, she tossed them in a wire mesh waste basket. Later, with luck, she could secret them inside her *bolsa*. She pivoted to face him. "Your office is small, *Señor*. I can clean it and the other rooms last thing at the end of day, after I finish cleaning my other—"

Perturbation creased a furrow across the high bridge of his arrogant nose. "No, no, you'll only be in the way. That's when I receive clients and wrap up my notes from my morning business calls."

"Then, I can come early, while you are out."

"No." He navigated between the armchairs to his desk, and his free hand grabbed her *bolsa* and thrust it at her. "Look, I'm already late for my first appointment." He took her elbow, hustling her toward the door.

She wrenched free, turned, and thrust her *bolsa* back at him. "You are as messy as your office, *Señor*." She took the pearl studs from him and, standing on tiptoe, fastened the studs to his collar. As he looked on, bemused, she lifted his free hand, and began inserting the cuff link at his wrist.

After finishing with linking the other cuff, she waved him toward the back room. "While you comb that bird's nest of hair on your *cabeza* and finish dressing, *Señor*, I clean your rooms here. In the mornings while you are out, I clean your office. You pay what you think I am worth—due at the end of the week, mind you. And, of course, I need a key."

Extracting a whisk broom and dust rag from her *bolsa*, she headed toward the credenza. Briskly, she began dusting around the telegraph and its register. Nervous, she hummed to herself like whistling past a graveyard. She tensed for an ordered, "Get out!"

After a too long moment, she heard his abrupt about-face and steps stomping to the back room. "No key," he called to her back. "And be here at 8:00 and out by 8:30, before I leave for my morning calls. Understand?"

She turned and grinned, "*Sí, Señor.*"

The door banged shut.

No key. Well, so much for a free roam of the place. She should tote her pail to the single bathroom shared by each floor's occupants, at the end of the hallway, and return with her water-filled pail to swab the floor.

But given the possibility he could change his mind at any moment, she switched her attention to the register's strip of tape with its embossed dots and dashes in Morse Code. They fashioned a couple of jumbled phrases, of which she could not be certain without further investigation. Were they German, Spanish, or English? He might miss the strips if she nabbed them.

She glanced back to the desk, where she scanned the barely legible yellow pad—only a few scribbled notes. Something in German, apparently about the local German-sponsored orphanage

Then she spotted the name, Adelaide—with a dashed scribbling and scrambling of letters and words that made no sense. She leaned closer over the lined pad, her fingertip underscoring the words. They were in blocks of five—like the most common-used method for ciphering text messages. She would need to recall the various enciphering brainteasers Silas had taught her.

From behind her came von Kloss's demand, "What are you doing?"

Feeling relieved his suite was rid of the plague, aka Pia Arellano, now pawned off on Dulcinea, Walt took a chair opposite Ed and Bobby for the usual late afternoon cocktail hour at Sheldon's downstair café.

Ed crabbed, "You're looking mighty pleased with yourself."

Bobby signaled the waiter for another Pass brandy. "You found Pia Arellano?"

His customary teapot and cup were already in place. "Found and hired." He reached for the creamer.

Ed's grizzled brows climbed his forehead. "Hired? I thought you only wanted to interview her?"

"Our Walt's sweet on her," Bobby jested but he was looking at Walt curiously.

Stalling, he took a taste-test of the tea, then added an additional splash of cream before replying. Intent on divulging as little as possible, he said, "Look, chaps, I am onto an entirely different lead story for *Collier's*."

He glanced at Ed. "You put me onto it—with your lead on Cisco Rodriguez. He and another man had kidnapped her. She was able to kill Rodriguez and escape, but—"

"Damn, she *is* a hothead!" Ed said and took a swig of his Lone Star.

"But I want to find out who arranged all this. I think it's a safe assumption that the trail leads back to our illustrious mayor. If so, he may make another attempt, and she's my bait." He was less concerned about the mayor and more concerned about the *Villista* she dubbed Jaw Man. He was still lurking out there somewhere.

Bobby was not going to give it up. "What does that have to do with your hiring her?"

"Well, until she can earn enough as a domestic here—a matter of a few weeks—to go out on her own, I am putting her up with a friend of mine. Meanwhile, I'm hiring her to do some snooping for me at the—"

"Excuse me, Mr. Stevenson," the waiter at Walt's elbow said. "There is a young lady in the lobby, asking for you. A Miss Arellano."

"Hell," Bobby said, thudding down his snifter, "this is one young woman I have to see."

Walt sighed, set aside his napkin, and with Ed and Bobby following his footsteps, climbed the stairs to the first-floor lobby.

At first, he did not recognize her. In one arm she restrained what he supposed passed for a dog but looked like a cross between a small, frenzied monkey and a rabid chipmunk.

She stood off to one side, near a cluster of tall potted fronds. A wide-brimmed straw hat banded with an olive-green ribbon shaded her upper face, and only loose spirals of red curls were visible around her sun-kissed jaw and neck. Looking taller in heeled pumps, she wore a tailored khaki jacket over a cream-colored V-neck blouse that exposed the pulse beating at her throat.

He dragged his gaze on down to her chocolate brown skirt that tubed her slight hips and fell well short of her ankles. He blinked. A vision of haute couture, she could have stepped off a page in *Vanity Fair*. And what was this, this sensual stirring within him ... when he had already seen her nude flesh in the bathtub?

Swiftly, he made the introductions. He wanted both men on their way before his ruse got out of hand. "Pia, this is Ed Bigelow, news editor of the *El Paso Herald* and Colonel Robert Michie. Gentlemen, Miss Pia Arellano."

Whatever discomposure she may have felt, she stunned Walt by extending a gloved hand and murmuring in impeccable English, "A pleasure to meet you both."

With gallant alacrity Bobby bent over her hand. "*Encantada*, Miss Arellano."

Walt all but rolled his eyes.

Predictably, Ed's face turned as red as raw, rancid steak, and he stammered, "Goo-good afternoon, Miss Arellano."

Tiny teeth bared, the dog she constrained under one arm let out a snarl that sounded like a couple of sneezes.

Bobby gestured toward the snipping creature. "And this fascinating pet—its name?"

"Perro—Spanish for dog." She smiled wryly and hitherto

unnoticed dimples appeared. "I didn't want to give the dog a name, because he was a stray I hadn't planned on keeping, and now I cannot imagine life without Perro." From beneath dense lashes, she cast Walt a sidewise glance and an off-centered grin. "Perro knows the good guys from the bad."

So he was still the bad guy? "Well, we must be on our way—got to get a leash for the dog," he said, hustling her toward the hotel's front door. "Pick up my share of the check, will you, chaps? I'll catch up later."

Once outside, she jerked her elbow from his grip. "¡Hijole, Walt! Slow down. I am hobbled like a horse in this silly tight skirt."

Well, his lungs felt tight. And it had nothing do with his brisk pace. He shortened his stride, but took her elbow again, propelling her along a sidewalk crowded with people hurrying along, most of them leaving work and heading to any one of the many bars. "What's this visitation about?"

Her mouth tilted to one side in a smirk. "Excuse me, my English, it is not so good. Did you mean 'visitation' in the negative sense of the word?"

Her erudition invariably caught him by surprise. "I most certainly did. Did you go to the German Consulate—" He cut her a sidewise glance and added, "Dressed like that?"

She flicked him a preening expression. "You like the outfit?"

"It's—it's noteworthy."

Irritation flashed in her eyes. The pale green of the Rio Grande's shallows. Her huff blew away a flame-red swatch of curls the desert wind lobbed across her nose. "No. I wore work clothes to the Consulate. And sí, I got the job."

"Swell!"

"And almost lost it."

"Oh, just swell!"

Taking her elbow, he assisted her down from the curb and across the street. He set out for San Jacinto Plaza. With the warming weather, the downtown plaza would be crowded that after-work hour. Less chance of being conspicuous or overheard. "What do you mean you almost lost the job?"

She hurried her shorter steps to keep up with him. "Von Kloss wants me to work only while he is there in the mornings, a mere half-hour. So, while he finished dressing—"

"Finished dressing?" Startled, he released his grasp on her elbow and eyed her.

Amusement lilted her voice. "Not like what you think."

"You do not know what I think."

She turned around to walk backward, facing him. Her expression was stone cold solemn. "I know you think you are still in love with this Cordelia, but—"

"How do you know her name?"

"You talked in your sleep. Besides, you would not have been happy with her."

Now, he was amused, sardonically amused. "And I gather *you* could make me happy?"

She grinned. "*Claro qué sí*. We are meant to be with one another, Walt." She tapped first her temple, then her chest. "I know this. *Qué lástima*, you do not!"

He stifled a groan of exasperation. "Back to von Kloss, if you don't mind. So what happened that he almost fired you?"

She swung around to walk in step with him again. "So while he was in the back room and I was tidying his front office, I tried to snoop. I did find a notepad on his desk with Adelaide Cardenas's name linked with what I swear may be a scribbled code."

"And?"

"And then, *Santísima Madre de Jesús*, von Kloss walked in on me!" She hurriedly crossed herself. "I explained I was only moving things around to dust. He ordered me to never again touch anything on his desk or I'd be out on the streets."

Walt extrapolated if von Kloss was doing something as chancy as sending and receiving messages that contained a code from his very office, something was obviously going down locally. This inside information beforehand might yet present him with both the identity of the master spy and his ticket to a bestselling book.

Her sly grin slid off kilter. "However, the telegraph machine, it is not on his desk but on the credenza behind it. So, it I can touch, *sí*?"

"Don't take any unnecessary risks." He made a mental note to arrange for a wireless listening service to be alert for any new local transmitters in the area.

"Ahhh, so. You do care about me."

He glared down at her. "I merely don't want to jeopardize this operation." He felt like a cad, dashing her hopefulness, which she failed to conceal behind a sangfroid countenance. But better she understand then and there that he had no intention toward her as a prospective wife.

At San Jacinto Plaza's bandstand, McGinty's Band, dressed in black and wearing silk hats, was tuning up for the first of its sundown concerts. Scores of people bundled in wraps against the late afternoon chill were gathered on the provided benches and folding chairs to listen.

The band launched into a vibrant rendition of one of the currently favorite songs, "You're a Dangerous Girl." Which was exactly what Pia Arellano was, Walt thought. She was too vibrant. Too distracting. She did not equate with contentment and serenity and orderly ease.

At his age, he had enough life lessons under his belt to know that while a heavenly shooting star was enthralling, earthbound it was nothing but a chunk of meteorite.

She inclined her broad-brimmed straw hat at a tilt closer to his trilby and spoke below the musical strains. Her eyes were watching his closely, as she talked. "Your Dulcinea does not like my Perro. She does not like his *popo* either. She has ordered us out of her place by tomorrow afternoon."

He stopped just short of the walled-off alligator pool. There was a throbbing behind his eyes. He had to remind himself that as much as Pia and her Perro staying at his place would be a purgatory, it would serve more easily as a repository for all the information gleaned. As resourceful as she was, right now he needed her more than she needed him. And this rankled him.

"All right, you can move in with me. But once my country announces it is at war with Germany, and it will be soon, von Kloss will likely either be recalled—or leave the country posthaste. At that point, your services will no longer be necessary. You're on your own. Out the door. ¿*Entiéndeme*?"

"*Sí*. But what if, just what if, I also find your master spy behind all this first? You will put the ten percent down payment for me on a home up on Mount Franklin?"

"That is what you want from life?" he scoffed. "You think that will bring you happiness? A brick-and-mortar home in an upscale neighborhood? The neighbors will look down their noses at you."

Her eyes flashed indignation, and her words snapped. "And is that what you do, Walt—look down your nose at me?" Then, before he could answer, she asked, "You think what you want will bring you happiness? Words on a page? Reviews soon forgotten? More money people like you have no need of?"

He stared with disgust at the raggedy dog cradled like a precious infant in her arms, then ferried his gaze back to hers. "First, I apologize. I didn't mean what I said like that. I don't feel like that about you."

A mollified smile hitched to one side of her mouth. "How do you feel, Walt?"

He ignored her. "Second, produce the master spy *before* the United States joins the war or a down payment on a mountain home is down the drain and you and your pooch are on the streets."

"Then come with me." She tugged on his coat sleeve and edged away from the plaza toward the streetcar stop, less than a block away.

"Where are we going?" he asked.

"To the end of the line—*La Plazita*."

La Plazita was the name the residents gave to Stormville, sitting atop the mesa. The community overlooked two cities, two states, and two countries. It also overlooked Smeltertown's sulfurous smoke-stacks.

Old man Storm had developed the site for the poor people who had lost their homes in the great Rio Grande flood twenty years before. However, El Paso considered Storm's addition on the mesa a public health nuisance, and most citizens gave it a wide berth in their hikes. With 75 houses built only of adobe, Stormville had no water, electricity, gas, phones, or sewers. It was rumored to contain about 500 people and twice as many dogs.

Walt helped Pia, toting her pugnacious pooch beneath one arm, off the streetcar in front of Stormville's only stone building, the small church, *La Iglesia de la Virgen de la Mercedes*. Surveying the place, he was appalled by its squalor.

He pushed back his coat flaps and, hands on hips, turned to confront her. "Look, Pia, as much as you want me to make a down-payment on a piece of land you can afford, you would not even qualify for a site here in this hell's half-acre. Mr. Storm stipulated those who live here have to be employed and be able to build their own adobe homes." He fixed her with a gimlet eye. "And, furthermore, the applicants cannot have a police record."

She tsked-tsked frosted breath. "Oh, it's not here I want to build my home." She pointed past him—west, farther up the road, where it dead-ended. A dirt track took up there and in the distance several masons were laying bricks. "I want a home in Kern Place."

He was sure his jaw dropped. The *El Paso Herald* described this newest development to feature horse trails and planned parks, for which Mr. Kern had already planted 500 trees.

He glowered down at her. Sunset's wind, brisker at that height, had tinted her cheeks a deep pink. "And you expect me to make the ten percent down payment on a site in Kern Place, do you?"

Happiness exuded from her. "Only if, as agreed, I discover the identity of El Paso's master spy, right?"

That, of course, she would never do—not when even Bobby's Military Intelligence out of Fort Bliss or Ed's informants who occasionally gleaned tidbits for the *El Paso Herald* or he, himself, for that matter, had failed. He just needed meanwhile to keep her spying on Günther von Kloss. Grudgingly, Walt nodded. "Sure thing, buttercup."

Elated, she stood on tiptoe. One arm bundling Perro, the other wrapped around his neck, she kissed his jaw. The mutt slobbered on his sleeve.

On sudden impulse, he angled his face slightly. His lips sought hers. They returned his kiss with a fervor that floored him. At once, he stepped back. The sweetness in Pia's kiss nearly crippled his façade. Affection, real affection—not expressions of a sexual nature—had been practically non-existent in his life since as a ten-year-old he had run away. His father found him and brought him back.

How could he bear to live, even if only for a month, with such a demonstrative, intrusive and invasive being as was Pia Arellano?

Chapter Twenty-One

February 2nd, 1917

The clatter of silverware and clink of porcelain masked the verbal volleys of Walt's two friends. In addition, the morning's early customers at the Hotel Sheldon's downstairs café were engaged in their own conversations.

The businessmen were chafing at the lack of workers crossing from Juarez, its population already greatly decreased by people deserting the embattled city through two decades of revolution there. Production was plummeting and as a result so were profits.

"We're doing all we can to choke off Villa." Bobby settled back in his chair and lifted his typical morning cup of steaming black coffee. "Last week we held up a trainload of coal bound for his trains in Mexico."

"We'll it hasn't stopped Villa yet," Ed poked. "And last I checked, the villainous Villa had two million dollars in American banks."

Walt admired how easy-going Bobby did not bristle. As second in command at the post, Bobby was kept busy not only controlling smuggling but operating the post as a reception center for Mexican refugees and a supply point for troops throughout the Southwest.

Ed braced his sweatered forearms on the table. "Look, Bobby, what can you tell me about the upcoming parade for Pershing and his Expeditionary troops?"

"Now you know, Ed, I can't share the parade's specifics. Security and all that rot."

"Come on, I already know the 8th Cavalry will provide the honor guard. And every wetback in the city will know its route come the day before." Ed dunked half a bagel in his cup, then chomped down. His mouth full, he mumbled, "I need to station a couple of photographers along the route ahead of time. You're damn well aware how long it takes to get all their equipment set up."

Walt should have been paying more attention to the banter at hand. But his mind was sidetracked by the mutt upstairs in his suite. He had to take the dog for a walk. Soon. Before the dog took another shit.

Then, too, he was distracted by Pia, off again to clean the German consulate's quarters this morning. She was certainly more high-spirited than her mangy mongrel, which presently had set up house beneath the rocking chair in Walt's sitting room. God forbid the pooch took a shit beneath the throne.

Despite the strategic placement of the settee's rolled cushions, Pia had claimed dominion of the better part of Walt's bed last night—and his thoughts. He could not imagine why. She was the proverbial thorn in his side. Until her arrival in his life, he had his thumb on every aspect of it. Everything was orderly and punctual and under his control.

And yet, when she had sallied forth in her bib overalls from his suite this morning, the well-appointed rooms seemed to have lost their luster. Whatever assumptions he had about her were being gradually dispelled.

"Besides," Ed grumbled, "you know the War Department will want Hollywood's cameramen there to film for propaganda purposes. That will require at least a day's setup in advance."

Naturally, the mention of the War Department waved a red flag in front of Bobby. With an exasperated sigh, he plunked down his coffee cup. "Well now, Ed, let me get back with General Bell and review the situation with him."

"And I have to get back upstairs with Pia's pet. Take the mutt for its daily outing." Walt finished the last of his cup's tea. At that moment, it tasted little better than the ersatz tea with its ubiquitous sand he had endured during the Pershing Expedition. He laid his linen napkin next to his saucer.

"I thought that riot instigator was staying with a friend of yours," Ed said.

"She was. Until her dog took one too many shits. Now I am saddled with her."

"Wait." Bobby grinned and placed a restraining arm on his coat sleeve. "Don't tell me you are becoming domesticated, old fellow."

"More like that domestic has commandeered his quarters," Ed said.

Walt could feel the heat rising above his collar, which all at once seemed too tight. He felt deepening disgust by the predicament into which he had gotten himself. Awakening this morning to find her washed stockings drying from his towel bar was as irritating as had been shaking out his shoes each morning with the rest of the doughboys for insects like centipedes and scorpions. "It's merely a temporary arrangement."

Between bites, Ed mumbled, "That's what all gullible males say at the beginning. You've gotten yourself into a fine fettle."

Bobby sent Ed a smug look. "Well, I for one think this would make an interesting tale for the *El Paso Herald*'s lovelorn column."

"Oh, criminy," Walt told the two, "hop off the squirrel wheel, will you."

"What are you thinking, Walt?" Ed demanded. "That girl has no self-control—she started that riot, right? She's a powder keg. Disreputable. Unstable. My advice is, get rid of her."

He rolled his eyes and stood. "Easy enough for you to say." He took up his hat and grimaced at the two men. "Neither of you have ever been afflicted by a human tick."

That outing with Perro took Walt longer than usual. He chided himself for being insufferably preoccupied with thoughts of Pia Arellano. Her attitude and behavior were uniquely her own. Spunky with a kind of whimsical high spirits, her subtleties bemused him ... alas, for his peculiar tastes, a very sensual femme fatale. She was like the desert scenery, what he would call nature laid bare—rugged, defiant and in an odd way starkly beautiful.

He and Perro, its ragged tail wagging happily, crossed the bridge to Juarez's Avenida de Comercio, where blocks upon blocks were lined with bars and restaurants. It took him only about half an hour of inquiry with various informants to track down Pia's remaining assailant.

He found Jaw Man, Pablo Alvarez, in a seedy bar on one of the backstreets off Avenida Laredo. The bar, at that time of morning empty, reeked of alcohol, urine, and vomit. He bypassed the grimy counter and went directly into the smoky back room, where three men were playing cards at a round, knife-notched table.

At once, Perro started snitting in that bizarre combination of a snarl and a sneeze. All right, so maybe the mutt, as Pia claimed, intuited the good guys from the bad guys.

One of the three men, with a black rolled-back mustache and prominent Adam's apple, eyed Perro doubtfully then asked, "You are wanting to sit in on our game, *Señor?*"

He scanned the next face—a narrow one with saddlebags beneath its eyes—and then landed on the face across from those two, that of a brutal-looking countenance with a jutting jaw. Walt addressed him in Spanish. "I understand you abducted Pia Arellano from jail, Alvarez."

Above the spread of cards in his hand, the man looked Walt up and down. Apparently ascertaining Walt did not appear to be armed, and rightfully so, he growled in English. "Fuck off."

Walt's peripheral appraisal of the other two men assured him he was in better condition than they and could have won the round if they decided to go up against him. But all three? Most doubtful.

Nevertheless, he flipped out his BI badge. "You broke the law, Alvarez. Let's go, amigo—to the El Paso Jail."

The Adams apple of the player with the rolled-back mustache bobbed erratically.

A venal smile appeared in the man's blue-shadowed jaw. He shrugged serape-clad shoulders. "The *Señora* Cardenas, she arranged for us to get the *puta* out of jail, so she could arrange to get me out, too, don't you think, *pendejo*?"

Walt struggled to refrain from gaping. Adelaide Cardenas? "You can tell that to the judge." Though how in the hell he expected to get Jaw Man to accompany him across the border peacefully was a matter of some concern.

At the same time Pablo Alvarez dipped his free hand below the table, the other two men jumped clear and backed away. Unexpectedly, Perro launched a flying attack at Alvarez's scuffed cowboy boot. Alvarez tried to shake off the mutt.

Walt seized the advantage. Grabbing the table's rim, he jerked it upward and slammed it against Alvarez. His chair toppled. His drawn revolver went off. And he slumped sidewise, the upper torso of his corpse protruding from behind the upturned table.

"Good dog," Walt said dryly.

Chapter Twenty-Two

The clash of cultures, occurring when the aristocratic, leisurely world of diplomacy encountered the rapidly industrialized world of telegraphy, required someone able to negotiate the tightwire between the two.

Günther easily passed himself off as an aristocrat. After all, as the starving son of a ragpicker in the squalors of Frankfurt, he understood clothing—the coarsest and the finest.

A quick learner, as a child he had gone from scavenging for rags at night to working by day in a rag shop for a dealer, known as a master ragpicker. The dingy room where eleven-year-old Günther sorted and bound bales of rags had smelled of clothes, damp from bad washing, long use, and embedded sweat, dung, and pee.

This master ragpicker in turn worked as middleman for paper factories. At fourteen, Günther was pulling a cart, delivering bales of better class rags to these paper factories. At one, he met the fifteen-year-old daughter of the factory owner. Helga was plump with sandy hair and pale hazel eyes that begged for attention.

Over the next year, whenever his deliveries chanced to cross her path at her father's paper factory, he made sure he gave Helga just that—attention. He was intuitive enough not to flatter her, only to comment appreciatively on her obvious assets: her rosebud lips, star-like dimples, and, most importantly, her intelligence. She was well-read, and he valued that, being nearly illiterate as he was.

By the time he was seventeen, he was running that particular paper factory—thanks largely due to his diligence but in part to importuning her father. As its manager, Günther learned that new culture, the industrial world of telegraphy.

Occasionally, Helga would drop by Günther's office with a basket of food—and a book or two. He was determined to educate himself, and he devoured these books as hungrily as he did her sauerbraten. And, likewise, her body. And he gave her more than attention now. He lavished affection. He was smart enough to ensure she experienced the sexual pleasure found between the brain's lobes as much as she did between the thighs.

"*Ja, ja*, my hero" she urged one particular afternoon, eager for the climax he purposefully withheld.

And that moment was a climactic one for him, as well, because he realized that was what he wanted, to be a famous hero, his name breathed with admiration on everyone's lips, not just Helga's. Even then, he was honest enough with himself to admit that adulation of others made him feel worthy, when he knew with a certainty he was not.

Fortuitously, about that same time a wheelchair-bound wealthy Berlin investor and his wife Sofia visited the factory to investigate possible acquisition. And Günther set about charming the middle-aged Sofia as he had the underaged Helga.

Leaving a furious Helga and her father behind, Günther became Sofia's lover. She taught him to play progressive euchre, and he learned enough French to pass as an elegant passé dilettante. From there, it was a hop, skip, and jump to navigating the salons of Berlin, known for its leadership roles in science, higher education, and government.

And, thus, eventually, he found himself here on the frontier post of El Paso with the lowly governmental position of honorary consul.

However, he was in the advantageous position of capitalizing on El Paso's geographical location—the flash point of growing international political tensions.

The mid-morning was early for a social call, but he was impatient. Adelaide had managed to obtain Pershing's parade route's details for him, most likely through one of her 'I'll scratch your back if you scratch mine,' canny ploys.

The snake-eyed Bao admitted him to the Cardenas mansion and taciturnly led him to the parlor where Adelaide greeted him. "Mr. von Kloss, so good to see you again." Her tone was polite and concerned but her eyes glowed with unsuccessfully damped passion.

He was perturbed that his lowly ranking of honorary consular did not qualify her to address him as Your Excellency. "And I you, as well, Mrs. Cardenas." He bent over her extended hand and skimmed its porcelain back with his lips.

"I asked you to come because I noticed a small portion of the Aubusson carpet you gave us is disintegrating. I am not sure if it is beetles or moths or what. Would you mind taking a look, please?"

"But, of course, Mrs. Cardenas. I would be delighted to."

He followed her up the flights of stairs to the attic landing. Once inside the room, lit only by sunlight sifting through the single window's shade, she turned to him, imploring, "I cannot possibly keep this telegraph station here, Günther. It is far too dangerous. My husband—or Bao—or even a wandering houseguest might come upstairs and overhear a transmission."

"Highly unlikely," he assured in a placatory tone. "These transmissions from the German Foreign Office do not occur that often." With one arm he encircled Adelaide's waist to draw her against him. Fortunately, Adelaide Cardenas was not hard on the eyes, unlike the corpulent Helga or the crepe-skinned Sofia.

Her brows knitted. "But since you last were here another message came in—late last night, Günther."

His heart skipped a beat. "Let me see it." A more important issue was at stake here than gratifying her passion. With a lingering kiss at the hollow of her collarbones, he captured her hand and tugged her toward the crocheted throw draped over the mound atop an old desk.

She shoved aside the throw covering the telegraph station with its headphones and telescopic antenna. She passed him the curling strip of tape. "I found it this morning."

He deliberated over its indentations that represented letters and numbers. Telegraphy was prone to garbling. And the war in Europe had created critical problems for Germany such as the danger of telegraphic espionage.

He lit up a cigarette. He knew he smoked far too much. He would not have been surprised if he disintegrated into a pile of ashes one day. If the cigarettes did not finish him off, then the malt liquor, which constituted his daily breakfast, would.

Cigarette in one hand, he picked up a pen from the desk with the other and turned to an old wall calendar, where he had decoded the last message from the German Foreign Office—old news, as it turned out, because Bigelow's contact had been already one step ahead by hours in receiving that order.

On the calendar's lower right portion, free of his earlier decoding, he began jotting—circling and crossing out letters and numbers. Minutes crawled by. Then, "*Scheisse!*" he muttered.

Standing behind him, she laid a hand on his shoulder. "What is it, Günther?"

He tore off that portion of the page, stuffed it in his jacket pocket, and ground out his cigarette with his highly polished shoe. He turned to her. "Britain has intercepted and decoded one of our telegrams." The message was incendiary. "It contained our Kaiser's offer to President Carranza, restoring the states of Texas, New Mexico, and Arizona to Mexico."

"Oh, no!" She looked shaken, although she could have but a glimmer of the magnitude of this disclosure.

Worse, was the German Foreign Office's 13040 code had been broken, putting his own mission at peril.

The transmission he held ordered him to resort to a backup in the codebook he had been supplied. Rather than keep it at his office, he had hidden it there in the attic along with the wireless station, from possibly prying eyes.

"*Liebling*, continue to check for any communiques and call my office immediately if one comes in. Mention something about the orphanage we're sponsoring, just in case of wiretapping. I'll understand."

She was gnawing her lip anxiously, as if she might be regretting getting involved. He could not allow an equivocating response from her. He gripped her shoulders and edged her backward toward the rolled out portion of carpet. "Meanwhile, *liebling*—"

She pressed a restraining hand against his chest. "Günther, my little son Richie told Bart he saw a man kissing me."

"*Verdammt!*"

"No, no—I was able to convince Bart it was but one of those platonic busses, bestowed the way Europeans do."

Relief eddied through Günther.

"But I cannot continue this risk."

"Where is your son now?"

"In the garage, watching my handyman Amado string electrical lighting."

Günther dipped his head and lightly kissed her throat. He could feel the flesh of her shoulders quivering through her georgette blouse. "You're right, of course. This isn't the right time. But soon ... very soon."

He could not afford to botch his assignment here. To return to the deplorable life he had known in Frankfurt was a fear that crushed his lungs. He could not permit himself to become slipshod.

But he was more concerned about Adelaide's reliability. Her current nervousness under pressure. Of course, for him, she was risking more now than ever. Her life, possibly.

She knew too much about his past. He genuinely admired her tenaciousness and sensed in her a repressed sexual appetite that could match his own. She was the first and only female among the many he had seduced with whom he felt a compatibility, a true and deep fondness. She understood him as none other did, not even his long-left behind family. He would sorely hate to have to dispose of Adelaide.

Chapter Twenty-Three

February 3rd, 1917

"See here—and here," Pia said, noting with one of Walt's pencils two disparate blocks of dashes and dots she had jotted on his notepad, "see the replications?"

No, what he saw, sitting next to her at his suite's narrow desk, was the way its lamplight gilded the graceful arch of her neck. What would her roped red hair look like if he reached behind her neck and removed the pins?

She was still dressed in bib overalls over a long-sleeve white pullover shirt, loosely rolled back at the wrists, what she had worn to clean von Kloss's place earlier that day. A fresh smell, a mixture of cleaning agents like beeswax, Palmolive soap, and lemons, enwreathed her.

Perro, curled upon the settee, did not smell so sweet. But, at least, Pia was steam-shoveling as rapidly as she found his fetid deposits.

Before commandeering Walt's desk, she had kicked off her lace-up boots. Oddly, the mere glimpse of her dainty wrists … her small stockinged feet … sweltered him. He had taken off the collar of his shirt, yet it still felt constricting. He ran a finger behind his shirt's top button, loosening it.

Over the last couple of days, he and Pia had been tethered in the hotel room except for the mornings she sallied forth to clean von Kloss's place.

Reluctantly, Walt acknowledged he and Pia had settled into a productive routine in the confines of the suite, learning each other's quirks and strengths. He detected an affinity between them he could not explain by logic.

She was intelligent and clever, with the exceptional ability to analyze in three languages. He admired her drive to better herself. And she could be funny, only that day asking while he was deep in the drudgery of filing a *Collier Magazine* expense report, "Do you know what they call pirate's earrings, Walt?"

"No, what?" he asked somewhat impatiently.

"Buccaneers." And then she had bestowed him with that lopsided smile that twisted up his better judgment. He was a sucker for crooked smiles.

They needed a break. She had never seen a moving picture. The Alameda Theater was showing *Bronco Billy and the Bad Man*. He thought about taking her to the theater, the pleasure he would derive in watching her watch the moving picture—and then wanted to smack his forehead with a, "What am I thinking?!"

He considered telling her about Jaw Man's disclosure and demise and thought better of it. Not until he had talked with Bobby. Found out what more Bobby knew about Adelaide Cardenas.

Instead, he mentioned attending the upcoming parade for the AEF, the next day. "It will be a good place to meet and greet," he paused to grin, "And seek a leak."

She hurled at him one of her wadded up sheets of paper she had retrieved from von Kloss's wastebasket, then laughed exultantly.

He noted the way she tilted back her head, her lips parted to emit her merriment. He was entranced.

She wagged her head in mock despair. "Walt, you and your espionage tactics. As for myself, I'd rather take in a game at the Rio Grande Ball Yard."

His brow jerked up. "You're interested in watching baseball?"

She laughed again. "I'd rather play it. But that's not likely to ever happen, not for us females."

While puzzling over the codes, Pia hummed, off-key awful. He whistled. Rather well, he thought. She thought not. "A rooting hog sounds better," she teased with one of her sassy grins.

She loved chaos, demonstrated by how she haphazardly discarded her clothing and belongings. They were strewn about, a stumbling impediment he had more than once tested and what he found maddening.

He loved order, which she smart-alecky denounced as anal, pointing out the way his pencils were sharpened to needle point and laid out on the desk in precise order, from the stubbiest to the longest.

While it seemed her impulsiveness translated into inspiration when it came to deciphering, he nonetheless craved structure, and justification—not Pia's randomness.

He was tired, his nerves frayed between juggling his job as war correspondent for *Collier's Magazine* and his undercover work for the Bureau of Investigation.

Walt thought of the merciless pathos and insupportable tragedies he had seen during the coverage of the Pershing Expedition. If the common people on both sides of the border—those unaffected directly by the revolution—had seen the sinister slaughter for themselves, would they have cried, 'Enough is enough!' and insisted their leaders negotiate for immediate peace?

It all had come crashing down earlier that day when Ed shared that the *El Paso Herald* had received a communique reporting the commander of Juarez's Fort Hidalgo had hanged yet another boy, this one a nine-year-old boy caught smuggling ammunition for Pancho Villa.

Walt was swamped by a wave of emotional turbulence and found himself suddenly thrust back to his own adolescence. His entire life had been colored by that one disastrous moment from nine-years onward.

Half a dozen years later, triggered by growth spurts and puberty changes, he had gotten drunk once and detested the feeling of not being in control. But right now, a drink was what he wanted more than a best-selling novel. A drink, one or a thousand, would never completely obliterate his childhood nightmare. He blinked rapidly, swallowed the knot of desolation pounding against the back of his throat.

He tapped the most recent sheet of paper mazed with Pia's pencil squiggles and asked in a quite controlled tone, "So, what bearing do replications have in deciphering?"

"Codebreaking is about noticing and then rearranging patterns, Walt. For instance, in German the letters E, N, I, R, T, and S occur more frequently. And in Spanish the letters E, A. O, R, S, and N, occur in that order. Silas—you know, the streetcar ticket master you talked to at Union Station—he taught me that most ciphers occur in groups of five. I bet he could hold his own against Fort Bliss's Military Intelligence."

He refrained from mentioning Silas was one of his paid informants. Always, the less said, the better. And a wooden expression to go along with it did not hurt. "Well, then, this should be easy enough."

"No, because each five-digit group can represent a letter or number, which in turn represents a word of phrase or even another letter or number, which is almost impossible to decipher without a codebook. But, trust me, I'll find it. And your master spy."

"Von Kloss is clever. If he has a codebook, he wouldn't hide it in his office. It could be anywhere here in El Paso—or Juarez, for that matter—and we don't have that kind of time required to look for it."

She reached up and removed his pince-nez and set it next to the brass desk lamp. Her small hands aligned either side of his chiseled face, which she turned down toward hers. "Walt, you have to stop looking with your eyes."

"What else is there?" he asked indignantly. He was damned proud of his observational skills.

"Your imagination. It's far more in-*sight*-ful than mere eyes."

He had to marvel at her play on the word. "You are much smarter than I originally gave you credit for, buttercup."

Her stiffening neck signaled she had taken umbrage again. Her palms released him abruptly. "You know, you could stand a touch of humility."

But it was his hubris that lessened his load. A load even his wide, muscled shoulders occasionally found too heavy to bear, despite time and swimming's cushioning. At these low ebbs of emotional stamina, he would feel sometimes he was going to die of sadness.

His sigh was as heavy as his burden. "How tactless of me." He braced his forehead with one hand, shadowing from her the perennial pain behind his eyes. His fingers and thumb massaged his temples. Don't think. Don't think at all. No, if you must think, think of something else. Cool Cordelia, like a cool drink of lemonade.

"Walt Stevenson, I believe you use your words like a soldier does a gun."

He raised bleary eyes. "God Almighty, a gun? Oh, I am very, very good with a gun, Pia. Cain and Abel have nothing over me and Thad."

She leaned in. Her whispered words were hummingbird wings, fluttering against his cheeks, his lips. "What are you talking about, Walt … share with me."

He found himself mumbling, "Not that much to share, except I was already angry at him."

"At Thad? What happened between you and Thad?"

He lowered his shielding hand. His eyes met hers, as if thereby permitting her to see into the hollowness of his soul. Something he had never let his parents, friends, even Cordelia see. "I killed my brother, my twin, Pia."

Such a bald-faced statement. He expected a gasp of horror from her or a demand for an explanation for his confession's outrageousness. Instead, she took his hand and drew him over to the rocker, where she nudged him down. She settled into his lap and nestled her head in the cradle of his neck and collarbone.

After a lengthy period of silence, he automatically began rocking. The repetitive creak of the rockers was a state of grace for him. Atop his waistcoat's left breast pocket, Pia's splayed her small hand and gently massaged his chest, where resided his heart ... had he one. Ages ago it had withered like a tossed piece of fruit.

A long time went by it seemed. He continued rocking. She was synchronizing her massaging with the rocker's motion it felt to him.

Then, staring into the darkness beyond the lamp's pallid light, his memory summoned forth the past. "Often my mother had to entertain guests ... government officials and their wives who called upon my father. So my widowed grandfather rocked me and my twin brother Thaddeus from early on."

He halted, cleared his throat, but seemed to have trouble forcing words up from his tight chest.

"Were you identical twins?" she prompted gently.

The words came. "No. Thad was fair, like our mother. In fact, he was the Golden Child. He was one of those rare individuals born with an easy charm and bonhomie that both young and old are drawn to."

"How difficult to be in his shadow then, *sí?*"

"Often, yes. But I loved Thad. Everyone did." He was finding a fury in voicing aloud his heart's heavy guilt. "When we were nine, Thad and I discovered an old pistol, an American Revolution holster pistol, hidden away in my father's closet. Hidden, I guess because my mother ... she was a Quaker ... was so against wars and weapons. Thad and I were each wrestling for possession of it like it was a rope in the Tug of War game."

He stopped rocking. The fury had subsided to a fear. A fear of finally giving voice to the past, giving voice to the pain. He tried to clear his throat again. It felt stoppered, like by a cork.

She did not let up on her soothing massage. "Go on," she said, her tone as tender and soft as a breath blown upon a dandelion.

He felt he must finish his painful recounting, intuited that somehow her quiet attentiveness might just save him from himself.

He resumed rocking, a little faster now, in time with his accelerating heartbeat. "After that, after my mother suffered a nervous breakdown, after my father devoted himself entirely to the demands of his political position ... my grandfather started rocking me again. My gangly legs hung over the rocker arm, but it made no difference to either of us. He rocked me off and on for maybe another year or ... until he died. After that, I ran away. Was caught sleeping in a cooper's backyard workshop. And then ... then a little later, when I was thirteen, my father sent me away, enrolled me at the New Mexico Military Institute."

"How I admire you, Walt ... admire your nobility and courage to carry on when it would have been so easy to, you know, to flounder through the rest of your life."

Stunned, he looked down at her luminous face. For him, that disastrous day had colored the rest of his life. "That ... your comment ... was not what I expected."

She left off her massaging and took his hand. "Come, *mi corazón*. We're both tired. The deciphering can wait."

He let her lead him into the bedroom. She drew him down alongside her on the bed and wrapped the counterpane over their fully-clothed bodies. There was no resistance left in him. He was drained. When she entwined him within the cocoon of her thin arms, he fell immediately asleep.

Much later ... it had to be near dawn, because a sliver of pearl gray light seeped from behind the bedroom's window shade ... he stirred awake. He could not remember sleeping so deeply; a restorative sleep it had been.

He was still dressed but realized his shoes had been removed. He shifted slightly on the mattress and peered down to find a fully-clothed Pia snuggled against him in the cradle of his arm and chest.

Her dark lashes fluttered, and she gazed up into his eyes, as if awaiting some response from him.

He bent his head, his lips skimming each of her eyelids. Her sigh whispered over her slightly parted lips, and he felt that sigh cutting through him, like an axe-sharp wanting. Wanting what he was not sure he was prepared to give.

After all, he knew so little about her. They had set eyes on each other only … what, was it seven or was it eight days ago? He had to remind himself that for someone so small she was so strong, so mulishly determined. For all he knew, she could be bestowing her affections in exchange for realizing her ludicrous dream of a grand home on Mount Franklin.

Pia's sigh surfaced from both instinct and experience, both rooted in the heartbreaking beauty that was life. Her sigh pined for a man who would never be hers. Walt Stevenson was an impassioned man, a man who was upright, direct, and concise. But his secret and its grief might never let her forge past them to his heart. Alas, he was storming the gates of her own.

"Will it matter … this is important, Walt … will it matter to you that I am not a virgin?"

He smiled ruefully. "Will it matter to you that I am not?"

She shook her head.

Shifting his streamlined torso to angle across hers, he propped on one elbow above her. His gaze studied her eyes, lowered to her lips, dipped to the wildly pulsing hollow at the base of her throat, and returned back to her eyes. "You have a soothing way, Pia, a soothing way that war never is." His voice was as raspy as a horseshoe file.

"Forget the damned wars and their killings," she whispered. "There is just us, here and now."

His lips skimmed her cheekbone, then muttered into the tangled hair at her temple. "This is all wrong … selfish of me … but I can't seem to find the will to save us. This has to be your decision, what *you* want."

She turned her face, inhaled sharply as her lips brushed his. His scent, sleep's muskiness underlaid with his wood-barrel soap's, flooded her nostrils and rationality. Not that she had ever been good at rational thinking. Josefina would likely attest that her spontaneous nature was her ruination.

And that heightened responsiveness of hers would surely be her damnation now. "*Sí, mi corazón ... sí ... sí ... sí.*" And she knew not whether she was pleading him to halt or continue his besieging of her thoughts and flesh.

He shifted his attention, which seemed never to miss even a particle of dust on his desk or a speck on his suit, to her hand only, nestled in the mat of his hair where the top of his wrinkled shirt was unbuttoned. He drew her palm up to examine it. He thumbed its hollow, then lifted each work-worn finger wonderingly, as if its very fingerprint contained the answers to the mysteries of the universe.

"Sandpaper is softer ... and yet I suspect your skin elsewhere ... the skin is so very soft ... as if hidden away, waiting to be touched." His light exploration, continuing along the rim of her ear ... and in the hollow beneath her chin ... and returning to her palm, jolted her like crackling lightning bolts of spring's thunderstorms. And, like spring awakening from a lifetime of winter, her body was springing to life, implored by his gift for words and knowledgeable touch.

With a lingering that was maddening, he began to divest them of their clothing. She sensed she was hurtling toward something of urgency, something her body was demanding, whether it was reward or punishment, she could not interpret. Driven by some mindless want, she clutched at his shirt front, yanking at its resistant remaining buttons.

"Patience, Pia," he murmured. "I want you to know the difference between being ravaged and being ravished."

She half sighed, half huffed. "I know my thesaurus quite well, *gracias!*"

"But do you know what it is to be filled with intense delight? To be enraptured?"

She could hear the faint amusement in his tone and in frustration she nipped his earlobe.

"Owww!" At once he leveled his entire weight fully atop her. Surely, only his forearms braced at either side of her head, prevented her from being crushed. "You do nothing halfway, do you, Pia? Your mind and body's need to experience the limit … and beyond?"

For her, his purposely selected words were the equal to opium for an addict. "When you talk to me that way—"

"We both get drunk on words, don't we, *mi vida?*"

Did he realize what he had just said, "*Mi vida?*" "Do your truly mean that, Walt—calling me your life—or is it merely a tossed out endearment?

"Kiss me, Pia."

So, his '*mi vida*' was only offhand sweet talk. At that moment, it mattered not.

She shoveled her fingers through his thick hair, capturing his head to draw those unyielding lips nearer hers. She stared up into his passion-dilated pupils with the fierceness of her own intent. "Listen, *mi corazón* … I want you to desire me as you have no other." When she knew what she really wanted was for him to love her as he had no other, not even his precious Cordelia.

Hoping wildly to impart a glimpse of the world that her love could give him, she obeyed then and kissed him with her heart's hunger. She had always felt certain that somewhere, sometime, somehow she would see someone, he would see her, and they would know in that instant they were meant to be. She knew now for sure. But Walt still did not.

"My God, Pia … you mess with my mind." His mouth slammed over hers, dominating her and devastating all thought. Then just as abruptly, his mouth shifted to rain kisses on her cheek, her chin, and below, where his shadowed jaw abraded her throat with his lingering love bite.

At this exquisite edge of unaccustomed pain, goosebumps erupted over her breasts and upper arms. A mewling eddying from the back of her throat sounded more like a feline's purr.

"Sorry ..." he was mumbling, "... your flesh will wear my mark tomorrow."

"I want ... I want ...." She who revered words encountered inadequacy now in expressing herself.

"I know, I know, what you want, Pia. You must trust me."

She did, which could well be her undoing. She could feel his erection pressing against her belly. "I *know* what I want," she breathed. "You, Walt. Only you. Now and forever."

Gently, a forearm slipping beneath her knee, he lifted it and began gradually nudging himself inside her. She was caught up with the intensity of his gaze, inches away, measuring and monitoring her changing expressions.

"I want to see that dreamy quality in your face." He delved ever deeper. He was giving her no quarter, so that she was drugged with mounting passion and unprepared to react with instinctive fear. "Move with me," he coaxed.

She could not have denied him had her mind even been in possession of self-will then and there, which it was not. Compliant, her body bowed within his fold, uniting with his own body's cadence. From that place of infinitesimal bliss, a crescendoing, exquisite pleasure erupted into a conflagration of unbearable sensations. They roared in smaller to wider concentric circles throughout her.

Abruptly, his powerful frame halted its stroking, which had been pure bliss for her. Once more, he began kissing her lips, her temples, her ears, her throat. Puzzled and feeling bereft, she turned her head slightly to the side to look up at him.

"I am merely delaying our gratification and extending our divertissement," he murmured.

"Divertissement?" she muttered in sheer frustration. "This I do not understand."

He allotted a male's triumphant smile. "The best is yet to come. No pun intended."

"Your American humor, it is ill-timed."

He laughed softly, and, while his hips began to rock hers in that immemorial way of coupling, he rained incendiary kisses over her face and throat and breasts that puckered in response.

Beneath her palms, she now felt the enormous tension mounding along his spine and shoulder blades. And, as if from afar, she heard herself making a keening noise that united with his mountain lion's growl.

Then, taking her by surprise, her limbs went suddenly rigid, and her head fell back. Her heart banged within her chest. Her breath rasped with a rapture that was setting afire her flesh.

As though her body signaled his, a seizure of spasms racked him. Her fingertips dug into his flesh, and her own body arched against his with a shuddering that seemed unending.

So that her scream of his name would not reverberate through the hotel corridor's other rooms, she buried her face against his damp, heaving chest. And she could only be grateful it was not the name of Cordelia she heard as he groaned into the mass of her disheveled hair on the pillow but the sound of his body's splintering ecstasy.

However, later on she did hear his gentle snoring … while she, nestled within the curve of his long, muscled body, reviewed the night's splendor. Sadly, she had to acknowledge that he had made love to her … but did not love her.

A world of difference existed in the mere phrasing of words, did it not?

Chapter Twenty-Four

February 4th, 1917

A towel wrapped around his midriff, Walt stood at the pedestal sink, beneath the beveled mirror. He did not look directly into the eyes reflected back at him. Could not bring himself to meet the possible derision lurking there. He sensed he had shortchanged Pia last night. And, worse, he knew she sensed it, too.

An hour ago, they had parted, she with a tight-lipped feigned smile, off to clean von Kloss's place; he with a lightly dropped kiss on her forehead. Their tender parting was more like two sparring boxers returning to their respective corners of the ring.

But, criminy, by now she should know him better than anyone, should know one could only give so much of themselves without shattering. He had survived shattering as a nine-year-old, he would not shatter now.

He stretched his bottom lip upward to create a razor path along his jaw. A noisy ruckus resounded from the suite's sitting room, and he sliced the cleft in his chin. "Tarnation!"

What was Perro destroying now? Already, the mutt had chewed ragged one edge of the bed's counterpane.

He whipped from around his waist the knotted towel and used it to dab at the blood beading on his chin. Slinging aside the towel in disgust, he strode from the bathroom, through the bedroom, only to step into something mushy. "Shit!" He plunged on toward the sitting room. "Hell's bells, Perro, just one more fiasco from you and I'll sell you off to—"

At the doorway, her mouth open, Pia dropped her *bolsa* from one hand and with a clunk the pail with mop and cleaning supplies from the other. She wore a pair of men's worn-out blue jeans so long the thick cuffs were rolled nearly to her calves.

At the sight of his nakedness, the flush of her face deepened even more—despite the carnal pleasure she had partaken from it only hours earlier. "To what, Walt? Sell Perro away to a slaughterhouse?"

What the hell?! At that moment, he could care less about his nudity. Between the mauling mutt, who now cowered beneath the rocking chair, and his raw feelings, he was in no mood to back down. "It's *your* country that sells butchered dogs at every corner *carnicería,* not mine."

Her chin thrusting upward, she mimicked his stance, her fists knotted on the slight curve of her hips. "And it is you Americans who buy the most dog meat—and opium, I might add."

An immense sadness dragged him under like a riptide. "Then that's what we've come down to, isn't it? Americans versus Mexicans."

"You brought it up—but, *sí,* might versus right."

Both of them were ignoring the elephant in the room. Their respective countries were proxies for their own intimate issues. He parried her attack with his own rapier thrust. "If you're accusing the United States of being the war monger, I might remind you that it was you yourself who started a riot, destroying public property, and assaulting public officials."

One elbow jutting, her hand went to the small of her back and rubbed it, as if the source of her anger originated there when he was all too conscious that his withholding was that source. "It was a protest

191

not a riot, Walt. How many times do I have to tell you?"

"It was war versus peace," was his verdict "War is wrong. And so is violating the law."

She closed her eyes. "So you claim … you who have never had to fight against your house being torn down, against your means of earning a living being denied, against your dignity as a human being rejected, "she paused a beat and swayed, "… against rape by people like Cisco Rodriguez and Jaw Man." The last broke on a metallic moan comprised of both wrath and pain.

At once, he scooped her up and carried her into the bedroom. He lowered her onto the bed, half kneeling over her. "What is it, Pia What's wrong?"

Her fine features drawn, eyes still closed, she whispered. "It's like the bad and the good, war and peace … my monthlies … ¡*Dios mío*! … they so hurt my back, low in its middle. I never even finished cleaning the consulate."

He lay down next to her and, turning the fairy-sized frame of her spine against his length, gently, tenderly massaged that tiny spot that was the small of her back. His gaze alit on the small bruise marring that side of her neck. He should have felt guilty but he recalled the pleasure they both had felt at the mark his mouth had stamped the night before.

"*Sí*, there … that's the right place, Walt." A delicious sigh shuddered from her. "That is the bad. The pain before my monthlies. And the good … for you I suppose it would be that I am hardly likely to be carrying our child."

His lips compressed. Could he blame his stymied relief? To father a child when his shutdown feelings no longer had the capacity to bestow love?

Pia had a courage he could only envy. The courage, the *coraje*, to live life's full spectrum, from joy to pain and back. In Spanish, *coraje*, meant from the heart … that kind of courage which his own heart could not sustain nor for that matter continue to function at all.

Chapter Twenty-Five

February 5th, 1917

Awakening early that next morning from dozing fitfully in a drugged stupor a full day and night, Pia found she was still fully dressed, although her boots had been removed. It would seem she and Walt were becoming adept at tucking one another into bed.

Quietly, she readied for work. Walt slept strung-out on the sitting room's settee. He wore only his trousers, his upper torso bare. She stood for a moment, admiring the beauty of his body. His shoulders and arms were roped with muscles, and his stomach looked like Mamacita's corrugated washboard. The squint lines fanning from his eyes were relaxed, so that he had a boyish look about him.

Her impressions of him were confused. He was just and kind, but also proud and so certain he knew what was right. As if to expose himself to others' opinions might undermine the sand beneath his very foundations.

As was his nature, he had been exceedingly attentive last night. He had coaxed her to eat chicken soup from the hotel's main dining room and plied her with cool water and pain powders he must have picked up from one of his 'sources.' She vaguely recalled his massaging her sporadically, from her temples, down her spine, to the arches of her feet. What an exquisite sensation. Had it been real—or only intensified by the laudanum?

And somewhere in that drugged sleepiness, she recollected him telling her, as he smoothed a sweat dampened tendril from her cheek, "Pia, you never have to worry about Jaw Man again. He's dead." She had been too drowsy to inquire how the man died. Certainly not at Walt's hand. He lacked a warrior's unsparing instinct to terminate the opponent.

Walt's next words muttered more to himself had seeped into her subconsciousness just before she fell asleep again. "We're as opposite as black from white, left from right, up from down, Pia. How did we get in a muddle like this?"

At the last moment, before leaving, she turned back to the settee, and, lightly brushing from his forehead a hank of brown hair, whispered, "It's because we can't resist each other, *mi vida*."

She would almost give him her soul ... she had already given him her heart. From the first, she had decided he was the one. But she could tell he did not have a clue about this thing he ridiculed, synchronicity. She had looked the word up in her *Roget's*. She might have been ignorant about the word itself, but she understood its meaning.

How could she not when every choice she and he had made, every road they both had taken, had led them time and again back to one another? She loved him so much, to the exclusivity of all else, it was almost sickening.

What if at their first crossing of paths at Union Station she had deboarded from the streetcar a minute later ... he would have missed noticing her. Or what if she had caught an earlier streetcar and missed that first sighting of him? What if he had arrived too late at the bath house fiasco to come within yards and sight of her being hauled away by the police? What if he had not made the decision to come looking for her after those two Neanderthals abducted her from jail … and what if she had chosen another desert footpath to lead her back to the main road running between Juarez and Chihuahua? She would have missed where the Hudson had crippled up. And missed out on Walt Stevenson.

His pin-striped shirt, waistcoat, and matching morning coat lay haphazard across one settee arm, when usually they were tidily hung in the tall wardrobe. So unlike him. He had to have been exhausted. Tenderly, she dropped the coat over his lanky, naked torso. Something small slipped from the coat's inner pocket, and she stooped to retrieve it.

Stupefied, she stared at the silver badge with its gold lettering. She reread the embossed words, thinking she might have misunderstood. But, no.

He worked for the United States Bureau of Investigation! All along, he had been deceiving her, lulling her into complacency with his yarn of wanting to write a bestselling story. She dropped the badge like it was a flaming match. He had been lying all the time.

What a *tanta* she was for loving a man like Walt Stevenson, a man who was too mummified to reciprocate. Too committed to the need to control. Control of himself. And this last—government control.

She felt as if her heart had been blown to bits in her chest. Alternately she wanted either to sink to her knees and weep or to hurl something breakable. She picked up the nearest object, her thesaurus, and slung it at the bundled muscles that striated his midriff.

"What—what the hell!" He sprang to his bare feet in an aggressive crouch.

She kicked the thesaurus where it had landed on the carpet toward him. "Work for the Department of Justice, do you, Walt? *Pues*, look up the various meanings of justice in the thesaurus, because you do not understand its true meaning."

He stared at her like she was a hissing rattlesnake disturbed from its nest. "Stop this ridiculous tirade, Pia. You are letting your female's monthlies get the better—"

That made her even madder. "I am talking about egalitarian justice. And after that look up words like integrity and honesty! You, who once told me you were so certain you knew what was right for you—like truth. Like honesty."

He tunneled fingers through his rumpled hair. "Now look, Pia, never have I lied to you."

Her anger nearly choked her. She swallowed hard. "Well, those who are godly might deem it a sin of omission."

"Godly? I doubt there is one single thing you hold holy."

She stared at him with eyes that felt a thousand years old. "Love. I hold love holy."

"There you go again. Look, let's not bring religion in to this. You should have figured out by now I'm agnostic. Oh, I would like to believe in some greater force, a Serendipity, at work in the cosmos, but science and a little flexing of mental muscle argue convincingly against it."

"Agnostic? Cosmos? Serendipity? You pompous ass! Flaunting your knowledge, as if that makes you superior. When you wouldn't recognize wisdom if it smacked you in your face. You are ignorant when it comes to people. *Estúpido, entiéndeme?!*"

A nerve flicked along his jaw. She could almost hear his teeth clenching and unclenching.

She grabbed her *bolsa* and pail and mop. "When I do find the identity of your master spy—and I will, *por Dios*—really, how can I expect *un cabrón* like you to hold to your word, to come through with the land in Kern Place when you have no integrity?"

She could tell she had stung him—attacking the only worthy trait he felt he possessed. In response, his own words might as well have been poisoned darts. "I may not have integrity, as you so piously claim, but wisdom I do have. I am wise enough to know a relationship between us would never work. Your education, your financial status, your social circle, well—" he shrugged.

That roiled her anger to its boiling point. "*Chinga tu madre!*" she spat and gave him the crude gesture of the *corte de manga* with angry

196

satisfaction. "No more will I let my heart ache over you! All this wasted time. I am finished being the sunflower, with you my sun."

She stormed to the door, fumbled with the knob, then slammed it behind her. On the street below, tears that threatened to brim her lids reflected the rising sunlight in blinding prisms, so that twice she bumped into businessmen hurrying to work. *Walt Stevenson is not worth crying over!* And yet her chest felt like a hand grenade had exploded inside it, shredding her heart into a thousand painful pieces.

Somehow, head down, stomach knotting, she made the trek to the First National Bank Building. With a scowl, von Kloss admitted her. A cigarette dangled from beneath one end of his rapier mustache. "You! You did not finish cleaning yesterday!"

"I—I got sick … to my stomach … and had to return home."

He eyed her red eyes, her weak smile, and they must have reflected suffering enough to convince him. "Be quick about it then. I have a client coming in twenty minutes."

She dipped the mop in the pail and mechanically swished the damp yarn on the floor, directly behind the expanse of desk. She felt the pain of Walt's deception as strongly as she still did the menstrual ache in her lower back.

Only a door separated her from von Kloss, readying behind it for the day's appointments. She turned her attention to the suddenly clicking teleprinter. She listened to its Morse transmission of dots and dashes that registered as pings and whines. She edged closer to scan its tape. Nothing she could make out yet. But on von Kloss's desk lay a mustard yellow telegram—this one with its every third letter circled.

Swiftly, she propped the mop handle against the desk edge and picked up the fountain pen. Its tip dashed ink across her palm as she jotted the telegram's circled letters.

Behind her, she heard the doorknob turn. ¡*Mierda*! She bumped the bucket, upending it. Whipping the dust rag from her shoulder, she dropped to her knees and swabbed at the pool of water. It rolled in a shallow tide around a nearby pair of Chelsea boots.

Her gaze traveled up the subtly striped pants and morning coat to collide with von Kloss's frown. She offered an apologetic grin. "Spats would help keep the water from your boots, *Señor* von Kloss."

"That does it! You—you are incompetent. I want you out of—"

The telephone rang. He grabbed the candlestick and its earpiece. "What?! Oh, Adelaide, my apology. What? A transmission? No, I warned you about teleph—forget it, I am on my way over."

He whirled back to where Pia crouched. "Out!" He jabbed a finger from the upturned bucket and mop to her *bolsa* on the credenza. "Get your things and do not come back. Understand?"

She understood all too well. So, Adelaide Cardenas was a part of the conspiracy. Not surprising, given her German ancestry and her husband's Mexican one. Both had reason to hold grudges against the United States. As she herself did. But she meant to turn her grudge to an advantage—the house at Kern Place.

Slinging the soggy dust cloth and the mop into the bucket, she grabbed her belongings and bolted out the door. A gust of near panic stumbled her toward the stairwell. At its bottom, she sighed huge relief. In her left palm, she held the key to her new home. Or rather written on her palm she held the key.

Outside on the street, she jumped aboard the next Union Station-bound streetcar and alit at the depot. Dodging travelers, she jogged across the numerous platforms to the streetcar ticket station.

At the sight of her, Silas' iron-gray mustache barely fluttered upward at the ends in what could be interpreted, in his case, as pleasure. "Well, gal, you've gone missing."

Breathless, she slid inside the little booth and stowed her cleaning gear below the counter, keeping only her *bolsa* with her. "Silas, I've been working at the German consular's office. I think he is a spy for Germany—and I just found a telegram on his desk that I think he may have partially decoded. Look!" She thrust out her palm—then gasped. The dust cloth she used to soak up the spilt water—it had smeared the ink.

Sadly, Silas shook his shaggy head. "Gal, you let your silly imagination run away with you sometimes, I swear. I should never have gone and got you started on telegraphy and coding." Like shooing away a fly, he flapped a veined and liver-spotted hand, gnarled by arthritis. "Now, skedaddle. Go on. Find some more productive outlet for your imagination."

Chapter Twenty-Six

At the Sunset Heights stop, Pia swung down from the streetcar and hustled up Corto Way to the Chateau Cardenas. Skirting the steps leading up to the imposing mountainside home, she veered off to the side. Here stately green poplars bordered the mansion and reduced the cloudy morning's chill.

She darted along the narrow line of trees until she reached the rear of the house and its carriage house-garage. She realized she was acting foolhardy, justifying Silas' judgment. Nevertheless, she was disappointed. She had thought he and she were alike, two square pegs that did not fit into round holes.

But then, she thought, bitterly, she was wrong about a lot of her assumptions. Wrong in thinking Walt was worthy of her love and devotion.

She worried she could run into Cheng, meandering about the vast premises with his gardening duties. But caution demanded time and time might well be in short supply. She was in a race with Günther von Kloss, and he was most likely already here.

Then she came upon the very person she was seeking. Using his trowel handle, the sombreroed Amado was nudging a red brick in place. For a moment, she felt that girlish giddiness she initially had at the sight of his handsome features, before the humiliation of the bath house.

She was no longer that girl—and he had not the power to disturb her, beckon her, challenge her … and hurt her, as did Walt.

Amado's head canted, and as if detecting another presence, he halted. Only his eyes shifted in her direction. Then he grinned. He removed his sombrero, dropped it and the trowel, and crossed toward her. He took her hands playfully. "Pia, what are you doing here?"

She squeezed his large-gloved hand with contrasting urgency. "You've got to secret me inside the Chateau."

"What are you talking about?" One black brow scrunched. "*¿Que pasa, bebé?*"

"I'm hoping, needing, to find a wireless set I think is hidden there."

"A what?"

"I believe Adelaide has a telegraph machine, Amado—most likely hidden somewhere high, near the roof, maybe in the attic. I think she's in league with that German consul, von Kloss." But certainly neither he nor the German *frau* could be the master spy. They were too caught up in their individual, self-absorbed agendas.

"I've been cleaning his office. And I think the two are involved in coordinating some kind of plot. Maybe sabotage. Maybe soon." Just hearing herself, she thought how loony she sounded.

Now that same black brow jacked upward, as if he might be thinking the same. "What has that to do with you?"

A lot. Now that von Kloss had fired her and she was persona non grata with Adelaide, this might be the final opportunity to earn that plot of land at Kern Place—if Walt was a man of his word. Word. For all he appraised their differences, they had that, at least, in common … their love of words.

"Walt Stevenson is paying me to keep tabs on von Kloss—for an investigative story he's doing for *Collier's Magazine*," she hedged, though she thought it disgustingly foolish for to protect his cock-and-bull cover-up.

"Uhhh, do you have to look for the wireless set now? Can't it wait?"

"*Sí* and no! This could be urgent. *Por favor*, Amado. Do this for me. *¿Por favor?*"

Amado rolled his eyes. "*¡Ay, caramba!* You don't make it easy on a man, Pia."

"You'd be bored with any *mujer* who did."

The man with this much machismo actually flushed. Squeezing her hand in return, he emitted an exasperated sigh tinged with excitement. "All right, then. I'll be your advance scout. Keep a decent distance behind. Your von Kloss, is here now, in the parlor."

"How long has he been here? Time enough to go upstairs?"

Discarding first one work glove then the other, he shrugged. "*¿Quién sabe?* I only noticed him when I passed through to take a look at a loose balustrade the *Señora* wants me to fix—five minutes ago, *más o menos.*"

She did not have to risk this, being caught, ending up in jail again most likely … or worse. Why do this, when she could live out her life in relative safety—and extreme poverty—in Juarez? "Lead on."

Amado took her by way of a side entrance. She paused at the laundry room and watched while he strode past the kitchen's swinging door and down the hall toward the backstairs. He halted, glanced up the steep staircase, then signaled her with a nod to follow.

He started up the carpeted steps, and she immediately slipped along the hallway to trail him. At the bottom of the staircase, she grasped the newel—and paused. Feeling someone watching, she glanced over her shoulder. At the kitchen door, Bao stood, her eyes slits, her lips stringent in her little wrinkled face.

A shiver rippled up Pia's backbone. There was nothing she could do now. Either Bao alerted Adelaide or she did not.

She hustled up the steps. Carefully, she kept a safe distance behind Amado, who had disappeared up around the next flight. She rounded the second landing, where the stairwell narrowed. Here, the light in the wall bracket's crackled amber glass was dimmer. She climbed to the next floor. Up ahead, Amado opened the attic door and turning back to her, beckoned with a curl of his finger.

Panting shallowly, not from exertion but anxiousness, she sidled past him into the attic room's near cavernous darkness. A single window permitted only marginal early morning light past the edges of its draw-down, fringed shade.

Amado's shadowy form groped above for the bare light bulb's pull chain. Next, weak buttery light pushed the shadows toward the room's perimeter.

The place smelled of mothballs. She had been up here only once, to store Richie's rocking horse. Atop an old desk, wedged beneath the window, was a new addition to the storage items. Haphazardly concealed by a crocheted throw had to be what was the wireless radio unit. Clearly visible was the antenna extension running from it to the window. A paper spiral of transmitted tape coiled nearby.

"There it is," Amado said, wonderment tinging his voice, "the telegraph set you were talking about."

"*Sí*, but now I need something else."

Simple deduction meant the transmission of messages over the radio would require telegraphic codes … which, in turn, meant a codebook had to be somewhere. It could be anywhere in the house. Logic said it would be up here, near at hand. And a code, if cracked, might just well divulge for her the identity of El Paso's master spy.

"A codebook of some kind." She sighed. "It could be a miniature book as small as a postage stamp."

She had read about a miniature etiquette book, *The Little Flirt*, where women learned to attract men by using items already in their possession, such as gloves, handkerchiefs, fans, and parasols. Maybe she should have read it. Maybe she should have flirted with Walt. Maybe, just maybe, he would have been more attracted to her.

She wove her way through the mound of storage—a cracked Tiffany lampshade, a scuffed duffle bag, a box of party supplies, and an old Victrola cabinet, its lid hanging from one hinge—to the desk.

She plopped her *bolsa* to one side of the telegraph set and opened the desk's drawers, one by one—all empty. But the bottom one. It contained an assortment of what appeared to be old bills, receipts, and such. She dropped to her knees to peruse the flakey and yellowing slips of paper. Their typescript or scribbled notes were all faded, indicative of years long gone by. Nothing, she noticed nothing that looked like anything out of the ordinary.

Amado picked up a fountain pen on the floor. She stood and eyed the pen. If it had rolled from the desk, where was its ink well? And more importantly, where was the paper used to write upon? Surely, Adelaide would not have carried the two, the paper and inkwell, up and down the stairs.

Pia's scrutiny did not have far to travel from the desk. It alighted on the room's single window, directly behind. In a corner, almost obscured by the lowered window shade's sun-bleached fringe, resided the inkwell. "Amado, the pen did not roll off the desk but the windowsill. If it and the inkwell were stationed there, why not the codebook?" Her fingers piano-keyed beneath and behind the window shade.

"Here, let me help." He reached above her head to grope along the shade's roller at the top and its brackets. "Nothing here."

He picked up the coil of transmitted tape, studying it with befuddlement. Exactly what she was feeling. She sighed and eyed the stored knick-knacks. "That means all that stuff to rummage through."

"Pia, we don't have the time!"

She glanced inches away, directly to the right of her temple, at the old calendar tacked beside the window. "Winchester Guns and Cartridges" advertised a cowboy astride his horse in the scrubland, his Winchester stock propped against his shoulder.

Below the artwork was the outdated calendar page for the month of March 1913, four years before. Interestingly, a portion of it the page had been ripped away.

Her gaze scanned the remnant of the calendar. Curiously, a variety of dates and letters in the days of the week were circled—recently, as indicted by the fresh blue ink. Did these letters and numbers contain a code? A checkmark was stuck inside the March 5th rectangle—and inside a couple of others, like March 15th.

"Amado, this calendar—it may contain the deciphering we're looking for." She flipped up the page to expose the previous month of February 1913—nothing. She flicked farther back to January of that year. Nothing, no markings or circlings, no checks.

She let the calendar's previous pages flutter back down to March 1913 again and stared. The markings here had to be a recently deciphered message. Memorize it she might, but she still needed the key—and the key had to be hidden in the room.

"Pia, hurry!" Amado hissed.

She darted a glance back down at the windowsill. She scooted the inkwell aside from the shade. Like most, its bottom rail had an end cap—and she had an idea. Rapidly, she screwed off the end cap and fingered inside the tube. Nothing. She could feel sweat forming between her meager breasts. Then, her fingers tripped over something. *"¡Híjole!"*

Amado hovered closer. "What?"

"There's something inside." Her fingers fell short of grasping the prize. "See if you can get it out."

She stepped aside, and he inserted his longer fingers, fished around, and drew forth a sheath of tightly rolled papers.

"Let me look at them." Rapidly, she unfurled one sheet after the other of the sheath he passed her. "*Sí*, Amado—I think this is the key, the codebook!"

"Pia!" he hissed, this time insistently.

She turned to look up at him.

"Someone's coming up the stairs."

"¡Mierda!"

They stared at each other in horror. They were trapped. She glanced around at the accumulated rubbish—nothing large enough to hide behind.

He grabbed her shoulders, slung her flat onto the floor. Fireworks cascaded in the back of her skull. Next his body fell splayed atop hers. The breath whooshed from her lungs at the same time that he began smothering her with kisses.

Then she heard from above, "Just what is this!" The heavily German male accent could only belong to von Kloss.

Amado looked over his shoulder. "Oh, *Señora* Adelaide, *mil perdones*. I thought we'd be alone up here."

"How dare you carry on like this," Adelaide flung out her hand, "In my house!" A tinge of jealousy overlaying her accent metamorphosed into suspicion. She glared down at Pia's partially exposed face. "You—I remember you!"

Pia rolled Amado from her and pushed erect to face von Kloss and Adelaide. Grinning foolishly, she tucked in loosened swaths of hair while edging toward the door—and hiding behind her in her other hand the rolled sheaths of the code book. "We were just leaving."

Amado closed the gap behind her. "*Sí, sí*. Again, my apologies about this, *Señora* Adelaide."

Von Kloss's eyes narrowed to dart points. "You're the girl cleaning my office. You've been spying on us!"

Amado shoved von Kloss's shoulders hard, and the man stumbled into Adelaide, throwing both off balance. Pia darted past them. With Amado on her heels, she fled down the flights of stairs. From behind, she could hear the thundering of pursuing steps amplifying.

She and Amado reached the bottom and streaked for the front door. Arms folded, the little Bao and glowering Cheng stood there, blocking it.

"Stop them," Adelaide screamed from the landing above.

"This way," Amado gasped. He swerved and headed toward the back hallway.

Pia sprinted just behind. He halted and flung open a door. Over his shoulder she saw that it opened to a steep stairwell. He flicked on an overhead light. It illuminated below a storage room. Skimming down the steps, he headed straight toward a corner, where a small fireplace was mounded with rubble.

At the sight of the dead-end, she hauled up. "*¡¿Estás loco?!*"

"No! *¡Sí! ¡Venga!*"

He drew her over the pile of rubble. "Follow me!"

In amazement, she watched him shove aside a metal panel. He stepped over the rubble and, hunching, wiggled with some difficulty past a narrow aperture on one side of the fireplace's sooty alcove.

She squeezed through more easily but nevertheless painfully scraped a shoulder. The basement's filtered light faintly illuminated beyond what appeared to be a tunnel, no more than an oxcart wide if that. He prowled farther, fading into stygian darkness.

"Amado?" Her whisper was tremulous.

A moment later, she felt his grappling hand. With her in tow, he plowed ahead, and like a blind person she stumbled behind through a cool, dank and musty passage.

At last, his footsteps slowed then stopped, and she collided into him. "What?"

She sensed he was listening. "Without a light, they will not follow us far."

In the distance ahead came the faint sound of scurrying little feet and short peeping squeaks. A chill shot up her spine. "And without a light, what do *we* do?"

He drew her to one side several steps at a time, as if searching for something. "Here!" Then he placed her hand against what felt like a wood brace, a railing.

"Where does it go?"

"Under the river to Juarez ... I hope." He moved on ahead of her, leaving her hand to grip the railing.

She had heard stories of such a tunnel connecting beneath the river the twin cities of El Paso and Juarez. She had never credited these stories. She still was not sure she did. In the dark, everything seemed unreal.

Suddenly, the tunnel sloped sharply downward. She clutched the damp-slick railing to keep from pitching forward. Even though she could hear Amado trotting at a fast pace directly ahead of her, she was terrified of letting go of the railing—until her hand enmeshed with some sticky fiber. She yelped.

"What?" demanded Amado from the death-like darkness ahead of her.

"Nothing." She shuddered. "A spider web, maybe." She hoped. "How much farther?"

"I don't know. I've never been this far."

Oh, *¡Jesucristo!*

The tunnel's steep decline beneath the mountain's flank was like plunging into the bowels of hell. Maybe fifteen long minutes later the tunnel began to level out. Here, the dense dampness felt cloying on her skin.

Amado halted suddenly, and she ran up against him. Her turn to ask, "What?"

"The railing—and the wall—they've ended."

"Now what?" she whispered, the same way one did in a graveyard at night.

"Grab hold of my belt."

Latching on to it, she could feel the faint swish of air from his groping arms.

"The tunnel seems to turn right." He swerved that direction.

"No, wait." She jerked on the back of his belt. "What if this is only a branch off the tunnel? Shouldn't we try to go straight ahead?"

He halted, and, like her, he had to be taking stock of their predicament.

She felt the same chill of fear he had to be feeling. "*Dios mío,*" she rasped, "we could be buried down here forever!"

"*Bien,*" he said, "we can't go back. We go forward then. If we encounter the tunnel's opposite curve of wall, we have to make a right, sí?"

"What if there is a left? Another tunnel branching off to the left, as well?"

"Mother of God, Pia, one step at a time, *por favor.*"

She gulped. The darkness exacerbated her confusion. Following him, hand on the back of his belt, she silently counted off ten paces while listening to any footfalls from behind.

Once more, his arms swished the blackness before them. He stopped again.

"I say we go straight ahead," she told him. "If the tunnel itself had veered to the right—or left—wouldn't we have run into the curve of its far wall by now?"

He forged on ahead Then, excruciating seconds later—"Found it, found the railing!"

Once again, the air around her head rustled. Shuddering, she fought back panicky screams and flailed her hands to ward off what had to be a bat.

Amado reached behind to grope for her hand. "Don't lose hold, Pia!"

She gripped harder. "That's not going to happen."

This was what approaching death must be like. After what seemed like hours, she noticed the ground beneath them beginning a gradual upward slope. Another twenty minutes or so brought them to a steeper incline that required they stoop to negotiate it. Then, she could make out, just beyond, a rectangular seep of light from above.

"A trapdoor," he whispered a minute later and latched hold of what in the dimness looked like one of several steel rungs anchored in the wall. But the trapdoor above didn't give at his upward shove. He shoved again. "It's locked from the other side!"

"What do you mean?" Her voice echoed more shrilly than she intended. She glared up at him. "You didn't know it might be locked?"

"Damn't, Pia. How would I know? I told you I have never explored the tunnel." He shoulder-butted the trapdoor several times, heaving all his slight weight against it. Chest heaving, he slumped against the tunnel wall. "Shit!"

Terror hijacked her breath.

Chapter Twenty-Seven

Walt used the excuse to walk the mutt for its early morning shit as a cover to check in with his various informants. He needed more details about Adelaide Cardenas. The U.S. Army's Military Intelligence might just have something. He could put a call through to Bobby about Jaw Man's jaw-dropping revelation, but that was something Walt did not want to share over Fort Bliss's PBX line, something that might be picked up by other entities.

Perro took the opportunity to lift a hind leg and piss on the brass hubcap of the taxicab idling before the Hotel Sheldon. A dry smile eased the groove at either side of Walt's mouth. He was becoming attached to the pooch.

His damp humor was short-lived. Because from thinking about Perro, Walt began thinking about the pooch's mistress. The razzle dazzle that was Pia Arellano had confused his life's committed course. He was analytical enough to understand her fury earlier that morning. He was willing to grant he had been less than up front with her.

In his defense, he was prohibited from sharing that he worked for the United States government. The BI insisted that be kept top secret.

But a niggling part at the back of his brain also insisted he face the truth, that his retort of brutal words had been unnecessary. Ironically, none of the cruel things he had said about her education or social circle or financial status carried any weight with him. This irrational blowup of his was so unlike him. His unflappable manner that Bobby admired had seen him through the worst of times.

He walked along trying to puzzle this out. As reluctant as he was to face the obvious, he had to acknowledge he had not fully fulfilled her expectations in relation to their intimacy last night. But if she could not countenance him as he was, then any expectation of taking their relationship to a deeper level was not worth his teetering heart's investment.

At that seedling of a thought he almost stumbled over a raised manhole cover. So much for keen observation.

His thoughts returned to Pia. Surely, he had not fallen in love with this firebrand of an agitator. The very idea raised the hackles on the back of his neck. If this was what it felt like to be in love … the emotions run berserk, the heart's vulnerability to pain … he wanted no part of it.

And obviously she wanted no part of him. And he could not blame her. But did he really understand this infuriating female?

How could he fathom her lunacy of declaring they were meant to be together simply because of electrical bolts arcing between them? When the obvious explanation was mere static electricity coming off them. He had hated to squash her illusion, but it took no towering intellect to know that.

At Walt's feet Perro strained on the leash and snarled at a mangy cat, nearly twice as big, that was slinking by. "I feel the same, pooch."

It was one of those high desert mornings that could not make up its mind whether to retreat back into winter or leap forward into spring. Earlier, the morning had started out chilly and overcast.

As he strolled toward Union Station, the blustery wind was backing off and the gray clouds crept away to expose the city's famed brilliant sunlight. Perfect weather for the three-o'clock parade. City workers were already at work, streaming banners from light pole to light pole.

Not that many people cued before the streetcar ticket booth. Walt waited his turn in the short line. When he reached the grilled window, he asked something he should have asked earlier. He was getting lax the last few days. "What do you know about Adelaide Cardenas and Pia Arellano's abduction from jail?"

Silas' brows pumped with uncommon nervousness. "That gal Pia stopped by a little earlier with some cuckoo idea."

What the hell! She should still be working at von Kloss's. "What's afoot?"

"Some malarkey about her spying at the German Consul's office."

Walt's eyes narrowed. "Did she say where she was going?"

Silas shrugged. "No one knows what that gal is about. Left her mop and pail here and vamoosed."

From across the way, the black-clad Wang Wei hailed him with a wave of his shoeshine rag. "Thanks, Silas."

While urgency compelled Walt to hurry, he forced his steps into an amble toward the shoeshine stand. Wang Wei held up for Walt's inspection a can of English Army Blacking shoe polish. Shaking his head, Walt pretended to disapprove the suggested offering.

"The Arellano girl, she went to Cardenas Chateau," Wang Wei whispered beneath his breath. "Cheng, he come to say Arellano girl and the bricklayer Amado, they run from the Adelaide woman and von Kloss."

Why would von Kloss be chasing after them? Unless ... had Pia actually managed to get the Holy Grail, the codebook? "Run where?"

"Down the Turtle Tunnel—half-hour ago, maybe more."

Walt nodded and once again headed off in what could be construed as a morning stroll but was more of a quick step. With the leashed dog, he covered the mile to the Rio Grande, crossing its bridge into Juarez in a good clip.

He bypassed the Black Cat, which a favorite writer of his, Jack London, had called one of the most degraded dives in the world. Even at that early hour, a ragtime tune drifted from the doorway, plunked out by some honky-tonk pianist and accompanied by ribald shouts and drunken laughter.

With Perro's paws clicking ahead of him on the morning's trash-littered sidewalk, he continued on down the avenue. He passed next a street vendor arranging jicama and mangoes on his cart and a juiceless man toting, not a Kodak camera, but a Graflex. The pallid-looking man had to be a spy. For whom?

Walt crossed the avenue twice, checking over his shoulder surreptitiously to see if he was being followed. Assured he was not, he then headed straight toward an old hotel in the heart of Juarez's commercial district. The Hotel Mena's façade sported bullet holes from a 1911 revolutionary battle—and above the arched entrance a brick configuration of a turtle.

With an effort at restraint, he sauntered through the lobby with its worn area rug and drooping ferns in paint-chipped *macetas*, and nodded casually at the desk clerk, in cautious conversation with the hotel bar maid. Was word already out on the streets about Pia and Amado's caper?

He extracted from his vest his pocket watch. Even at an all-out dash through the pitch black of the tunnel, surely Pia and the bricklayer could not make it that quickly from the heights of Mount Franklin down under the river and back up to the center of Juarez.

Tugging Perro along, he continued along a hallway and down the back flight of stairs at the far end of the corridor. In what had once served as the hotel garage, reinforcing steel bars protruded here and there from crumbling cement walls. Through a dusty haze, he skirted debris and headed toward the shadowy outline of what was a 1914 American Eagle seven-passenger touring car.

Last year, Jorge Reyes, a Juarez informant for the BI, had given him a rundown of the short, honeycombed tunnels that were more prolific in El Paso's Chinatown. "But no one would start to build a tunnel like the one from Turtle House, requiring so much labor and material, *Señor* Stevenson, without it serving some significant purpose."

Incredibly, the Turtle House tunnel exited through the basement's trap door beneath the abandoned parked motor car. The touring car's frame had once supported an engine. Only as Walt neared the automobile, did he perceive the figure bent over its opened hood. A thudding from below it had concealed Walt's approach.

But sensing it, the figure spun. Walt inhaled startled recognition. From beneath the brown fedora Mickey O'Bannon, El Paso's former mayor, stared back. In his hand was what looked to be an old Colt1911. He appeared as startled as Walt. Mickey jerked his handgun up and leveled it at Walt's chest.

Perro's muzzle drew back into a frenzied spate of snarls. Dropping the leash, Walt raised his hands. "You do not want to do this, Mickey."

"Silas says differently."

Silas? He had no time to process that revelation. No, in that half-second, Walt felt his life's recollections whirl liked a kaleidoscope behind his eyes: Thad's and his tussling with the revolver … Cordelia's cool reception to his first, less than ardent kiss … and his out of control reception to Pia's wild, heated kisses. And something within insisted he recognize that he had been simultaneously cheerfully repelled and morbidly enchanted by that inexhaustible dust devil that Pia was.

Mickey's forefinger curled inside the trigger guard—and at that Walt raised a questioning brow at the snipping Perro.

The mangy mutt launched at Mickey's ankle. Trying to shake off the ferocious little teeth, Mickey hitched his knee up but lost his balance. He flung wide his arms and toppled head over heels into the engine's well.

Walt sprang to the American Eagle. Inside its tight and empty compartment, the man lay at an awkward angle. From above his paper collar jutted gristle … an obscene portion of the neck's cervical column. His unblinking eyes would never see again.

How justly ironic. The symbol of the United States' might, the American Eagle, had come to the rescue.

Well, the American Eagle and the mutt. "Good dog," Walt said, heaving the corpse over the fender and out of the way.

The trapdoor above swung open, and dusty particles powdered down. Light from directly above Amado momentarily blinded Pia, several rungs below him. Squinting upward, she made out the shadowy outline of a head just beyond that of Amado's.

"Pia?"

"Walt?" Confusion at finding him there battled with both her fury and her misery, all over this one imperturbable, stoved-up man who clearly rated her as little more than one of his job's perks … sleeping with the hired help.

He thrust down a hand to Amado. "Quickly. We don't have much time."

Amado scrambled up and, squatting, turned to lend her a hand. She emerged and looked around, astounded. She and Amado and Walt were wedged inside the front of what appeared to be a giant touring car's skeletal hull.

Walt cradled on one arm a vigorously woofing Perro. "I want you both to get out on the side opposite me."

"Why?" Amado asked, then glanced over the fender. "Fuck, man, what did you do to the guy?"

"He stepped on a crack and broke his back." He thrust Perro at her and, completely encircling her waist with his two hands, lifted her up and over the fender. Once again at his touch, she felt that tingling shock. Apparently, he did not. His countenance stone cold, used his stilt-long legs to clamber out of the hull, landing lightly on his feet beside her. "Now let's get moving before someone discovers our late friend here."

She glanced over the motor car's far side and shuddered. The tail-wagging Perro was licking her cheek. Burying her face in the shaggy fur, she mumbled, "How did you know where to find us?"

"My contacts."

"But no one knew we fled down the tunnel," said Amado, following Walt up the staircase. "Except maybe old Cheng and …"

"Exactly. And Bao."

In the lobby, she fell into step alongside him and Amado. After they exited onto the noisy street, busy with morning rush hour, Amado boasted to Walt, "Pia found the codebook!"

With not a little pride, she paused in walking and opened her free hand. Stunned, she could only gape—her palm was empty. She was stunned by her stupidity. "I must have dropped it in the tunnel."

Walt's eyes rolled upwards.

"What about the wall calendar?" Amado prompted. "You thought it might have deciphering scribbled on it. Can you remember any of it, Pia?"

Trying to focus, she looked up into the sand-dusted sky, where a single kite dipped and surged above the cathedral several blocks over. Slowly, she shook her head. "I can't recall anything right now." She fought back fruitless tears.

Walt clasped her elbow, guiding her along. "No worries, buttercup. There's a smoke shop next door." He sidestepped a pair of boys, rolling a tireless bicycle rim between them, both who paused to stare up at his inordinate height. "In its back room, we can try to sort out the—"

She hauled up short and shook her head. The two men also stopped to stare at her quizzically. "I want to go home."

She simply wanted to let go of everything, as she had the damned codebook. Wanted to let go of her foolish yearnings to rise like the kite above the restrictions of earth's borders that could confine an impoverished lifestyle.

Instantly, Walt's palm was at the small of her back, steering her away. "All right, then, I'll see you to your mother's house."

Amado scowled, and she parried off both men. "I want to go home, just Perro and me."

Amado looked dejected, Walt, vexed. Unable to conceal her own conflicted feelings, she pivoted and darted between a horse-drawn wagon and a motorcycle to the street's far side.

How had her heart come to crash into oblivion, all over Walt? Such arrant nonsense.

216

Arrant—that was a word in her *Roget's* that had both stumped her and appealed to her. And arrant nonsense applied quite rightly to that singular moment she tore the console from the streetcar and threw it into the river.

And yet, that disastrous rebellion had both unleashed her tumultuous feelings for Walt and the destructive secrets her family harbored. More importantly, she understood better now the meaning of friends and community, and her place and role within it.

As far as Amado and Walt were concerned, she sternly reminded herself that she and Amado had much in common. She and Walt, nothing. Amado and she were close to the same age; Walt older by eight years. Amado made her grin, Walt made her think. Amado made her feel affectionate, Walt made her feel amorous. Amado was a raffish spirit, like herself. Walt, well, she pegged him to be the efficient, hold-the-line kind of man.

Taken in balance, Walt was not at all suitable for her. Yet it was him with whom she was inexplicably, incomprehensibly, and irrevocably in love.

But more important was: what did she want?

Crazy, how she had thought herself so independent, so correct in her stance for dignity and equality and independence; when right now, she could care less about the suffragette movement, the bath house humiliations, or even the horror of another possible war there on the border. She wanted nothing more than to crawl like a child again into the safety of her mother's arms.

So, like carrier pigeons returning to Fort Bliss, she was returning home that morning.

Chapter Twenty-Eight

Stifling a sigh that was half chagrin, half something else, and Walt did not know exactly what that something else was, he watched Pia dodge Avenida de Comercio's late morning traffic.

Resolutely, he turned back to Amado. "You're on your own, pal." He saw a rattletrap of a taxicab approaching. "As for me I'm catching the first outbound taxi for El Paso and Fort Bliss."

"Why?"

He went to hail a taxicab, but it hurtled on past with its passenger. "To get Colonel Michie to issue an arrest for Adelaide Cardenas as a German spy." With martial law declared, a warrant would not be necessarily required.

He waved down the next taxicab in the traffic rush. It passed him by.

Amado grinned, jammed his hands in the riveted front pockets of his blue jeans, and watched and waited.

Meanwhile, another taxicab flashed past. As did yet another. Walt huffed. Precious minutes wasted. Precious minutes that would hurtle him that much closer to nailing the master spy orchestrating minions like the Cardenas woman and von Kloss.

After that bit of BI business was wrapped up … well, Walt was returning his ancillary focus to his passion, writing … and adios to that infatuation that had momentarily derailed him, Pia Arellano.

"*Buena suerte*," Amado said, finally. "As for me, I am headed to the *Plaza de Toros*."

Walt shot him an inquisitive look.

"Dulcinea will be there, practicing with her *cuadrillos*."

Walt peaked a brow. "Ahhh, so. I take it you are enamored with her—and not Pia?"

Amado smirked and gestured at Perro. "I love dogs. And I love cats, too." He shrugged. "If a dog does not fancy me, a cat just might. But right now, more importantly, Dulcinea's Model T speedster is at the *Plaza de Toros*. Interested, mi amigo?"

Walt had to give the younger man due credit. He was no slacker. Affably, Walt clapped him on the shoulder. "*Vamonos a Plaza de Toros, mi amigo bueno*."

The bull ring was only blocks away. Morning's eerie pink sunlight, forecasting a sandstorm, splashed against a Spanish advertisement bannered on a curve of the empty arena's wall. Within the arena's circumference, wind swirled the dirt.

At the arena's center, with all the grace of a ballerina, Dulcinea made passes with a caped muleta and a fake sword in front of a pair of horns held by one of the *cuadrillos* who charged in and out around her. Two other young male assistants were observing.

Her mahogany hair was caught back in a single braid, and she wore a dusty pair of tight, white matador pants that accentuated her very feminine physique and a loose, embroidered white camisa. When she spotted him and Amado, she passed the muleta and sword to her assistant and sauntered across the dirt-filled arena, careful to avoid its divots. "¡*Hola!*"

Walt was not certain for whom her flirtatious smile was meant, Amado or himself. Not that it mattered that much anymore, if it ever had. "I need the use of your Speedster, Dulcinea."

Her chin tucking, her brows arched, implying he had lost his mind.

"It's important we get to Fort Bliss," Amado supplied, as if he were an official part of Walt's BI investigation. "To report a German spy."

She tossed her head. "Not without me at its wheel, hombres."

Minutes later her red Ford Speedster, crammed with the three of them and Walt's knees jamming his chest, was hustling along Avenido de Comercio. Dulcinea drove with the speed and skill of any Indianapolis Motor Speedway contender—until a plodding donkey cart mounded with brightly painted pottery decided to venture into the sand-hazed intersection.

She fish-tailed the Speedster into a 180-degree swerve. The rear bumper plowed into the cart, skidding it. Pottery shards went flying. Next, the Speedster's front bumper careened into a light pole.

On impact, Amado and Walt were pitched forward. His hands jammed against the dashboard, he looked back, saw that the donkey looked as startled as its sombreroed driver—and saw a pistol-packing policeman hoofing it toward them.

"¡*Carajo*!" Dulcinea cursed.

A frisky Perro tugged Pia along in its beeline for her mother's barrio home. Above it danced the kite, fluttered by a brisk wind heralding the approach sandstorm. Six-year-old Rosita stood in the alley behind their adobe home and tussled with the tossing kite. At her side, on one knee, Josefina played out the remnants of the ball of twine.

Pia came up from behind Josefina and knelt alongside her sister. Her plump shoulders jerked with surprise at this unexpected presence, and she dropped the ball of twine. Her head angled upward at Pia. "What are you doing here?"

The ache for what was not welled in a geyser of pain. Her sharply indrawn breath was nearly a sob. Instead she wafted in the spicy smell of roasted green chiles, tomatillos, and cilantro. She pushed to her feet. She realized it was approaching the noon hour, and she had not eaten. Disconsolate, she managed a tremulous smile. "Mamacita's *chilaquiles* were calling my name."

Rosita glanced around to see Pia and released the kite string to run to her and wrap her tiny arms around Pia's thighs. "I have missed you, Tia Pia."

Except, Pia thought, she was not only Rosita's aunt but her sister. "And I you, Rosita Bonita."

Her mind's eyes pictured a substantial home in Kern Place, a home that had a separate bedroom for Rosita, Josefina, Mamacita, and herself—and a kitchen with all the modern appliances for Mamacita. Never again would their mother have to peddle her woven handicrafts through monsoon springs, broiling summers, and bone-chilling winters at a street corner's pavement.

Pushing wind-whipped hair from her face, Rosita broke loose from anchorage on Pia's thighs to stare upwards. "Oh, noooo!"

All three now were looking upward as the kite took flight over the city. They stood watching until the red haze of sand blurred the diamond shape from view.

Pia recalled a distant memory with its image of Josefina, one knee anchoring crosstie sticks of woven *lechuguilla* fibers while she fashioned a kite of brown butcher's paper and a tail from strips of a sheet too threadbare for normal use.

Rosita was sniffing at her loss, and Pia draped a consoling arm around the girl's prominent shoulder bones while Josefina collected the remains of the kite project. Silently then, Pia and Josefina traipsed into the house, with Rosita moping behind.

Mamacita was concentrating on sautéing tortilla pieces in the old and heavy cast iron skillet. With her bare fingers she flipped the pieces. Handling foods made with caring fingers seemed to enrich food, releasing its digestive juices.

The odor of the heated oil reminded Pia of earlier days, when Mamacita used the *aceite volcánico* for a sprained leg or arm. She had that kind of healing hand for fixing hurts, whether it was patching a scraped knee, removing a mesquite thorn from a cat's paw, or padding wet dirt on a bee sting. And that was why Pia had returned home.

At the sight of Pia, her mother's expression altered to a glorious smile of relief. "¡*Mija*!"

Stifling a sniffle, she ran to embrace her mother. She inhaled her mother's familiar scent of spices and flowers and herbs like they were antidotes for all her fears and hurts.

Her mother stepped back and searched her flushed face. She might have asked Pia half a dozen pertinent questions, like "Are you all right?" Or "Are you coming home to stay?" Instead, with a motherly instinctual insight, she said, "Your man, *Señor* Stevenson, where is he?"

Her mouth gaped. "How do you know about Walt?"

"He brought us a sack of food."

"Cookies and strawberry soda!" Rosita interjected.

Mamacita went on before Pia could fully digest that information. "And you are in love with him. I see it in your face, *Mija*."

Her throat tightened. "You're wrong, Mamacita, I don't even like him."

"You don't have to like someone to love someone. You are hurting, I can see it, and love is the best medicine in the cabinet."

She was not ready to deal with that heart-stabbing hurt. With a sickening realization, she pulled away. "¡*Maldita sea*! I left my *bolsa*, with my *Roget's*, back at the Chateau Cardenas." And the valuable bankbook with its promise of a brighter future.

Rosita's wail joined hers. "And my kite—it flew away, Abuelita!"

Pia remembered as a child asking her mother why one had to run with the kite against the wind. "Because, *Mija*," Mamacita had replied, "that is the only way anything can hope to soar—kites, dirigibles, these new aeroplanes … and our spirits."

Pia told Rosita, "Josefina will build another kite. Your mother is the best kite maker in all of Juarez."

Josefina was stashing the kite's leftover strings, strips, and sticks. She paused to eye Pia suspiciously, but it seemed her compliment eased the barbed wire-taut tension between them somewhat.

"Josefina, you used to make kites for me, too," she reminded her.

"That was long ago."

"I still need your help." Then added on a whisper of wings, "I still need you."

Josefina's rounded shoulders hunched defensively. "How so?"

She shrugged, helpless with where to begin. She handed Perro over to a mollified Rosita and dropped into her accustomed chair at the old pine table. The chair's ripped thatched seating creaked as she took her time settling into its concave. "Well ... with what's going on now, Josefina."

Warily, her sister approached the rickety table. "What now, this time?"

"*Oyes*, I know I am impetuous, saying and doing things without thinking, and now I am on the run again."

It was as if Josefina did not hear the last. "And look where your self-preoccupation has gotten you—and the rest of us. Our family? The women who rebelled with you at the bath house? We're still submitting to the fumigations, unless we want to go without work." She went to sit in her chair, opposite Pia, and leaned forward on one fist-clenched forearm. "Nothing has changed." Her mouth formed a harsh smile of rancor. "Except worse for you. And now you want our help, do you?"

Pia slumped further in her spindle back chair. Lids lowered so as not to reveal glistening eyes, she mindlessly drummed her fingers on the scarred tabletop. How much lower did Josefina want her to sink? No matter where she turned, were there always mishaps awaiting? She was so weary of her well-meant but misguided intentions flinging her soul's wealth away. "It's not just about me this time."

"It's always about you, Pia."

Where to begin? she leaned forward and began talking in an abbreviated explanation—starting with Adelaide's setting her up to be abducted from jail to next working for Walt to help locate El Paso's master spy. Added what she knew of Adelaide's spying for Germany. Shared about the attic's calendar with its notation and the miniscule codebook.

Finally, she wound up with the flight through the tunnel with Amado and the loss of the codebook, before emerging at the tunnel's end at the basement of the old Hotel Mena.

"So what?" Josefina grumped, appearing unaffected by her harrowing recount of her and Amado's escape. "A codebook, a calendar—next it'll be a cookbook or bankbook."

Bankbook! In a flash Pia recalled the calendar's checked date of March 15th. It was the Roman deadline for settling debts. Was there some kind of debt here that Germany was hell bent on settling?

"I am not sure, but I think Germany is planning some kind of awful disturbance here in El Paso. But I can't figure out what or when. If I could, I would be closer to nailing the identity of the agent provocateur here that Sommerfeld planted." And closer to building her own home there in Kern Place.

Josefina hmphed and the mole dipped with the downturn of her lips. "Agent provocateur? This is so like you. Big words and big drama."

Mamacita hobbled from the stove to plop into her chair. "Life *is* drama, Josefina." Then to Pia, "You think Germany is plotting to arouse the people here to stage a protest. Some kind of violent action of some sort?"

She was relieved to have her outlandish suspicions accepted as plausible, at least, by her mother. "I think Germany would have to be fomenting something worse than a protest."

"Like throwing a homemade hand grenade at City Hall, right?" Josefina scoffed.

Trying to imagine what storm could be brewing, she stared off into space—and her eye alit on the Trujillo *Farmacia* wall calendar above the pie safe. Rising from the table, she untacked the calendar and snared the pencil stub from its string.

She returned to lay the calendar in the table's center. "I can recall a few of the jottings on the attic's calendar—an old one, March 1913, it was. Certain words were circled. Some dates were checked. But without both—the codebook and the calendar's encryptions—it'd be easier to decipher the petroglyphs at Hueco Tanks."

Josefina's eyes narrowed. "The *what* at Hueco Tanks?"

"You know, those rock drawing on the cliffs there." An upheaval of a rocky fortress in the nearby desert, the Hueco tanks contained imprinted on its granite walls handprints, dancing figures, horses, weapons and human stick-like figures in European-style clothing.

"All I remember are the nests with their white bird droppings on the cliffs," Josefina groused.

Deep in thought, their mother's knotted forefinger was tapping the calendar page, featuring the present month of February. Her sigh implied the same thing Pia was feeling—thwarted by the lack of so few clues.

But then she was befuddled by so much that had happened topsy-turvy in the mere week or more since Walt had walked into her life. The true nature of her feelings about him cried for consideration. And that she could not bring herself to do. Not now. Maybe someday in the far future.

She scrubbed a hand over her face. "All I can recall clearly was that the dates March 5th and March 15th—and, oh, yes, March 20th—were checked off, not circled."

"*Pues*, what do you think that could mean?" their mother asked.

She waggled the pencil in helplessness. "I don't know. It just doesn't make sense, does it? Linking 1913 with 1917? A coincidence—or on purpose?"

Josefina leaned forward to squint at the calendar. "But those words and numbers that were circled, some dates and days—they would remain the same in either year, sí? 1913 or 1917. Like holidays—you know, like Saint Patrick's Day."

With surprise, Pia blinked at her sister. "Why, you're right, Josefina!"

In return, Josefina blinked with pleasure at Pia's affirmative response.

She tapped the March 15th rectangle. "I remember now. March 15th is more than just a deadline for settling debts."

"What else is it?" their mother asked.

"That's the Ides of March."

Josefina cut her a look. "So?"

Pia glanced at their mother, her expression also clueless. Both were clever women but at a loss here. Neither had pursued further education, as had Pia. "When bad things happen," she explained, summarizing Julius Caesar's assassination.

"Silas would know how to unscramble all this," she muttered. "Codes usually come in blocks of five. Look for patterns, he says. Patterns in the blocks."

Caught up in the cerebral jigsaw puzzle, Josefina suggested, "Then these words—or letters or numbers—they can even be rearranged, sí?"

"Yes—but they could also stand for other letters or numbers. If we had a series of transmissions, we could reduce the possibilities by comparison." She sighed. "What we need is that damn code book."

"Can you recall anything else on the calendar, *hermanita*?"

Josefina's old term of endearment offered a tiny hope for reconciliation, but Pia could only shake her head in despair. "No. No, I only had an opportunity to glimpse it."

"But, *mira*, Pia," Josefina persisted, "what if we work with what we do have? Like the letters or numbers in Saint Patrick's Day—the March 17th date. Or March 20th—the beginning of spring, the calendar says?"

Pia bowed her body over the table to better scrutinize the calendar and began a mixture of jotting and doodling, striking out and rearranging, in the allotted square space below the calendar date of March 20th, the beginning of spring. And nothing. No patterns that could be construed into a word.

Then she found one. "Here—if you take the pattern 5-3-3 and apply it to the note under March 20th—'spring begins.'"

The other two women leaned forward to study where she tapped her pencil as reinforcement on the letters she had circled—*sprinG bEgiNs*.

"And run the same pattern on March 17th, Saint Patrick's Day. "The letter following the fifth—the 'P' in Patrick's."

"*Sí*," Josefina said, "but then, by that rule, the next, three over, would be an 'r.' GENPR. You're the smart one, Pia. Explain what that could mean."

She sighed, more at her sister's snide tone than her own frustration with her attempts at decoding. "It could mean anything—or nothing—because we also have to take in account whether this could be further translated into German or Spanish."

Her eyes returned to the calendar page heading—MARCH. "Wait a minute." She tapped the pencil on that word. "On the other calendar—the month had been only partially circled, like someone might do in a rush. I believe the letter 'M' had been omitted from March. If so—" with the pencil she re-looped that portion of March, "—we now have the word 'arch.'"

"That could mean a lot of things," Mamacita said. "The arch of a foot? A rainbow's arch?"

"A cat arching," Rosita said, coming to her mother's side. Pia had been unaware the girl had suspended playing with Perro to listen in on the adults.

"Then there's eyebrows arching," Pia offered half-heartedly.

Grinning, Josefina hugged her daughter to her. "Or arches like a gazebo's."

The suggestions seemed to Pia to require a far stretch of the imagination, but then that was what deciphering was about, was it not? Stymied, she sighed more heavily this time.

Mamacita tapped the calendar again, her scarred fingertip landing in the checked square of March 5th. "Today is the 5th of February. Could that mean something could be happening today?"

Pia perked up. "Oh, *Jesucristo!*"

"Pia!" her startled mother said. "Watch your mouth."

"There's a parade this afternoon, at three-o'clock. Downtown, where the San Jacinto Plaza is—and its bandstand! Josefina, you are a genius."

Both women stared at her uncomprehending. She rolled up the calendar and shot to her feet. "The bandstand has arches, don't you see? Like a gazebo."

"Where are you going?" her mother asked anxiously.

"Back to Union Station. Silas can break this cipher and maybe whatever is going down at the parade can be stopped."

Josefina shot to her feet. "You'll have to submit to fumigation at the bath house. Something you swore you would never do."

Was that a note of glee Pia detected in Josefina's voice? Pia's shoulders sagged. Even if she did submit to undergo the dehumanizing procedure, time was at a premium. If what she, Josefina, and their mother had gleaned from the calendar's secrets was an actuality, she could not spare that horrid half hour or more.

Josefina grabbed her shawl. "I'm going with you."

"Why?"

"A diversion is needed while you crossover to El Paso."

Stunned, Pia could only stare. "My *bolsa*—I don't have it. I'll need some money."

Despite the weighty mole, Josefina's lips threatened to wrench upward. "I owe you some—what I took from your Cracker Jack box."

Was this Josefina, the practical, no-nonsense sister? "You think another riot is needed on the bridge?" Pia asked, grinning and rolling up the calendar.

Their mother crossed herself. "*Jesucristo*, what rebellious daughters I have raised!"

Pia was not sure if that was a lament or boast. She smiled and leaned over to hug the little woman. "Mamacita, watch your mouth!"

Chapter Twenty-Nine

Bracing against a dust-filled wind, Pia and Josefina arrived at Avenida de Comercio and Trujillo's Pharmacy. They darted inside and, while Pia waited for her call to go through to the Hotel Sheldon's switchboard, she watched Josefina sneak behind the counter to hug the handle-bar mustachioed Guido.

Odd, yet two more prosaic people in Pia's madhouse of a life and yet two stalwart souls that added stability to it. She envied what they had. Of which it was becoming clear she was unworthy. She had chosen the wrong man to love. What a most hopeless situation.

But there was still the consolation prize, Walt had guaranteed—the house on the hill—if she came through with their objective, unmasking El Paso's master spy.

Outside, the streetcar clanged to a stop, and Pia had only time to leave Walt a message that Günther and Adelaide were in some way connected to a disruption of that afternoon's parade honoring the AEF.

At the last second, she and Josefina raced to board the streetcar. They were forced to stand shoulder to shoulder with other passengers, many who it seemed were leaving early enough to attend the three-o'clock Grand March.

Advancing dust and debris were drastically reducing visibility. As the streetcar passed *Asuntos Internos Municipales*, the old city hall, she peered out at its tower clock. Two twenty-nine.

When the streetcar reached mid-bridge and then the fumigation plant, Pia's stomach began to churn noisily. Her belly was cramping with fear. She realized in that instant that Josefina was the brave one and all those like her who daily trudged to work under the most difficult circumstances on behalf of the ones they loved ... whereas she merely walked away if it did not suit her.

After the streetcar came to a halt, Josefina demonstrated that courage. When it came Pia's turn to get off, her feet refused to shuffle forward, and Josefina edged ahead to step down from the streetcar—at which point she collapsed on the pavement. Her arms and legs twitched, her eyes rolled, her protruding tongue swashed. She groaned an otherworldly noise, something between a gargle and a snarl.

Nosey people hurried to gather around her. "*Dios mío, un ataque epiléptico!*" a fat, sweating man muttered.

Immediately, a Public Health Agent rushed forward. But all the agent did was to hail a Mexican guard from the other end and turn to Pia. "She's with you?"

She stuttered. "*Sí.* She's an epileptic." Epileptics, idiots, and homosexuals were not allowed to cross into the United States.

At once, Josefina leaped to her feet and started beating her fists against the back of the white-clad agent and screaming epithets. Pia had to grin. Here, it was Josefina who had described *Pia* as all drama?

She edged away from the crowd. Not wanting to attract attention, she set off at a moderate trot to the El Paso side. Ahead, waiting on the American side of the bank, several armed border guards watched from in front of a parked army wagon that obstructed easy passage.

Nervous heat tingled her skin. She did not have the bath house ticket, proof of recent disinfection. Fortunately, the guards were eyeing the fracas in front of the bath house, and she rushed to slip past the wagon and between the obstructing sawhorse barricades.

"Halt!"

She froze, then slowly turned. A first base away from her home base, one of the two guards, a square-set soldier, pointed the barrel of his Springfield at her and shouted, "Your ticket?"

Though the duster was now blowing hard, perspiration instantly dampened her temples, and sand clotted on her skin. If she landed in jail, if Adelaide learned of it, Pia's days were numbered. She managed a sickly smile, fumbled in her jeans back pocket, and drew forth the rolled calendar. She flashed it, blew the soldier a kiss, and pivoted away.

Feeling the spot between her hunched shoulder blades a bullet's target, she forced herself to walk at a sedate pace in the direction of Union Station. Few passengers came and went at the train depot itself. Most people were headed a few blocks over, in the direction of the parade route, its light poles already festooned with red, white, and blue streamers.

Above Union Station's entrance the giant clock indicated two thirty-six. Desperation oozing out of every gritty pore, she slumped into Silas' booth and gasped, "You have to listen to me, Silas." Fatigued, she leaned against the counter and slapped her hand on it. "I know you'll never believe this. But I think I may have figured out what that German telegram is about."

His grizzled brows jerked up. "You're joshing me, gal."

"No, no." She hauled herself onto the high stool beside him. "Adelaide is a German spy, Silas. She has a wireless set that Günther von Kloss helped her install in her attic. There was a calendar tacked on its wall where I found clues. Look. I have been working from memory on my mom's calendar." She unfurled it and jabbed at the March 20th date. "See—the five-letter groupings I figured out here."

He humphed. "They could mean anything or nothing."

"But I remember March 5th was also checked on the attic's calendar—today is the 5th."

"Of February, gal, not March.

"And March 15th," she continued, unrattled by his interruption.

"That's the Ides of March, so I can't reconcile that date with March 20th, the beginning of spring."

"Exactly. This calendar or Frau Adelaide has nothing to do with a German sabotage."

She frowned at his hopped-up insistence. "But I think it does, Silas."

"Look, gal, once again, you've let your imagination get away from you. However, give me the calendar and let me study it for a few days."

A part of her could not accept defeat so easily. That was most likely her largest flaw. Not able to accept criticism, constructive or otherwise. "No, wait just a minute." She jabbed a finger at the calendar. "Look here. When I use the 5-3-3 method you taught me, I came up with G-E-N-P-R-K. I know it is illogical, but I still think that there is a ciphered message here."

He scowled, but she was suddenly remembering. "The other calendar, Adelaide's—it was smaller, less space. It said, not 'Saint Patrick's Day' but 'Saint Pat Day.' So the next three over would be a space, not an R or K." She struck those two letters from the 5-3-3 sequence of letters.

She searched her mental dictionary and blinked. Five seconds later, the skeletons of the words leaped out and made her jump. "Silas, without the R or K, the message is Gen P—General Pershing!"

He huffed. "Simply indicating the parade honoring the American Expeditionary Forces that Frau Adelaide has been putting together for today."

"No, don't you see? It's General Pershing the Germans are planning on assassinating today—like the assassination of Julius Caesar on the Ides of March."

"A bunch of hooey, gal." His arthritic claw tugged down the two shades that effectively closed the window grills. Outside, waiting passengers grumbled their protests.

Triumphant with the result of her deciphering, she swung back toward Silas and, shocked, stared down at one of his prized souvenirs—the barrel of the Luger revolver's sound suppressor. She nearly leaped out of her skin. Her mouth opened, closed, then got out, "Why?"

"You know why—the United States took everything from me. My health, my wife, my savings, my life even. At least, the Germans can restore some of that. Sorry to do this gal. I liked you."

He raised the barrel, and she felt its cold metal press against the bridge of her nose. She could not assimilate this, make sense of it. She blurted, "You don't want to do this. That silencer will still make a pop. The passengers outside will hear."

"When the Oregon Line Streetcar pulls into the station," he glanced up at the timekeeper's clock, "well, in seven seconds it'll make noise enough to cover your plugging."

She took advantage in that instant of his distraction and flung the booth door open against him, knocking the Luger from his hand. He grabbed her wrist. She jerked free, sprang from the booth, and darted through the assembly of passengers.

"Stop her!" He yelled. "Stop her—she stole money!"

Startled, people turned, watching. She risked looking over her shoulder. He was chasing after her. That one glance back cost her as she kept running, right onto the track. The arriving Oregon Line streetcar began clanging wildly.

After four hours at the *Asuntos Internos Municipales* and a hefty fine of three-hundred and fifty pesos, Dulcinea's battered red Ford Speedster limped from the old city hall, to cross the bridge into El Paso and then out along the dusty road leading to Fort Bliss.

Once beyond its guard house gate, the roadster passed the outer ring of peaked tent camps. Bumping over a railroad's spur track to a supply depot, the Speedster crept past the Officers Club and wheezed to a halt at the Army's stately two-story headquarters.

Eventually, Walt, Amado, and Dulcinea cleared the Army's own guardians of the gate and were admitted to Colonel Robert Michie's office.

Brows raised in puzzlement, he came around from behind his desk to greet them. "Great to see you, Walt!" He clapped him on the back. With an even more quizzical expression, he nodded at Dulcinea and Amado.

"Miss Dulcinea del Jardín and Amado—" Walt broke off the introduction, realizing he did not recall the lad's surname.

"García, Colonel Michie, sir," Amado said, his reverent tone betraying how impressed he was with the silver eagle pinned to Robert's shirt collar. "Amado García."

Bobby glanced pointedly at the tall grandfather clock that indicated thirty-seven minutes past two o'clock. "My apologies, Walt, but I have to be at the Grand March in a quarter of an hour, no later than fifteen hundred hours. And I am already running late."

"I don't have much time either, Bobby." Walt reached inside his coat pocket and pulled out his BI badge.

Collective gasps issued from all three—Dulcinea, Amado, and Bobby, who growled, "All this time and you never let on to me and Ed that—"

"This is a Federal case. Listen, Bobby, whatever it takes to issue an arrest for Adelaide Cardenas—for espionage against the United States of America—do it immediately."

Bobby's dark brows fairly flew up into his short haircut. "On what charge?"

"To begin with, Pia says there's a wireless station in the woman's attic."

"Now, Walt, that's all well and good, but you know I need evidence for such a charge."

"Come on, Bobby, something's going down—and soon."

"Sorry, but I can't go on word, alone—immediately—even if you are with the Bureau of Investigation." This last was uttered with some disgruntlement that he had been omitted from Walt's confidentiality.

"I got proof!" Amado declared. He dug into his jean's pocket and produced a coil of telegraphic tape. "This came from the telegraphic station in the Cardenas attic."

Dulcinea hooked her arm under Amado's. "Olé! A hero you are, *mi amor.*"

The lad preened like a damned peacock.

Bobby glanced from the luscious looking Dulcinea back to Walt. "We'll find Adelaide Cardenas at today's grand parade. But there is something else you should know. I just received a report that your Pia's sister, Josefina Arellano, was arrested about half an hour ago for starting a disturbance on the International Bridge."

His Pia? Walt sighed. "The penchant for disturbance must run in their family."

Chapter Thirty

Pia made a desperate leap and cleared the track. Silas did not. The sound of screeching steel wheels, followed by horrified screams, and then the ghastly sight of the mangled body pursued her.

Breathless, arms pumping, she speared another glance at the Union Station Depot clocktower—two forty-one—and sprinted toward Oregon and Mills Street. She had fifteen minutes before General Pershing, astride his horse, would set off to lead his troops along the parade route.

She dodged pedestrians, a flower cart, and a bicycle to cut across Mesa Street traffic, already blocked off for the parade. Desert winds flapped buildings' and street signs' flags and banners. The approaching sandstorm already dusted the air with a dreadful vellum of sand that stung her face.

She felt sure the assassin would be with Adelaide and von Kloss and other notables on the review stand, adjacent to the San Jacinto bandstand, where the military band was warming up.

Its booming march music, combined with the din of the cathedral's pealing bells and factories and locomotives' whistles, now signaled the start of the parade. The din of discordant sounds was deafening, making it difficult to think sensibly.

The stand had been erected where once three decorative cannon had kept lookout. A large-bladed steam shovel that had razed the area now reposed next to the fence surrounding the alligator pond. Inside, seven alligators bellowed in a stand-off with the threatening mechanical monster.

It was another monster Pia was searching for. She wended her way through the curbside crowd with its waving boater hats, bobbing parasols, and wind-whipped feathered and flowered chapeaus, which anxious females' gloved hands anchored to their heads.

At the front of the three-tiered reviewing stand, Mayor Lea and his wife sat center stage. Directly behind Mayor Lea and his wife sat a score or more spectators, obviously of the El Paso elite.

On the mayor's left, Adelaide smiled vacuously and patted her husband's stout arm, linked in hers. On Lea's right, von Kloss's handsome features were strained into an attentive expression as Mrs. Sturtevant chattered, though it was unlikely he could hear her above the noisy crowd's ecstatic energy.

At the end of the bleacher Don Horst Heinrich hunched like a giant bullfrog. His mane of red hair curled from beneath his derby. Not a word of acknowledgement to her, his own daughter, although she was sure he had seen her. Her heart ached. Was the yearning for love forever to be punctuated by arrows of indifference?

Just beyond her father, at the bottom of the platform steps, Ed Bigelow waited with his photographic equipment ensconced on a tripod to capture the moment for posterity. She sidled up close, yanked on his sleeve. "Mr. Bigelow, can I beg a moment of your time, please?"

Aggravation reddened his face and lowered his bushy brows. "Yeah? What is it, Miss Arellano?"

She felt silly just saying it. "I think someone is going to kill General Pershing today."

As though buying time to form a reply to her outlandish statement, he brushed the camera pan's white flash powder from his ill-fitting coat. "Miss Arellano, I am quite positive there are a lot of disgruntled soldiers who would like to take a potshot at their commander but none would dare."

"No! The assassin—I am almost sure—is somewhere here in the review stand. Working for the Germans. Several people in fact." Of Adelaide and Günther, she was certain. But they would never take that ultimate risk. It had to be someone else dictating it. The master spy she sought.

"Have at it." He flicked a fleshy hand toward the stand at his left, as if he wanted to brush her off as quickly as he had the flash powder. "Go take a gander."

At that moment, the mounted troops, with Pershing at the forefront, clip clopped in precise formation from around the corner of Mills Street. A mighty cheer went up. The military band launched into the stirring "Washington Post." Fireworks began to explode noisily overhead. Their colored sparkle and trailing white smoke contrasted with the blood-red sky. Confetti showered from skyscraper windows only to be blown away by the sand-laden wind. Everyone pushed to their feet, craning their necks to better see through the dusty haze.

Then, from the opposite direction, a short block away, a military staff car barreled around the corner, followed by—and at this, Pia's mouth dropped open—Dulcinea at the wheel of her Speedster. It looked to have been wrecked—and Amado sat beside her.

Both cars were headed straight for the promenade, now directly in front of the review stand. At once, General Pershing's gloved hand shot up to halt the procession. At the impending collision of man and machine and animal, bystanders retreated back from the curbs with terrified screams. The area erupted in chaos.

At the last moment, the Cadillac staff car yawed with a screech of tires to an abrupt stop. At the wheel, Colonel Robert Michie flung wide his door—as did Walt on the passenger side. In the back, the two MPs distinguished by their white-on-black brassards scrambled out close behind. The four closed in on a wide-eyed Günther and Adelaide.

"See here," blustered her outraged husband, Bartolomé Cardenas, "what is this all about?"

Günther was struggling and Adelaide shrinking from the determined MPs. The noise now was nearly ear-drum shattering, and Pia barely heard Lt. Michie shout, " ... under arrest ... espionage against ... United ... America."

The entire review stand broke out into mayhem. Its score of spectators scuffled to clear from the stand. One large-hatted woman fell or was pushed from the second bleacher, and Dulcinea sprang to assist her.

"God have mercy!" Mrs. Sturtevant screamed.

Mayor Lea was yelling for order, and the Provost Guard was rushing to control the crowd along the street.

The panicky surge emptied the stand within seconds. Only Pia and her father remained. She stood on the bleacher's second tier, he just below, so that she was almost on equal height with him.

He looked as if he wanted to speak to her, then turned away, turned back toward Pershing's honor guard, trying to restore order among the screaming people—and in their midst Pershing, still on horseback.

At that point, she spotted Walt's trilby. His needle-like focus was sweeping the crush of street crowd—then fixed on her. He shouldered past Mayor Lea, who appeared to be arguing indignantly with Colonel Michie, and sprinted along the length of bleachers toward her. Her heart lurched with passionate pain. What could he possibly say or do to change the way things were between them?

Suddenly her father's gargantuan form interposed between her and Walt. In disbelief, she watched Don Horst Heinrich reach inside his coat and pull out a pistol. Next, his outstretched arm pointed in the direction of the rack of brass medals adorning General Pershing's chest.

Holy Mother Mary, her father was the master spy?

Abruptly, he swung around, aiming at her, instead. She froze. No, his arm continued the arc of its swerve—past her, to below and right of the bleachers. At what?

And then she heard it. POP-POP! So close, coming from behind her, that her ears rang.

But it was her father who staggered. Released the pistol. The small hole off center of his forehead forecast the fanned burst of blood from the back. He crumpled.

"Nooo!" She scrambled down from the bleacher to kneel beside him but was violently shoved prone.

Slamming atop her father's massive stomach, she heard at the same time Walt hiss, "Stay!" Then from her peripheral vision, she watched him lurch from her to dive for the pistol.

He sprang into a crouch in front of her, the retrieved pistol's barrel pointed somewhere beyond. She twisted to look up over her shoulder. The newspaper editor held a revolver. She realized then it was Ed Bigelow who had shot her father.

"Drop your pistol, Ed," Walt shouted.

"You won't ... your old friend," was the little she could hear of the newsman's reply above the screaming crowd, oblivious to this sideline drama. "... know ... against killing."

The tendons in Walt's neck stood out. He white-knuckled the pistol grip. Its muzzle wavered, almost imperceptibly.

She knew he would never shoot. And he, so in tune with her, surely knew she knew. "You'll never get away with this, Mr. Bigelow," she yelled, diverting the editor's attention back to herself.

The ends of the dumpy man's brushy mustache fluttered with his grim smile. She strained to hear his response above the uproar in the streets. "... you two died ... trying ... stop Heinrich."

At the same time she heard the ripping bamm-bamm of multiple shots, she saw Bigelow's arm and shoulder shunted backward as his pistol got off its own shot. Then he spun, taking off in the opposite direction.

Walt faltered to one knee, a small spot blackening the crease of his trousers above his knee. He flung away the gun, a look of pure self-disgust darkening his features.

"Walt!" She crawled the short space separating them. His face a rictus of pain, he ignored her. Struggling to his feet and, hobbling, he gave chase.

But Bigelow was far ahead and clearly was going to get away. Madre de Dios, a short dash to the river and its border, and the master spy was home free! Momentarily, when he dashed behind the workmen's steam shovel, she lost sight of him. Then he reappeared again.

From somewhere behind her, Amado sprinted past both her and Walt. Bigelow glanced over his shoulder, spotted Amado in pursuit … and seemed to hesitate but a mere second, as if calculating his next move. Obviously, Amado was younger and in better condition and would quickly gain on him.

It appeared, rather than lose time circumventing the large pond, the newspaperman chose to cut across it. Hands braced on its balustraded concrete, he catapulted over the pond's wall. For a brief second she glimpsed the raw terror on his face.

At that point, in the blur of wind-whirled sand, he was lost from view … but not sound. The screaming and floundering in water of man against beasts seemed strangely anticlimactic after everything else.

But who was she to question providence?

Pia descended from the ambulance and, alongside the attendant assisting Walt, entered Providence Hospital. She watched as he was ushered through double doors to have his wound stitched.

Then she sat on a chilly metal bench in the waiting area. Within a few minutes, a woman in white of indeterminate age but who must have seen all of life's dramas played out there in the hospital emerged from those same double doors. She seemed to be able to find it within herself still to dole out pity. "Mr. Stevenson said to tell you your sister has been arrested, Miss Arellano. To tell you to go on and attend to her."

Pia's heart felt as cold as the cavern-like waiting room. Sighing, she left the hospital. How Walt must hate her for forcing his hand, forcing him to fire the pistol. And she could not blame him.

Well, Walt knew what he wanted. And it was not her. Had never been her.

She made one stop, just before the bank's closing time. The same balding teller who had assisted Walt and her last time rose to greet her. His fawning manner was replaced by skepticism that she wanted to close her account and withdraw her funds when she possessed no identification, not even a purse, much less her bankbook. Apparently, though, Walt's business with the bank overrode the teller's reluctance.

By the time she had withdrawn her funds, the sandstorm had abated. A chilly twilight was spreading its gray tarp over the city. She traversed the intervening blocks to the El Paso City Jail. As she walked down its long, subterranean corridor leading to the book-in area, her clunky work boots thudded a rapid staccato beat that echoed her own heart.

At the police counter stood a tired-looking older man, derby hat pushed back. The interchange between him and the officer behind drifted back to Pia. Apparently, from what she could overhear, the man was posting bail for his son, arrested for stealing a sawhorse from a construction site. Farther along the counter, a very pregnant negro woman with a harried look on her face filled out a slip required for visitation.

When Pia's turn came, she forked over the wad of money in her blue jeans back pocket, her entire earnings that Walt had paid upfront for her spy services.

How preposterous, how unimaginable, that Silas, who had inspired her to invest in real estate, had been a part of that group bent on destroying that dream of so many. And how unimaginable that the frumpy *El Paso Herald* editor could be Sommerfeld's master spy.

She positioned herself on a wooden bench across from the counter but near enough the heavy metal door that she could see Josefina immediately upon her release. Fifteen long minutes later, the door opened and Pia saw that precious brown face was both haggard and relieved.

Josefina hugged Pia, and she could feel her sister's rounded should-ders shuddering. "Thank you, *hermanita*. I know this cost you everything."

"Family is everything." She sighed. Truth was not always palpable to the palate. "Come along, Mamacita will be worried about us."

She expected for them to catch the next streetcar outward bound for Juarez. Instead, outside the city jail she found a glum-looking Amado. He was waiting next to a hired hackney drawn by a horse giving off a snorting neigh while plopping a pile of shit at the curb.

"We'll take you home, Pia."

Home. "We?"

"Silvestre and Dulcinea and me. Not enough room for all five of us in her Speedster. Besides, a donkey cart has crippled it."

"So that's what happened," she marveled.

"Only *un pequeño choque*." He assisted Pia and Josefina up the step into the rear of the vis-à-vis hired carriage. From its dimness came both Perro's yapping greeting and Dulcinea's throaty purr. "If I have to put up with your pooch one more time, Pia, I swear I'll either shoot it or myself."

With amusement, Pia noted the woman was restraining an excited Perro with calming, even affectionate strokes. "*Por favor,* don't kill yourself today," she said, sliding in next to the *matadora* and relieving her of Perro. "There's been too much killing already."

With the sound of hooves clopping against brick pavement, the carriage lurched forward in several jerks. She noted the way Amado, sitting directly across from Dulcinea, reached a palm to steady her outthrust hand. A wry smile tipped the ends of Pia's mouth. The young stud would not pine long for lost love.

Silvestre, sitting directly across from her, cleared his throat and adjusted his ascot. "In reference to that—killing, as you mentioned—I went to the city morgue a few hours ago to identify our father's body and then met with his *abogado*, a probate attorney, to arrange for a burial that complied with the Last Will and Testament."

She fumbled for words of consolation. "Our father died making the hero's choice, Silvestre."

Beside her, Josefina grumbled, "There is so much I could say that is not heroic about our father."

A heavy sigh uttered from Silvestre. "I regret my father and I were never able to come to terms."

"*Sí*," Pia agreed, "it is sad that your opposing political views got in the way."

"But more so my lifestyle." The sound of the carriage wheels rumbling over the international bridge was as hollow as his words. "You know this. It shamed him. That is the real reason he disinherited me."

Soon they would be home. Mamacita's home, rather. "I understand, and I am sorry. Truly sorry, Silvestre."

He leaned forward, tapped his cane between his patent boots, and stared intently in the carriage's dimness, first at her, then at Josefina, and returned to focus back on her. Unaccountably, she felt the intense attention of Amado and Dulcinea, as well, focused upon her and her sister. Something momentous was portending.

"Pia—Josefina, our father's eight-million acres along with their cattle and oil and pueblos belong to either Carranza or Villa, whoever triumphs ultimately in Mexico. What you may not know is that, according to our father's *abogado*, he recently changed his will. He left his hacienda and its acreage he still owned in Chihuahua City to you and Josefina."

"What?" she and Josefina gasped in unison.

"I think his sins weighed heavily on his heart."

Still scarcely unable to comprehend this windfall, she murmured, "Then you must know?"

"That we are half siblings? I always suspected. The attorney merely confirmed it. Of course, the paperwork to finalize the will could take months, but Pia—Josefina, you'll never have to cross the bridge into the United States, never have to be forcefully fumigated again."

She felt scalding tears brim and blinked them back. She leaned forward and squeezed the gloved hand atop his cane. "Thank you."

"Oh, *Dios mío*," Josefina cried. "Can this be true? Not a dream?"

She began to weep noisily, and Pia hugged her sister's spasming shoulders.

The carriage halted before their home, and Amado helped her and Josefina down. Pia waited until it rattled off down the unpaved street before telling Josefina, "I'll be in soon. I'm taking Perro around back to poop." She was buying time.

"I understand," Josefina said, and Pia knew her sister understood her very well.

The gentling of night had found its way to the back side of the adobe. Releasing Perro, she slumped down next to the galvanized tub. The steady drip-drip of the water spigot and sweet smell of the *yerba buena* nestled with the watercress in the spongy soil calmed her turbulent thoughts.

Perro came pattering over to lick the back of her hand, damp with tears that insisted on being shed, slowly, one by agonizing one. She gathered him up against her chest and, sighing into his fur, stood to go inside. She glanced down at the drowsing *yerba buena* and watercress, and it dawned on her it was Walt who had added the spice to her life.

But she had forced his hand, forced him to go against his highest principal, his damned conviction against bloodshed, and she was miserably conscious that she had forfeited him. But then he had never wanted her. Not really. Not in the sense that she was his all, his everything.

Well, he was the fool. And she was finished being a fool, striving toward something that was but a mirage of her imagination.

She reminded herself of the intrinsic reward she had received—a house far grander than any of those on Mount Franklin. She would go on with her life, as Walt would with his. Their love affair, if it was even that, had been but a few days hidden from time.

Chapter Thirty-One

February 6ᵗʰ, 1917

That next day, Pia sat at the table, across from her mother, and determinedly wove the *lechuguilla* strands into a rounded mat used to fan fireplace flames. She wished she could so easily fan the flame incinerating her heart to cinders.

Josefina had left for work at El Paso Laundry fifteen minutes earlier, just after sunup. Behind Pia, Rosita was trying to teach a tail-whipping Perro to sit up for a breakfast treat, a piece of the morning's honeyed sopapilla. In an hour she would leave for parochial school, its nuns' tutelage overseen by Father Ignatius. Pia intended first thing, after the hacienda inheritance came through, to procure a *Roget's Thesaurus* for Rosita.

The tedium of the weaving should have had a soothing effect on Pia but instead it gave her too much time to think, to question what she could not quite pinpoint. What was she to do with the rest of her life?

Her mother cleared her throat. Peering up from the tough fibers her gnarled fingers so effortlessly plaited, she asked, "You want more than this from your life, do you not, *Mija?*"

So, her mother was doing it for her, steering her to the precipice's edge where she feared to approach. She shrugged. Already her hunched shoulders ached from the continual sitting. "This is good enough for you."

"But it is not what I wanted. I wanted Carlos Herrera. And out of fear I waited too long. You want this writer, this Walter Stevenson, *si?*"

"Carlos Herrera wanted *you.*" Her shoulders hunched even more over her fan taking questionable shape.

After a pause, her mother said, "*Donde hay amor, hay dolor.*"

A leave's prickly point jabbed Pia's fingertip, and she winced. "*Sí,* Mamacita, where there is love, there is pain. So, I choose to forego the love and thus the pain. It is that simple."

Her mother tsked. "But then you would miss out on the sweet joy that the heart—"

Josefina burst through the door. "Pia, you have to come. Quickly!

Frowning, Pia halted the braiding of the leaves. "What?"

Josefina half-pivoted, and, waving for her to follow, gasped, "Now!"

Pia dumped her weaving, grabbed a shawl from the peg, and hurried to catch up with Josefina, already bustling across the street and heading a block over to Avenida de Comercio.

Pia thought her destination was the *farmacía*, that maybe something had happened to Guido, but Josefina passed it, then the phonograph shop next door. Her skirts flapping about her ankles, she kept up her walk-run toward the International Bridge still several blocks off.

Along the way, a barber tossed aside his scissors. A hatmaker dropped her pins. A *carnicero* yanked off his bloody butcher's apron. All joined in the rush to the middle of the bridge. Two Public Health officers were leaning over its metal railing and shouting and waving their arms.

"Mira, there!" Josefina said, wedging space for them among the spectators gathered at the guardrail. All stared toward the United

States' riverbank. From that side of the Rio Bravo, amidst swirling dust and a whirlwind of debris, came a growling, grating sound. Directly over the origin of the booming noise, the dust cloud cleared momentarily.

Pia spotted a steam shovel, its massive blade repeatedly ramming a portion of the fumigation plant's brick wall—and she saw the steam shovel's driver. Below a brown trilby, he was wearing dust goggles, but there was no way she would not know that military stiff, ruler-straight spine.

Then the wall collapsed, and in the explosion of dust Walt Stevenson vanished.

"My telephone has been clanging with questions about your demolition fiasco by everyone who can get on the line." Bobby wore a uniform of olive drab wool with gold piping and black dress shoes. Hands gripped behind his back, he paced a circle that encompassed a functional metal desk and the hardback armchair in which Walt sprawled his length like some bored king.

Walt said nothing.

"What the fuck were you thinking, Walt? Did the Mexican drug trade at last trip up your brain with opiates?"

He could no longer cling to his conceit. Too late, he had realized there was a glory in Pia's randomness and a stagnancy in his systematic order. And, oh, so much more—a galaxy of wonderment he would have missed had he not chanced across her ten days before.

Or had he? Had he *chanced* across her. Had something serendipitous been at work?

He flicked a desultory hand. "You know me better than that, Bobby. Listen, lay it out. The charges I face under martial law—and the penalties."

Bobby did the sharp pivot required in a foot drill to face him squarely. "It was the Mexican beauty Pia Arellano who tripped you up, wasn't it?"

"She's not up for discussion." He had not intended his words to sound so harsh, so defiant. But then this latest act of his stretched what he had ever imagined his capability of defiance might be.

He could offer no sane justification … or maybe that was it. No justification but justice. He wanted to see justice done, at least, in this one case, for someone whose own act of brave defiance he knew would go unremembered in history.

Regrettably, Pia would remember not only his stiff-necked nature but, also, his last spat of unforgivable words. He could think of no redeemable quality of his that was worthy of her.

Why had he not attuned to that sense of recognition when first crossing paths with her, that strong sense of yearning, that acute awareness that forces were at work beyond his control?

Bobby planted his palms on his desktop. "Well, then, I'll fire away. Thank your lucky stars that the city is under martial law. Because that might give you a modicum of leverage with Pershing. And under the Articles of War, which we are, you might get a reprieve timewise. With but seventy-two hours allotted for preparation, the commission is required to prove that you, the defendant, acted willfully and maliciously."

"As I told you, I offered the investigators at the review stand yesterday to move the steam shovel from the crime scene for them." He steepled his fingertips and shrugged. "My foot slipped on the sand-caked pedal and then the steam shovel careened off down the hill."

Bobby shot him a narrowed look, and he snorted. "And then the steam shovel reversed and shot forward repeatedly, all by itself?"

"Like, I told them, I am not all that familiar with heavy machinery."

"Damn't, you razed the disinfection plant on purpose!" The fire and fury went out of Bobby then. He grunted. "Look, Walt, I'm trying to help you. Here's what you're looking at—up to ten years' imprisonment, a fine of up to $15,000—or both. And that doesn't include the damages to the bath house and what civil fines could be brought against you for that little escapade of yours."

He shrugged again, tilted his head back and closed his eyes. It could be worse. Adelaide and Günther were still incarcerated. Their hearings were to be held at a federal court on charges of espionage. The penalties were stiffer for both, twenty years and $25,000—or worse, execution.

He was still stunned in discovering that not only was his pal Ed the master spy he had sought but that fossilized Silas Wright had been a double agent. So much for Walt's touted observation skills.

Burnt in his brain was the image of Pia's disappointment that he had not outright killed Ed. Walt had never wanted to kill anything, but that did not mean he would not lay down his life for something that was of a larger issue—like justice, like love. He returned a stalwart gaze to his friend. "Tell them to bring it on, then, Bobby."

Chapter Thirty-Two

February 9th, 1917

Another revolution of the clock, Walt noted. Because the U.S. was teetering on war with Germany, the swiftness of his court martial, a mere three days, was backed by the Articles of War. No time was allotted to seek clemency.

On the plus side, Pershing had given a nod to a public court martial hearing. It allowed the support of public opinion, which weighed heavily in Walt's favor—not that the military was likely to take that into consideration.

The hearing was convened inside Fort Bliss's main repair facility. Maintaining the newly motorized division of the Punitive Expedition and boasting the largest truck-repair complex in the entire War Department, the repair facility was the only place on the post with the capacity to hold the crowd, gathered by word of mouth, for the trial. Three-ton tanks, trench destroyers, and a newly designed Jeffery quad—a four-wheel drive, had been shoveled to one side.

The day was drizzly and humid. Even though the weather had not reached July and August's furnace-heat, many were patting perspiration from their faces with lace handkerchiefs and bandannas.

Walt sweated no less as he watched his hastily hired defense attorney approach the bench. The air crackled with impending doom.

Utilitarian tables, chairs, and benches had been commandeered from throughout the post. The attendees occupying these seats were troopers, civilians, and members of the press. Some faces in the press corps he recognized—Jules DuBois from the French press and his old acquaintance, Reginald Armstrong of the British Reuters. Numbering among them was Amado, who was sketching the proceedings for *La Reforma Social.*

Among the spectators, most of them from the working class, he spotted Dulcinea. She was chewing on a fingernail. Next to her sat a worried-looking Bobby and his wife Ellie.

And Walt recognized another face—Pia's. She was seated on the other side of Ellie. Since Pia was adamant she would never submit to being fumigated again, Walt speculated Bobby had provided a pass for her today. Walt looked at her face as long as he dared.

Then the defense attorney, speaking in a high, nasally voice, reclaimed Walt's attention. He felt grateful that Bobby had wrangled from Pershing a civilian lawyer in lieu of a military one, since a civilian lawyer had no higher chain of command and did not have to adhere to certain rules as strictly as high-ranking military personnel.

And this civilian attorney was none other than Silvestre Salinas, who had foregone expenses to volunteer. "Even should you find that Mr. Stevenson intentionally razed the disinfection plant," he was saying, "that cannot be constructed as malicious but rather a protest against injustice."

"Objection, your honor." The prosecutor shot to his feet. Perspiration glinted on Lt. Grundy's high forehead. "This cannot be misleadingly construed as a mere act of protest. The charge is sabotage against a federal facility."

The military judge, looking like a huge black crow in his judicial robe, snapped, "Overruled. That determination is why this court has been convened."

Salinas spread his palms in supplication, looking with his pointed beard like Jesus blessing the multitudes. All eyes were glued to the slight and dapper man.

"I beg then the military commission consider my worthy opposition's introduction of the term 'sabotage.'"

The judge nodded and revolved his hand in a gesture to get on with it.

"I studied law in Paris. The very word sabotage derives from an old French form to describe, in regard to class struggles and labor disputes, the wrecking of machinery. This was originally done by poor workers wearing wooden shoes called sabots, which they would throw into machinery to disrupt production."

"Counselor," the judge said impatiently, "your point, please?"

Walt could see Salinas making a monumental effort to keep his expression neutral. "Yes, Your Honor. Thus, I contend that even were the actions of my esteemed client to be deemed intentional, they were, indeed, in the form of a protest and not a malicious act. In fact, beginning with the Boston Tea Party, destruction of government property has played a long and proud part in America's illustrious history."

"Strike that last remark," the judge ordered.

Salinas shrugged and returned to the small desk facing the judge's bench to sit alongside Walt. "Well, I blew that, my friend. I should have saved that for my summation. Not that it will make a difference." With an apologetic grimace, he said, "I have not the experience of a seasoned civil lawyer nor the background of a military attorney. I fear our case is lost."

"You did your best, and for that I am grateful."

Apparently, Silvestre Salinas was not the only one to feel the trial was all but over. With heavy dejection Walt watched a disgusted-looking Pia rise, maneuver past the knees of the seated spectators, and exit the building. Well, so much for any hope of loyalty, much less love. Depression settled around him like dense fog.

He thought of one of the corrido's *La Cucaracha* many improvised and humorous lyrics, translated into English: "When a man loves a woman but she doesn't love him back. It's like a bald man finding a comb in the street."

Humorous failed to describe the state of his mind ... and heart.

The judge must have felt likewise that the trial was all but over. He rapped his gavel on his desk. "Court is hereby recessed to reconvene promptly at sixteen hundred hours. Attorneys, be prepared to wrap up your case with your closing arguments."

Those two hours Walt waited in the recess room gave him time to review his life. The mess he had made of it. The grudge he had held against his old man, raised with equal harsh discipline by a Civil War Union officer, had served no purpose whatever. What a wastrel, Walt thought, what a fool he had been. He, with all his self-righteousness—that he alone knew what was right and civil.

At last, the posted guard opened the door to admit a grim-faced Salinas. "I have been sequestered with the judge and the prosecutor, trying to reach a plea bargain, based on your lack of a record, but the evidence against this charge is simply too overpowering."

Walt stood. "Well, let's face the music then." How ironic, he thought, recalling how the Mexican Federal bands drummed during executions. At one such execution, thronged with people as if to a fiesta, dramatic selections from Verdi's *Aida* had played until the executed soldier fell like a scythed wheat stalk.

As the judge lumbered to his desk, everyone rose. At that same moment, a little girl ran up the aisle to pass an envelope to Salinas. Quickly, his beringed fingers tore it open. He perused the first page, then scanned the second.

"What is it?" Walt asked.

Salinas ignored him. The papers in hand, he stepped forward with alacrity. "Your Honor, I request permission to meet with you and the prosecutor in your chambers."

The judged glared. "The Court does not like surprises, Mr. Salinas."

The prosecutor jumped to his feet. "Your Honor, I protest. This time was to have been allotted for closing arguments."

Salinas circled the table and approached the bench to confer with the judge. The judge's grizzled brows climbed his patriarchal forehead.

What possibly could be transpiring? Walt sweated from his temples to his balls.

Finally, the judge nodded grudgingly. "A five-minute adjournment then," he told the court. "Mr. Salinas, Lt. Grundy, you will follow me."

While the three closeted themselves in the judge's chamber, which was an office of the repair center, no one moved from their seats.

Walt sat perplexed. Taking off his pince-nez, he rubbed the high bridge of his nose with his thumb and forefinger while he rifled through the files of his brain. He was almost certain the pigtailed girl who had delivered the message was Rosita, although he had seen her but that once.

In what seemed an inordinate length of time the judge and the attorneys reappeared. All around murmurs ran through the press of people. Once more everyone stood, and Salinas took his place next to Walt.

"What is going on?" he mouthed to the elegant little man.

An emptyhanded Salinas sent him a sidewise glance. "I negotiated a plea bargain for you."

Surprise, then anger, shot through him. "Without consulting me? You can't do that!"

The judge hammered the gavel for order in the court. "The prosecutor has agreed to a plea bargain by the attorney on behalf of his client. The defendant will pay both the maximum fine and reparations of the disinfection facility, a cost estimated at $82,000 in exchange for a dismissal of the penalty of imprisonment."

Surprised rippled like a riptide through the room.

Nonplussed, the judge continued. "The defendant is released on his own recognizance until such fine is paid." He tapped the gavel again. "Case is closed. Court is dismissed."

Walt sat stunned, feeling nothing ... then relief followed by confusion and then vexation bordering on anger once more. He turned on Salinas. The dandy was stuffing his notepapers into his briefcase. "You know I don't have access to that kind of money."

Silvestre looked up at him gravely. "But someone does. You are a smart man. You work it out." He smiled, pumped Walt's hand, then shouldered his way through the people surging forward to congratulate Walt.

After accepting the hearty pats on his back and praise, then signing off on a plethora of legal documents, he fled from the building. He did not like being considered a hero. The sky was now a rain-washed pure blue. He should be ecstatic. He was a free man. Howbeit, a free, aimless man. Both *Collier's* and the BI had dismissed his services.

He jammed his hands in his pockets and started walking ... yes, aimlessly, he admitted to himself.

Of course, this anonymous benefactor befuddled him. No one he was familiar with had that astronomical sum of money on hand. Oh, he was on speaking terms with some fabulously rich men, connections of his father's, but none who would be willing to part with some of their cherished money for his sake. And he would have rotted in jail before he asked his old man.

He looked up and realized he had walked the entire length of Fort Bliss and arrived at the Cassidy Gate. Here others also congregated to wait for the streetcar to take them back to El Paso's Union Station hub. The vivid memory of first sighting Pia there, thirteen days ago, the jolt he had felt when his eyes connected with hers, assailed him—and he was jolted again.

Work it out, Silvestre had said.

Backtracking the events of the day and by deduction, Walt arrived at how the case has turned in his favor after the girl had approached Silvestre with the envelope. If the girl was, indeed, Rosita, then somehow Pia had finagled it! Was she capable of pulling off such a feat? Time and again she had astounded him with her resourcefulness and resilience. But this? Was she capable of this grand gesture?

His heart was hemorrhaging—hemorrhaging over this authentic and quite recherché young woman, this firecracker who brought out the goofiness, the silliness, and the depths of love he had thought had died with his childhood. Something about her had made him fall in love with life again. Fall in love with the enthusiasm of a child's fresh perspective.

He had to find out, one way or another; face her, even though she might want nothing to do with him. If she had, indeed, made this grand gesture of rescuing him, had it been out of a sense of duty—a debt she felt she owed for his rescuing her that night in the desert? He wanted to believe—no, had to believe—it was more than that. He had to believe that he had a chance with her, because to think otherwise was intolerable.

At Union Station he waited impatiently to transfer to the El Paso-Juarez streetcar. By the time he disembarked at Avenida de Comercio, dusk was closing off the tumultuous day. A ring embossed the Sugar Moon and fire flickered in the myriad stars.

He had been to Pia's house twice now, the first time the night he found her in the desert when he had dropped her off. Or rather, she had found him in the desert. At the memory of the armadillo she had startled, what might have passed for a slight smile tipped his lips.

The smile faded as he tacked toward the lopsided turquoise door. For a man with purpose, he was certainly unsure of himself now. He was a floundering fool. He did not know what to expect. After all, he had only known the vibrant young woman that was Pia Arellano a short thirteen days in time.

At his tentative knock, there came from inside Perro's ferocious barking.

Pia's mother opened the door. Her strong features were sculpted with the same proud dignity as those of Pia. "I don't know if you remember me. I am—"

"I know who you are." Her lips, thinned by age and weather, bestowed him a warm smile. "We've been waiting for you."

To cover his confusion, he leaned over to pick up the vociferous dog, whose slobbering tongue proceed to avidly swipe his face. Ugghh. "You have?"

She stepped aside. *"Entra, por favor."*

The savory smell of baked enchiladas—of green onions, black olives, and cheddar cheese—greeted him, and his stomach growled. He realized he had not eaten since yesterday. By habit, he swiftly scrutinized his surroundings.

The room was sparse in furnishings but warm with the vivid colorings of a red-and-orange striped serape that served as a door curtain to another room; of a blue-robed Virgin Mary wooden santo in a niche; of a faded purple, once plush velvet sofa; of a red geranium in a brilliant blue pot.

And here in hand-painted chairs of variegated colors, reposed people, most of whom he recognized.

The strutting young cock Amado had his arm draped around Dulcinea, who was uncharacteristically giggling girlishly.

Bobby, sitting next to his wife, played slap-hand with the pigtailed girl, who had delivered the envelope earlier.

On the sofa, Salinas talked with his usual flourish of beringed fingers to a rather stout mustachioed Mexican. This had to be Guido. He, in turn, held the hand of a young plump woman, Josefina. She was deep in conversation with Pia.

She was the first to glance up. She bit her bottom lip, then excused herself and rose to navigate the chairs and stand in front of him. She looked up at him. He, who loved words, was at a loss as where to begin and stupidly blurted, "Hello, *hola, hallo*, and cheerio."

Her characteristic grin did not lop up to one side. She was not amused. "You know what you want, Walt?"

The room went silent. Everyone was expectantly watching the two of them. "Uhh, can we talk, privately, Pia?"

She nodded and gestured toward the back door. He did not know what he expected. A tiny courtyard, maybe. A semi-darkened alley, it was, with a strip of sparse green abutting the desert sand-brown adobe. She slid down its pocked wall.

He set Perro free to sniff the alley's refuse and, imitating Pia, decamped to the other side of a spigot and galvanized tub, aromatic with mint. His long legs were jacked up to his chest. He wrapped his arms around his knees. The question burst from him. "You sprang for the fine, plus reparations—$82, 000 or more?"

He saw her nod. She was staring ahead into the evening's shadows. The air was redolent with the promise of sweet vegetation.

Proficient speech failed him. "How? Where? Where did the money come from?"

"My father—in his will Don Horst left me and Josefina his hacienda. With her consent and with some quick finagling, I managed to mortgage my half."

"Why? Why did you do this for me?" This was what he had to know, more than anything else.

She looked directly at him now. "Many times I have helped you, even though I had decided you knew what you wanted. Something more than me. And there was no use in giving my love to a man who did not value it. But when you razed the bath house ... it was like finding the exact ingredient that you have not realized was missing in a favorite dish. I realized I had not made a mistake in the beginning. A man who would risk it all—for abstract words like justice and love—this is the man I must have."

For the second time that day, he sat stunned. A lump was in his throat and a stinging in his eyes. Such love and generosity overwhelmed him.

Her pale skin and green eyes, grave and intent, glimmered in the moonlight. "I ask again, you know what you want, Walt?"

For a moment he was silent, considering her question. "For now, yes. But that could change."

Her sharp inhalation crackled the glorious night air's stillness.

Swiftly, he numbered off on his long fingers. "For now, number one, I want the vacant job as editor in chief of *The El Paso Herald*. For now, number two, I want to save enough from the job and my writing royalties to build that mansion at Kern Place, the home you always wanted."

Her equally sharp exhalation of relief rustled the tub's plants and scented the air with mint.

He reached across the tub to cup her nape where tendrils of her red hair tickled his fingers. He drew her closer, so close he could feel her vital warmth. "But for always, it is you I want. I have always wanted you. This want of you has driven me insane."

"Insane enough to raze the bath house, *sí?*"

Did he detect relenting humor in her voice? "Pia, I need your love to humanize me. I need a homelife, like the one your family has created here. I need you for my wife. And I want lots of children."

She hesitated. "But what about that great American novel you wanted to write?"

"The greatest story I could ever write is right here … about you, my social warrioress."

"That is good, because I plan to run for political office once we are married."

He scanned those gamine features so precious to him, then brushed his lips back and forth across hers, seeking her *joie de vivre* that gave the joy to his own life, and murmured, "I expected no less from you, *mi vida.*"

Her imperfect grin was perfect. "*Te amo, mi corazón.*" She captured his long face between her hands and began raining little love kisses on his jaw, his temples, and his cheekbones.

"Keep it up, buttercup."

Author's Note

I was halfway through writing a first draft for a novel set in the Pass in the 1800s, when, while researching, I chanced across an incident in El Paso that set my mind's wheels spinning. I knew here was a story I had to write—now! I set aside my other story.

In 1917, a seventeen-year-old redhaired Mexican housemaid, Carmelita Torres, started a riot on the El Paso-Juarez bridge to protest being forcibly sprayed with chemicals for typhus by the Public Health Department. The riot made international news.

It eventually involved over a thousand protestors and shut down traffic both ways on the bridge for three days. Dubbed the Redhaired Amazon by newspapers, Carmelita was arrested that day—and then abruptly disappeared from history and time.

No one knows what happened to her. It's believed that she was killed. And that's why I wanted to write a happy ending for this intrepid young woman.

Unfortunately, the disinfecting of Mexicans at El Paso continued for another 40 years. Ironically, the Spanish Influenza pandemic that spread across the United States a year later, in the fall of 1918, taking its toll also of soldiers stationed at Fort Bliss, proved far more deadly to border residents than the perceived fears of typhus.

As for the illusive and wily Felix Sommerfeld, in June 1918 he was interned in Fort Oglethorpe, Georgia as an enemy alien. He was released in 1919. A few trips of his back and forth to Mexico were recorded in the 1920s and 30s. However, the German agent disappeared in the 1930s—like Carmelita Torres—without a trace.

The rest of the bath house story is far, far more mind-blowing.

A 1937 German scientific journal specifically praised the El Paso method of fumigating Mexican workers with Zyklon B. Then, at the start of WWII, the Nazi party began practicing this Zyklon B fumigation formula at its concentration camps. Later, when the Final Solution was put into effect, the Germans used Zyklon B in their gas chambers not only to exterminate lice but also millions of human beings.

Another reason I wanted to tell the story of Carmelita Torres and the horrible way the citizens of Juarez were treated, is to make sure nothing like this ever happens again. We have to remember the atrocities of history, to ensure they are not repeated.

In researching Reluctant Rebel, I am most grateful for David Romo's *Ringside Seat to a Revolution* with its detailed accountings of this deplorable period in history, as well as Heribert von Feilitzsch's *In Plain Sight: Felix A. Sommerfeld, Spymaster in Mexico*, Antoinette May's *Passionate Pilgrim: The extraordinary life of Alma Reed*, and Madeline Gallego Thorpe and Mary Tate Engels' *Corazón Contento: Sonoran Recipes and Stories from the Heart*.

About the Author

Parris Afton Bonds is the mother of five sons and the author of nearly fifty published novels. She is co-founder and first vice president of Romance Writers of America, as well as cofounder of Southwest Writers Workshop.

Declared by ABC's Nightline as one of three best-selling authors of romantic fiction, the New York Times best seller Parris Afton Bonds has been featured in major newspapers and magazines and published in more than a dozen languages.

The Parris Award was established in her name by the Southwest Writers Workshop to honor a published writer who has given outstandingly of time and talent to other writers. Prestigious recipients of the Parris Award include Tony Hillerman and the Pulitzer nominee Norman Zollinger.

She donates spare time to teaching creative writing to both grade school children and female inmates, both whom she considers her captive audiences.